Sudden uneasiness swept over Tobas as he saw a thin, pale wisp of smoke rising from a high, jagged heap of stone. An instant later, the dragon's head reared up from behind the jumble of rocks. It was looking directly at them.

Even as they realized this, it clambered out of concealment, spread its great wings, and took to the air, flapping clumsily toward them. The dragon's great blue-green wings seemed to block out the entire sky as it swooped upward over their heads, apparently intending to drop right on top of them. Petrified, they stared upward, certain they had come to the end of their adventures.

The monster opened its mouth in what looked almost like a mocking grin. Then the dragon's face erupted into yellow flame, and it screamed with fury.

By the same author

The Lords of Dûs

LAWRENCE WATT-EVANS

With a Single Spell

Grafton

An Imprint of HarperCollinsPublishers

Grafton
An Imprint of HarperCollins*Publishers*
77–85 Fulham Palace Road,
Hammersmith, London W6 8JB

A Grafton Original 1988
9 8 7 6 5 4 3 2

ISBN 0 586 20009 6

Set in Times

Printed in Great Britain by
HarperCollinsManufacturing Glasgow

Dedicated to my mother,
Doletha Watt-Evans

Chapter 1

The little cottage at the edge of the swamp wherein old Roggit had lived out his life was not, strictly speaking, a part of the village of Telven. However, located as it was just over a hill from the edge of town, it was near enough that Roggit had been accepted as a Telvener; no one had protested when his apprentice, Tobas, had called on the villagers to attend his master's funeral.

Of course, quite aside from any fine distinctions about the village boundaries, it was never wise to anger a wizard, or even a wizard's apprentice – not even one as untrained as Tobas surely was after merely a year or two of study under a man who had been in his dotage and on the verge of senility for as long as anyone remembered.

As a result of these considerations, in addition to the usual morbid curiosity natural upon the cremation of one of the area's older and more eccentric inhabitants, the ceremonies drew a good crowd, with more than half the townspeople in attendance. As Tobas saw them all silently departing after the fire died, he realized glumly that he could not say a single one, old, young, or in between, had come out of honest friendship or sympathy for either the dead wizard or for himself, the surviving apprentice.

He had had friends in his younger years, he told himself, but they all seemed to have drifted away when his luck went bad. Since his father's death he had been considered a creature of ill omen, not a fitting friend for anyone.

He watched the villagers wander away in pairs, trios,

or family groups and then set out alone, back over the hill toward the cottage. The sun was still high in the sky. The pyre had burned quickly, as the weather had been dry of late.

As he topped the rise he tried to decide whether he, himself, actually grieved over Roggit's death and found himself unsure whether his distress was on Roggit's behalf or simply a reflection of his worries about his own position.

His own position was still, to some extent, in doubt. As Roggit's apprentice at the time of his death, Tobas was heir to everything the old man had owned that had not previously been settled on others; and as far as anyone knew, Roggit had had no children or relatives or even former apprentices to leave anything to. What little there was all went to Tobas.

That, however, was not necessarily a great comfort. Roggit had not been wealthy. He had owned a small piece of land, too swampy to be of much use, and the cottage, together with its contents, and that was all.

At least, Tobas thought, he hadn't been left homeless this time, as he had been when his father died. And the house still held old Roggit's magical supplies and paraphernalia, including, most importantly of all, his Book of Spells.

Tobas would need that. It was all he had left to depend on.

When he had first convinced the old wizard to take him on as an apprentice, despite the fact that anyone not half-blind and half-senile could have seen he was at least fifteen, rather than the maximum apprenticeable age of thirteen, Tobas had thought his place was secure. He had expected to live out his life quietly, earning his bread as a small-town wizard, selling love potions and removing curses, as Roggit had done. It had seemed easy enough. He had been initiated into the primary mystery of the Wizards' Guild – he unconsciously touched the hilt of the dagger on his belt as he thought of it – and had learned his first spell without difficulty when, after months of delay and apparently unnecessary preparation, Roggit had finally seen fit to teach him one.

Tobas had thoroughly and beyond all question mastered his first spell and practiced it until he could do it perfectly with no thought at all; when Roggit had at last admitted that the lad had mastered it, he had promised to teach Tobas a second within the month. The apprentice had been looking forward eagerly to this next step in his education when, just two nights ago, the old man had died quietly in his sleep, leaving Tobas with his house and his Book of Spells and his jars and his boxes and his mysterious objects of every description – but with only a single spell learned, and that nothing but the knack of lighting fires.

The old man had called it Thrindle's Combustion, and Tobas had to admit that it was very useful to be able to light a fire anywhere, at any time, under any conditions, regardless of how wet the fuel was or how fiercely the wind blew, so long as he had his athame – as Roggit had called the enchanted dagger that was the key to a wizard's power – and a few grains of brimstone and something that it was theoretically possible to burn. Since learning it Tobas had made it a point never to be without the knife and a supply of brimstone and had impressed people occasionally by setting fire to this or that. He had used the spell to light Roggit's pyre, and that had added a nice touch to the cremation ceremonies, an appropriate farewell; the villagers had murmured approvingly.

Of course, not every use of the spell had gone so well,

he remembered wryly; he had once embarrassed himself by trying to ignite a black rock he had mistaken for coal. The only result had been a shower of ineffectual sparks. Fortunately, the girl he had been showing off for had not realized any more was intended and had been appropriately amazed.

Useful as it might be, Thrindle's Combustion was not the sort of spell a lad could build an entire career on. It would not earn his bread, nor convince anyone to marry him – most of the village girls had been noticeably cool of late, though he was not sure why. He had never expected to wed for love, of course – hardly anyone did – but he doubted, under the circumstances, whether any of the available females would even consider a marriage of convenience.

He needed to learn more spells, quickly, and establish himself as the town's new wizard. If he failed to secure his position as soon as possible, someone might well invite in a foreign magician of some sort, leaving him out of work. The cottage garden, with its handful of herbs, would not be enough to keep him alive if that happened.

Fortunately, he did have Roggit's Book of Spells. But as he picked up his pace, hurrying down the slope to the cottage, he found himself unwillingly imagining reasons why he might not be able to use it. Had Roggit written it in some esoteric wizardly tongue? Would the spells he needed call for ingredients he could not obtain? The Book was old; might the pages have faded to illegibility, leaving just enough to remind Roggit of what he already knew? Was there some important secret he did not know?

He intended to waste no time. If he lost even a single day in mourning poor old Roggit, something might go wrong. He would open the Book of Spells as soon as he got home.

He crossed the dooryard impatiently, lifted the latch, and stepped into the cottage that was no longer Roggit's. This was his now.

He looked around, reacquainting himself with the place. His own little bed, a pallet, really, which he would no longer be using, lay in one corner; Roggit's narrow bed, where he intended to sleep henceforth, stood in another. A fireplace yawned at each end, both empty and cold; the weather had been mild, and he had not bothered to do any cooking since Roggit's death. The lone table, used for cooking, dining, and as the wizard's workplace, stood in the center. The long walls on both sides were jammed with shelves, cabinets, and cupboards, all packed with the necessities of the wizard's simple life and arcane trade. The ceiling overhead was the underside of the thatched roof, and the floor beneath his feet was packed dirt. The Book of Spells lay in solitary splendor atop its reading stand.

The cottage wasn't much, he thought critically, but it was dry and, when the fires were lit, warm. It was not at its best at present – the mattress on the bed was bare, as the only blankets had been wrapped around Roggit's remains atop the pyre, and the woodbin and water bucket were empty, as Tobas had not paid much attention to the details of everyday life since the catastrophe of Roggit's demise. A few spells that Roggit had cast might still be going here and there, and a few potions or philtres might be tucked away somewhere in the clutter, but no sign of anything magical showed. It looked much like any drab, ordinary cottage.

Still, it was his.

His gaze fell on the Book of Spells and fixed there. That, too, was his. Alone of all Roggit's possessions, that was the one he had never been allowed to touch. The old

11

wizard's sorry handful of semiprecious stones was hidden somewhere in the cottage, hidden even from his own apprentice, but Tobas had been permitted to handle them freely on the occasions when, for one reason or another, they had been brought out. Only the Book had been forbidden.

He stepped over to the reading stand and studied it.

It was a large volume, and thick, bound in hinged tin plates of a dull, dark blue-gray; a single large black rune that Tobas could not identify decorated the front. He knew most of the pages were blank, but Roggit had boasted that it held more than thirty different spells, and Tobas had glimpsed several. This book, he was sure, would be the key to his future.

He hesitated, the force of the old man's prohibition still lingering, but then reached out for the dented metal cover. He was well within his rights, he assured himself, and acting in a perfectly reasonable manner in reading the Book of Spells he had inherited, so that he might teach himself more magic and make a living. It was his now.

He stroked the book gently, as if expecting to feel its magic, but it felt no different from the side of the water bucket. He smiled at his own folly in thinking he might be able to feel the Book's magic – if it even had any of its own. At last, more excited than he cared to admit even to himself, he grasped the worn edge and pried at the heavy tin-coated cover.

Without warning, the black rune on the front exploded loudly and violently in his face, throwing hissing gobbets of orange flame in all directions; none struck him, though one seared away a stray hair as it passed.

Astonished, Tobas simply stepped back at first, staring at the smoldering, blackened face of the Book of Spells. Roggit had, it seemed, put a protective spell of some sort on it to frighten away thieves. Then the scent of smoke reached him, and he realized that the fireballs had not been pure illusion.

Puzzled and dismayed, he looked about; scattered sparks were dying on the hard-packed floor, and one had singed the tabletop, but seemed to be expiring without doing much damage.

Where, then, was the smell of smoke coming from?

He sniffed again, then looked up at a faint crackling sound, and saw that one of the fiery projectiles had set the roof afire, right up near the ridgepole. The dry thatch was already burning vigorously.

On the verge of panic, he spun his head about, looking for some way of extinguishing the blaze before it spread. He had not bothered to fetch water; that meant that he had none on hand to douse the fire, and, by the time he could make a trip to the well, or even the swamp, half the roof might be gone. He snatched up Roggit's old spare tunic from a nearby shelf, but could not reach high enough to beat the fire with it. The large blanket, which might have reached, had been on the old man's pyre.

He clambered atop the table, the tunic wrapped about his forearm; as he reached upward, one of the legs snapped beneath his weight, dumping him roughly back to the floor. He rolled aside, unhurt, then got to his knees, looking for something else he could stand on.

There was nothing. The chairs, he saw instantly, would not be tall enough to help.

He had to do *something*; the cottage was almost all he had. He was a wizard, more or less, yet he felt utterly helpless as he watched the flames, a few feet out of reach, licking at the age-blackened ridgepole.

The sight of the spreading fire spurred him to frantic desperation, and a thought occurred to him. He was a

13

wizard; he knew a spell, just a single spell, and it was a fire spell. Didn't the proverbs say to fight fire with fire?

Quickly, he snatched the dagger from his belt, fumbled in his pouch for brimstone, and flung his spell at the burning thatch.

The resulting explosion dwarfed the first; half the roof vanished in flaming shreds, and the force of the blast knocked Tobas to the floor hard enough to daze him.

When he recovered his wits the whole cottage was ablaze, dripping bits of burning debris on all sides. Panicking, he forgot all concern for his inheritance and for anything except saving his skin; he ran out the door, calling wildly for help.

Chapter 2

He watched disconsolately as the cottage burned. The entire structure was going up in smoke, its complete contents with it, and he could do nothing but sit and watch.

This, he thought sorrowfully, beyond any possible doubt, beyond any chance of recovery or hope of salvage, marked the end of his apprenticeship – *any* sort of apprenticeship. As if his master's death had not been bad enough, taking away the last person in all the World who cared a whit for him, now, just a few hours after the funeral, he had accidentally destroyed everything the old man had left him. His home and all his worldly possessions, save the clothes he wore and the few precious items on his belt, were vanishing before his eyes, being reduced to smoke and ash.

Roggit's Book of Spells was certainly gone, and just as certainly no other wizard would take him on as an apprentice. He was seventeen – what sort of a wizard would take on a lad of seventeen under any conditions, let alone one who had as yet learned so little of the arcane arts? He had learned the basic secret of wizardry, true – that secret was the nature of the athame, the ritual dagger that each wizard prepared and that held a part of its master's soul. Beyond that, though, he knew only his single spell. What could a wizard do with a single spell?

He had little chance of finding any other employment in Telven or the surrounding area; even an advantageous marriage was more than he could hope for, since he had no favors to call in, no close relatives who would help in arranging a betrothal, and no prospects for a love match. He was quite sure that nobody who knew anything of his past would want anything to do with him – especially after this latest disaster – for fear his bad luck might be contagious.

He sighed. He hadn't *always* been unlucky – or at least he hadn't thought so, but now, as he mentally reviewed his life, he wasn't so sure. Certainly it had been a bad sign when his mother died bearing him; that was hardly an auspicious start for any child.

Other than that, however, he had done well enough until he was fifteen. He had been happy with his father's cousin Indamara and her husband, the two of whom had raised him in his parents' absence, and he had gotten on well with their children, his second cousins. He had had no more than the usual number of childhood mishaps – falls from trees every so often, almost drowning in a farmer's pond once – nothing out of the ordinary. He had missed the plague that killed a few of the neighbors when he was eight and had come through a bout of pox unscarred. Life had been good to him throughout those years; he had played in the fields with the other children, taken long walks with his father whenever the ship was in port, and generally lived the normal, happy life of the son of a successful pirate.

Privateer, he corrected himself; his father had been a privateer, defending the Free Lands of the Coasts from the tyranny of the Ethsharites. That was what all the neighbors said.

He had never quite understood how robbing merchant vessels kept the overlords of the Hegemony of Ethshar from reconquering the Free Lands and ruling harshly over them, as they had ruled long ago, but everybody said that it worked, so he had long ago stopped questioning it.

His father had never worried about polite names, never bothered with excuses; to the neighbors' dismay he had insisted on calling himself Dabran the Pirate, rather than Dabran the Privateer, and had told anyone who asked that he was in business to make money, not for the sake of patriotism.

Dabran had been careful with his money, too. That was a major reason his son Tobas was now penniless. The pirate's entire fortune had been aboard his ship, *Retribution*, when he tried to board the wrong vessel and got sent to the bottom of the Southern Sea, along with his whole crew.

From that stroke of monumental bad luck had descended all the rest of Tobas' misfortune. Who would have expected an ordinary Ethsharitic merchant vessel to be carrying a demonologist capable of summoning such a thing? The witnesses on the shore had agreed on very little in their descriptions, save that the thing that pulled Dabran's ship under had been huge, black, and tentacular.

Tobas sighed again. He missed his father. He had never seen much of the old man, even in the best of times, but at least he had known that Dabran was alive, out there somewhere plundering, until the demonologist had brought that thing up out of nowhere.

He tried to cheer himself up by telling himself that it could have been worse. At least he hadn't been on board *Retribution* when she went down. If he had accepted his father's offer of an apprenticeship, in addition to the eventual inheritance of the ship and money, he would have been with Dabran right now, moldering on the bottom of the ocean. His own laziness had saved him there – he had intended to use his inheritance to set himself up in some comfortable business, which he would let employees run, rather than carrying on in his father's rather strenuous trade. He had had no interest in going to sea.

He remembered that awful day when the news of his father's death had arrived. The weather had been horribly inappropriate, a beautiful sunny spring day, the fields warm and green, the sky a perfect blue strewn with fluffy white clouds. He had been lying on the hill behind the house, doing nothing in particular, just lying there enjoying the weather, when his second cousin Peretta had come trudging up looking for him, her hair tangled and her face serious. He had known right away that something was wrong; Peretta was *never* serious and would leave her hair unbrushed only for the direst of emergencies.

She had wasted no time, but simply announced, 'There's bad news from Shan. Your father's dead; a demon got his ship and pulled it under. There were no survivors, and no salvage has been found; it's all gone.'

He had stared at her, he recalled, just stared at her; her words hadn't seemed real. Not until her parents packed up his meager belongings for him and told him to be out by sundown did he really believe that his father was dead and his old life gone. No one would have dared to offend Dabran while he was alive, but when he was gone and no more support money was to come, they were all too eager to be rid of his lazy, worthless son. Family ties don't count for much, compared to silver.

That had hurt. One disaster had come right after another.

Well, he told himself as the flames roared loudly up among the overhanging branches of the swamp trees, at

18

least this would be the last disaster. He had nothing more to lose.

Times had been bad at first after the ship went down, after his cousins threw him out, very bad indeed; he had slept in a few doorways and cornfields and gone without several meals. Old friends had quietly ignored him. He had thought it a great stroke of luck when, just sort of resigning himself to a lifetime career of theft or beggary, he had convinced old Roggit to take him on as an apprentice, despite his age.

Tobas was not quite so certain, as he watched the cottage burn and in its burning destroy his second inheritance, that the apprenticeship had been good luck, after all. He was homeless again, older and with fewer prospects than before.

A particularly bright flame rose up for a moment with an intense crackling, followed by a muffled explosion; Tobas caught an odd smell, one he could not place. The flames must have reached more of old Roggit's combustible supplies, the special sealed boxes he had carefully kept well away from the more ordinary wizardly necessities, such as powdered spider and tannis root.

Tobas frowned slightly. Trivial as such a detail might be in the face of catastrophe, he was irked to realize that now he would never know what all those things had been *for*.

He heard shouts and rattlings and turned to see the fire brigade from the village finally arriving, far too late to do any good, at least half an hour after he had sent his nearest neighbor calling for help. He recognized most of them: old Clurim, who, with his two wives, was the subject of most of the bawdy jokes told in Telven; Faran, the village's only blacksmith and expert on fires of all sorts; and Vengar and Zarek, who had been his compan-

19

ions as children but had avoided him since his father's death. Tobas sighed; they had come too late to do much good. He had long since given up any hope of saving anything beyond the foundation and perhaps the outer walls – and even as he watched the brigade arriving, he could see that the walls were going.

After he had come shouting out the door, had gathered his wits somewhat, and had found that helpful neighbor and sent him puffing off over the hill toward the village, he had struggled briefly with the thoughts of a heroic dash into the inferno. His common sense had quickly prevailed over his daring, however. After all, he told himself, what would he have saved? The Book of Spells would have been almost the first thing to go, since it had been directly beneath where the fire had started, and the only other items whose value he really knew were the athame that hung on his belt and the vial of brimstone in his pouch. Roggit's semiprecious stones would perhaps have been worth retrieving had Tobas known where they were, but the old man had hidden them well.

It occurred to him now, far too late, that a change of clothing and a pair of boots might have been a good idea. The water pail, too, might have been of service in fighting the blaze.

Tobas had to admit that, once they had arrived, the people of Telven had set to willingly enough, filling their buckets from the swamp and flinging the water on to the flames, where it hissed and sizzled with little visible effect. Those who had no buckets, like himself, stood by and watched, admiring the pretty colors that erupted here and there as the old wizard's arcane powders, one by one, fell from their heat-shattered jars and burned away, filling the air with a variety of perfumes and stenches.

For the most part the villagers avoided the old man's

unfortunate apprentice, quietly ignoring him. Tobas was not so insensitive as to miss this, or misinterpret it, and he accepted it as the final proof that the time had come to do what he had been resisting for years. The time had come to leave Telven, leave his native village behind forever, and go out into the wide World to seek his fortune.

He shuddered. What an awful thought!

He had never wanted to leave. He was a homebody, happy with the people and places he knew, with no particular desire to see any others. Telven had been his home. He had always chosen to stay in Telven when his father went off to sea, though time after time, before every voyage from infancy on, Dabran had invited Tobas along. He had stayed in Telven when his father had died, lingering in the village even while homeless, struggling to find a way to remain in the only place he really knew. He had had no career, no steady girlfriend or prospects for marriage, and no close friends, but Telven had still been home. He had succeeded in staying by convincing Roggit that he was still young enough to qualify for apprenticeship.

When he had accomplished that bit of deceit, Tobas had thought that his place was secure and that he would live out his life in his native land. Right up until he had opened the Book of Spells, he had thought he would stay.

Who could have known that the old man had put such powerful protective spells on the thing?

He shook his head in dismay. He still didn't know exactly what he had done wrong or how the protective spell had worked; he had never noticed Roggit speaking any countercharms or doing anything special when he consulted the book. The old man would simply reach over

21

and open it, as he would any other book. Tobas had just tried to do the same.

But the protective spell had obviously been there, and here he was, watching the fire destroy his last link to the village.

All he had ever wanted was a home and a quiet, comfortable life; was that too much to ask of the gods?

The front wall of the house sagged, bent, then crumbled inward with a grinding crash, and Tobas turned away. He had nothing left here, nothing and no one to keep him in Telven, and no way to live if he stayed. It was home no longer. He saw no point in drawing out the ordeal; he trudged off into the gathering twilight, away from the heat and light and sound of the fire, with tears in his eyes that, he told himself firmly, were caused by the smoke.

Chapter 3

The sun was well up the eastern sky when he awoke. His first waking thought was surprise at finding himself curled up in a field of tall grass rather than in his own bed in Roggit's cottage, but he quickly remembered the events of the previous day and night.

After leaving the swamp, he had wandered aimlessly in the dark with no thought to where he was going, until at last he had collapsed and gone to sleep. Now he was awake again, stiff from sleeping awkwardly, utterly dejected over his loss, and still with no idea where to go.

He sat up, the grass rustling beneath him, and rubbed the sleep from his eyes. He tried to think. Where *could* he go? He had no skills that would earn him a living; he was not particularly strong or fast or even handsome. A little thin, just over average height, with ordinary features and dull brown hair and eyes, there was nothing unusual about him at all physically, nothing that would suggest a career. As far as his education was concerned, he had learned the usual basics of reading, writing, and arithmetic and had heard the stories that made up Freelander history and religion; but except for his apprenticeship to Roggit, his learning and experience were nothing in any way special. He had never been more than three leagues from Telven in his life, save for one short voyage his father had taken him on out of Shan on the Sea, along the coast for a few leagues and then back. He knew what little geography every boy in the Free Lands learned, but no more. To the west and south was the ocean, to the north and east was the Hegemony of Ethshar. If one went far enough to the southeast, along the Ethsharitic coast, one reached the semimythical Small Kingdoms that had once been Old Ethshar. If one went far enough north, one reached the barbarian nations. Beyond those, the northern edge of the world was sealed in ice, the eastern edge was burning desert, the west was wrapped in fog, and to the south the ocean went on forever, so far as anyone knew. He had heard descriptions of mountains and forests but had no idea where such things might lie; all he had ever seen were the familiar rolling green hills, graveled beaches, and villages of the Free Lands and the vast empty ocean to the south.

Shan on the Sea, the only real town he knew at all, was less than a day's walk to the southwest. But if he went there, what would he do? A dozen people in Shan knew him as his father's son and would undoubtedly spread the word about his bad luck – or, worse, try and collect on his father's old debts, both real and imaginary. They would know his history, know that he had nothing to offer. He was now far too old to fool anyone into offering him an apprenticeship; even poor, half-blind, sometimes-senile old Roggit had been suspicious about his age. He couldn't go to sea any more than he could take an apprenticeship; he had heard that among Ethsharites a sailor might start as late as age sixteen, and he might have passed for that, but in the Free Lands the captains preferred to start their people young, at twelve or thirteen.

He needed to go somewhere no one would know him, that was obvious. Anywhere in the Free Lands someone might eventually recognize him.

That meant he would have to go to Ethshar. The Hegemony of Ethshar was the only nation sharing borders with the Free Lands.

But how could he do that? The border was dozens of leagues up the coast, he was sure, and such a journey would mean days of walking, days in which he would have to beg for his food or starve. And once across the border, where would he be? In an enemy land! In the wilderness! He knew little of Ethshar but was fairly certain that nothing of importance lay anywhere near the Free Lands.

A league to the south lay the ocean, and every ship sailing the coast of Ethshar passed by here – the survival of Shan and the rest of the Free Lands depended on that fact, since, without the plunder brought home by the privateers, the town would starve. No Ethsharitic ship ever put in at Shan willingly, and no ship sailed from Shan bound for Ethshar, so he could not board a ship in town. But what if he were to intercept one while at sea? He would need a boat of some kind – swimming out to a ship was not practical.

Could he build a boat? He asked himself that question and immediately knew the answer.

No, he could not. He had always intended to live a fat and lazy life on his inheritance, whether his father's gold or his master's spells; he was forced to admit to himself that he barely knew how to hold a hammer.

In that case, he told himself, he would obviously have to find a boat that had already been built and acquire the use of it somehow.

Well, he thought, that sounded simple enough and shouldn't be too difficult. He got to his feet and turned southward, thinking he could already smell the salt of the sea on the gentle breeze that ruffled the grass.

The sun was almost straight overhead when he finally topped the last little rise, a row of dunes, and staggered down on to the beach. A league had never seemed like very much when he had been sitting at home talking or dreaming – three miles, a mere six thousand yards, nothing much – but walking it in the hot sun, with no breakfast, wearing shoddy house sandals rather than boots, had proved to be an exhausting enterprise for one so out of shape as himself. His tunic was soaked with sweat, and he wished that some other garments, in addition to what he wore, had survived the fire. He sat down heavily on the pebbles and stared south, squinting at the blazing midday glare on the waves, his stomach growling. The breeze had died, and the damp, still air did little to cool or dry him.

When he had caught his breath and his eyes had adjusted to the brilliance, he turned and looked first east, then west.

He saw no sign of a boat and sighed heavily. More walking would be needed.

He got slowly to his feet, brushing off his breeches, then paused to choose a direction.

Either way, if he walked far enough, he would eventually reach Ethshar; the Free Lands bordered on nothing but the ocean and the Hegemony. To the west, however, he suspected it would be a good deal farther, and Shan was in the way. Besides, the richest Ethsharitic cities were said to lie to the east.

He turned east and started walking.

He had gone less than a mile when he suddenly stopped again to reconsider. He didn't want to walk to the border; he wanted a boat. Shan's docks were full of boats. For all he knew, though, there wasn't a boat to be had between where he now stood and the nearest Ethsharitic city. He glanced back.

The beach back that way, with his footprints drawing a lonely line across the sandy patches, was too familiar. He couldn't face it. No more looking back, he told himself;

face forward! If he had to walk all the way to Ethshar, he would walk, but surely – if he didn't starve first – he would find a boat eventually. He glanced out to sea.

A sail was visible on the horizon, far to the southwest, but working its way east; apparently a little wind was still moving out on the water, as it was not ashore. An Ethsharitic trader, he guessed, already safely past Shan and its privateers; if he could only reach it, he would be well on his way, but he had no boat as yet. He trudged onward.

Scarcely a hundred yards farther along, as he rounded a dune, he spotted a boat pulled up on the sand some distance ahead. He stopped, astounded by his good fortune.

It was a small boat, without sails or deck so far as he could tell; it was either a rowboat or one intended for magical propulsion. It was the right way up, which was encouraging.

No one was in it, and he could see no one anywhere nearby; a gull cried overhead, startling him, but he saw no people.

He wondered why the boat had been left where it was, untended. He saw no house on the shore above it. Probably, he thought, it was an old wreck, and he had neither the means nor the knowledge to repair it.

Or maybe, it occurred to him, it was propelled and protected by magic, so that its owner could leave it anywhere without needing to worry about it.

Why here, though? He could see nothing that anyone would want on this stretch of sand.

No, it was probably a wreck, or a ship's boat washed overboard in a storm and cast up here.

It was certainly worth investigating. He tried to work up some enthusiasm, breaking into an awkward trot –

awkward because his feet hurt from their unaccustomed efforts, and because the battered sandals were not meant for such use.

As he neared the boat, his hopes rose steadily; by the time he reached it, he was actually cheerful. His luck had obviously changed. The little craft looked quite intact indeed, more than adequate to get him out to sea, where he might still catch that trader he had spotted. The boat was even partially equipped; a sound pair of oars was neatly tucked under the thwarts, and a canvas sack of some sort was wedged into the stern. He could still see no one around who might be the owner. If there were any magical protections on it, of course, he might not be able to use it. In that case, he might need to rely on his status as a fellow wizard to avoid trouble – assuming the owner was a wizard, and not a witch or a priest or a demonologist or one of the mysterious new warlocks or some other sort of magician.

His heart suddenly plunged into the pit of his belly. The owner – no, owners – had not vanished without a trace and left him their boat, after all. The lines of footprints wound their way across the beach and up the nearest dune.

Something looked odd about those footprints, however. He stared at them, puzzling.

One set was large and deep, the other smaller and shallower. They were very close together; not on top of each other, as they would be had one person followed the other, but very close to each other and exactly parallel. Not straight, by any means; they wove back and forth like a snake's spine. In two spots the lines were broken by a small trampled area.

Tobas stared, and realization came to him, accompanied by a slow smile. He knew why these two people

28

had pulled up on this lonely stretch of sandy beach, so far from anywhere in the middle of the day, and why they had walked up over the dune, leaving the boat unguarded. People in love did foolish things – that well-known fact was why most people avoided romance and married for comfort and money. These two had probably had their arms about each other, accounting for how close their steps were to each other's, and the trampled areas were undoubtedly where they had paused to kiss, an appetizer to the main course that was surely under way somewhere in the dunes, inaudible over the hiss of the surf. An open boat, he imagined, would be too crowded and too unsteady a place.

They might return at any moment, though. Hurriedly, he shoved the boat down into the water. The keel scraped heavily over the sand, then floated free on an incoming wave. Tobas pushed it out until he stood knee-deep in the surf, then grabbed the gunwale and steadied it.

He was just clambering in when a bearded, black-haired head appeared above the dune where the foot-prints had led.

'Hey!' the man called, plainly upset by what he saw.

The woman's head appeared beside him.

Tobas ignored them both and yanked the oars from their stowage.

'Hey, that's our boat!' the man called. He was clamber-ing up the dune now, tugging his sandy tunic into place.

Tobas got the oars into the oarlocks, splashed their blades into the water, leaned forward, and pulled, refus-ing to worry about any damage he might do if the oar blades caught on rocks hidden in the sand.

The boat slewed out into the water, and Tobas pulled harder on one side, turning the bow out to sea. Each stroke moved him visibly farther from shore; the bottom

29

dropped off quickly, so that, by the third or fourth pull, the oars were no longer in danger of striking sand.

'Come back!' the woman cried, running down the beach toward him. 'Come back with our boat!'

Tobas found himself facing her as the boat swung around. He smiled at her as she stopped at the water's edge, already several yards away; she was very young, surely not yet eighteen, perhaps younger than himself, and handsome despite her rumpled brown hair and sandy, disheveled skirt and tunic.

'I'm sorry,' he called out. 'But it's an emergency. I'll bring it back if I can!' A twinge of guilt struck him. Teasing young lovers was a long-standing tradition in Telven, but stealing their boat might have serious consequences. 'Listen,' he called. 'If you go a mile west, then a league due north, you'll reach the village of Telven; they'll help you there! Tell them T – ' He stopped, hesitant to give his right name, but then shrugged and went on. 'Tell them Tobas the apprentice wizard sent you!'

'But . . . our boat!' the woman cried, ankle-deep in the foaming water. The man stood beside her, knuckles on his hips, glaring silently at Tobas' receding figure.

'I'm sorry,' Tobas repeated, 'but I need it more than you do!' That said, he devoted his entire attention to rowing and paid no more attention to the boat's rightful owners. He had a ship to catch.

Chapter 4

What little wind there was came from the northeast, helping Tobas along and hindering the ship he sought to intercept. He quickly found himself well out at sea, the coastline a vague blur in the distance. He glanced back over his shoulder and caught sight of the sail, far off his starboard bow; the ship was still hull-down on the horizon.

He looked back at the fading land again, and his nerve failed him. If the wind shifted, or if the ship decided to gain more sea room by running south, he would have no chance of catching it, and he dared not lose sight of the land completely. He was no navigator; he might be lost at sea. Generally, of course, he could find east and west by the sun, and he knew that the land was to the north, but there might be clouds, or a current might carry him west into the endless western ocean that extended from the south edge of the World to the north, uninterrupted by land. He looked at the sail, decided that it was, in fact, coming closer, and pulled the dripping oars inboard. He would wait. Why tire himself out and go farther out than was safe or necessary?

After a moment of sitting quietly, hearing only the faint slapping of the waves against the sides of his boat and the water dripping from the oars into the bottom, he remembered the canvas sack in the stern. This, he decided, would be an ideal time to see what was in it. Moving very carefully – he was out well past the breakers, but the sea was still rolling the boat gently, and he did not care to capsize it – he pulled the bag out and opened it.

A wonderful aroma wafted out at him as he peered inside, and he wasted no time in pulling out its source – half a roasted chicken. It was cold, to be sure, but he was hungry enough that he would hardly have hesitated were it raw.

As he gnawed on the drumstick, he explored further and hauled out a loaf of sweet golden bread, a bottle of cheap red wine, and an assortment of fruits.

He felt he was with the gods in Heaven as he poured the wine down his throat, close behind a good-sized chunk of chicken.

He devoured almost the entire meal, obviously intended for two, in short order, despite warning twinges from his stomach. At last he settled back as best he could and let his food settle.

It didn't; he had eaten too much too fast after too long without, and his belly ached. The boat's motion did not help at all. His conscience, too, was uncomfortable. He had stolen the boat and the food from the couple on the beach; he was a thief.

'Serves them right, losing their dinner,' he said aloud in a feeble attempt to laugh away his guilt. 'Imagine bringing *red* wine with cold chicken!'

He didn't laugh at his joke. It had been Indamara who had taught him that one should drink white wine with poultry – his father's cousin, the woman who had largely raised him and who had thrown him out as soon as Dabran was dead. She had also taught him not to steal, or at any rate had tried to, and he had never before stolen anything more than a few ripe apples from a neighbor's tree.

He had once brought up the question of theft when

32

talking with his father. After all, Dabran had made his living stealing.

'Piracy at sea is a special case,' Dabran had said. 'We rob merchants who are fool enough to sail around the peninsula close in. They know we're here; if they risk sailing our waters anyway, then they deserve what they get. They have plenty of money to begin with, or they'd not be fitting out ships and loading them with cargo, but they try to make more by sailing their goods through dangerous waters; that makes them greedy fools who deserve to be robbed. That's not the same as taking something from someone weaker than you who was minding his own business, or sneaking about in the night, stealing. We do our taking out in the open and we risk as much as they do. That makes it not so much theft as gambling, and I'll defend to the death a man's right to gamble away whatever he's got – even his life.'

Tobas had never been sure he accepted this justification entirely, but he agreed that a man had a right to gamble with what was his. Well, Dabran had gambled and lost his life, sure enough, and his son had turned thief as a result, stealing a boat and a picnic dinner from an innocent pair of lovers. Tobas quoted one of his father's axioms to himself as comfort. 'A man has a right to do anything that will keep him alive.'

He still felt rotten and wished the Ethsharitic ship would come pick him up so that he could let the boat go. It might yet wash up on the shore where the lovers could salvage it, minus the chicken dinner.

He looked around; the ship was definitely nearer now, its sleek, streamlined hull visible beneath a great panoply of sails, but still a long way off. He settled back, his head on a thwart that dug in uncomfortably, hands clutching his belly, and wished that he could convince himself that

33

everything that had happened since he turned twelve was a bad dream.

The next thing he knew he was being rudely shaken awake; his exhaustion had caught up with him once he had stopped moving and no longer had his hunger keeping him awake.

'Who are you?' demanded a deep, oddly accented voice.

'Tobas,' he said. 'Tobas of . . . of Harbek.'

'Harbek?'

'In the Small Kingdoms.'

'Never heard of it.'

Tobas could think of no answer to that, since he had made the name up on the spur of the moment, assuming, foolishly, that the questioner would know no more about the Small Kingdoms than he did. He looked up blankly at a broad, sunburned face surrounded by thick black hair and beard.

'What are you doing here?' the man demanded.

'Uh . . .' Tobas was not yet sure just where he was.

'Oh, never mind; come aboard, and the captain can ask you the questions.' He pulled Tobas to his feet and half led, half dragged him across his little stolen boat to the side of the Ethsharitic ship, where several hands reached down to haul him up over the rail on to the deck.

It was a shock, somehow, to see that the ship's deck bore very little resemblance to what he remembered of *Retribution*, his father's lost ship. *Retribution* had been built for speed and for fighting, long and narrow, with rope catwalks and platforms from which archers could fire and boarders could leap down on to the enemy; this ship was fat so as to cram in as much cargo as possible and, instead of platforms and walkways, it had nettings hung along the sides to make boarding more difficult. Several immense hatchways took up a large part of the deck, and much of the tackle on the spars overhead had nothing to do with the sails, being intended rather for use as cranes in loading and unloading. Furthermore, the deck was not one continuous surface, but in three sections, with bow and stern higher than amidships.

Half a dozen burly, blue-kilted sailors surrounded him; what he saw of the ship he saw in glimpses between shoulders or under arms. They smelled of sweat. 'This way,' one of them announced, jerking a thumb in the direction of the stern; he, too, spoke with a heavy accent.

Tobas followed silently and was escorted into a large, luxurious cabin hung with silken draperies and heavily carpeted, where a sweet scent Tobas did not recognize hung in the air. A plump, balding, red-clad man sat behind an ornate desk, two sailors standing on his right and a slender, white-gowned woman on his left. The woman stared at Tobas intently; the seated man's gaze was less intense, while the sailors almost ignored him.

'If this is a pirate trick,' the seated man announced in the same odd accent the sailors had, 'we'll make very sure you die before anyone can save you.'

'It's no trick,' Tobas said. He had had a moment to think as he was brought here. 'My name is Tobas of Harbek; I was accompanying my master to Tintallion when our ship was rammed by a privateer out of Shan. When she heeled over, I was thrown clear and found the boat; I didn't see any other survivors. The privateersmen didn't notice me, I guess.'

'Privateer?'

Tobas, thinking back over the conversation, suddenly realized his error. 'Pirates, I mean; my master used to call them privateers.' In the Free Lands they were considered privateers, whatever Dabran might have said, and Tobas had long ago acquired the habit of using the polite term with strangers and the more accurate description with his family. Among Ethsharites, though, it appeared they were known as pirates.

'Who was this master?'

'Roggit the Wizard,' Tobas replied boldly. That was true enough.

The red-clad man glanced at the woman, then drummed the ringed fingers of one hand on the desk. 'What ship?'

'*Dawn's Pride*,' Tobas improvised quickly.

'And?'

Puzzled, Tobas said, 'And what?'

'Where did she sail from, boy, and where was she bound?'

'Oh! Out of Harbek, bound for Tintallion.'

'Where's Harbek?'

'In the Small Kingdoms.'

'I gathered that, boy; *where* in the Small Kingdoms?'

'Ah . . . in the south?' He wished he had given a different origin; he knew almost nothing about the Small Kingdoms.

The man stared at him for a long moment, then leaned forward, elbows on the desk, and announced, 'I never heard of your master, your ship, or your homeland, boy, and no ship from the Kingdoms has any business sailing past Ethshar of the Sands, let alone so far as Tintallion, but I won't call you a liar yet; some fool from some worthless little corner of the south might just have tried it. Let me suggest a possibility, though. Suppose that a lad in the Pirate Towns wanted to seek his fortune – and in a wider world than his one little corner. He might want to get on board a ship bound for one of the Ethshars. If he managed it, he'd have to account for himself once he was on board. Knowing little of the outside world, he

36

would make up a story as best he could, rather than admit to being one of the Hegemony's enemies, but he wouldn't do a very convincing job of it. He wouldn't even realize that he was speaking Ethsharitic with the accent of the Pirate Towns, which is nothing like anything spoken in the Small Kingdoms, not even where they think they're speaking our tongue rather than one of their own strange languages. I think he'd look and sound a lot like you, Tobas of Harbek, who claims to be a wizard's apprentice.'

'I *am* a wizard's apprentice – or I was. My master is dead.'

'And the rest of it?'

'Uh . . .' Tobas fell silent.

'You had a good pair of oars in that boat, they tell me, and you look fit; why didn't you row for shore?'

'Uh . . .'

'You wanted to get aboard this ship, didn't you?'

'Yes,' Tobas admitted after a moment's hesitation, seeing no alternative.

'I thought so. And I don't think it's because you were afraid of what the Pirate Towners would do to you, either, not with that accent you have.' He sat back and looked up at Tobas, his hands pressed together before his chest. 'Well,' he continued. 'Wherever you're from, I'd guess you're pretty much alone in the world or you wouldn't be here; and whoever you are, I don't mind letting you work your passage to Ethshar of the Sands, or even Ethshar of the Spices. You will work, though. The overlords have decreed that castaways and refugees are to receive free passage; and if I'm wrong about you, you can go and complain to old Ederd the Fourth when we reach Ethshar of the Sands, but until then you'll work. If you don't, we'll put you back in that boat we found you in. Fair enough?'

Tobas nodded mute agreement and did not dare to ask for an explanation of the difference between Ethshar of the Sands and Ethshar of the Spices or who Ederd IV might be.

He allowed himself to be led meekly away and assigned a hammock. He was on his way to the galley to help the cook with the crew's dinner when it finally sank in that he had made it, despite the failure of his concocted story. They were not going to hang him as a pirate, nor throw him back in the sea. He was on his way to Ethshar to seek his fortune and find a new home!

He smiled. His bad luck was obviously past. He had needed a ship and here he was on a ship. He had needed a boat to reach the ship and he had found one.

Then he remembered that he had stolen the boat, which the ship's crew had hauled aboard and lashed down on deck, and the smile faded. Some day, he promised himself, when he was rich and powerful, he would pay those two lovers back for their boat and for the trouble he had put them through.

And for the chicken, too, while he was at it.

Chapter 5

The first port of call was Ethshar of the Sands, and at the sight of the city Tobas, already unsettled by the strange, flat landscape they had been sailing past, lost his nerve completely. He had not realized that a city could be so large. He had known Telven wasn't much, but he had thought that Shan on the Sea was a good-sized town, with a population he guessed at a thousand or more.

The entire population of Shan on the Sea could be lost without a trace in Ethshar of the Sands.

Tobas had first begun to have misgivings when they left the familiar hills and patchy beaches behind, passing league after league of almost featureless flat coastline, flat as a calm sea, an endless plain of sand and grass. He had not realized that land could be so flat; never before had he seen any sort of terrain but the gentle hills and graveled beaches of his homeland.

And when he glimpsed the Great Lighthouse in the distance, even before he realized its actual size, that did not help at all; the single huge tower thrusting up from this strange, level world had seemed almost threateningly out of place. As the ship drew nearer and the palace dome appeared, followed by the endless expanse of red-tiled roofs, his uncertainty grew steadily. Row after row of buildings lined the sandy shores, leagues of them, it seemed, as the ship worked its way up The Channel, past the Outer Towers, past the Outer Docks, past the Inner Towers, and into Seagate Harbor.

The city even smelled strange; an odd, hot scent

reached the ship, compounded of smoke, fish, and tight-packed humanity as well as other things he could not identify. No place in the Free Lands had smelled like that.

He stood at the rail, fending pole in his hands, and stared in dumbfoundment. How could there be enough people in all the world to fill so many buildings? What did they all do? Where did their food come from, with no farmland inside the walls?

A fishing boat drifted uncomfortably near, and the next man aft from Tobas fended it off, then cursed the Telvener roundly for his negligence. Tobas woke up enough to turn his eyes from the shore to the surrounding water, but even that was mind-boggling; more shipping was crowded into this one harbor, he was sure, than could be found in all the Free Lands of the Coasts put together.

It was all too much for him, and when the ship was safely docked and the captain called for all who were going ashore, he remained where he was, hanging on to the rail and staring at the bustling streets.

A few moments later, the captain – Tobas had learned two days out that the captain's name was Istram and the ship's was *Golden Gull*, but he still thought of the man simply as 'the captain' and the vessel simply as 'the ship' – came up behind him and asked, without preamble, 'Aren't you leaving the ship?'

Tobas jumped. 'Ah . . . no,' he said. 'I think I'll stay on, if you don't mind.'

The captain shrugged. 'An extra hand is welcome – if you pull your weight. You weren't much use with that pole coming into port, and you have yet to show me any of the magic you claim to know.'

'It's all fire magic,' Tobas explained defensively, his hand falling to the hilt of his athame. 'What use is that on a ship?' He had settled on this explanation when taunted by the crew and had gone so far as to use his single spell to ignite his worst tormentor's bedding to prove his ability. After that, no one had bothered him, but apparently word had not reached the captain. 'I've been lighting the galley fires, but what else can I do?'

'We don't need a wizard to light fires!' Istram said scornfully.

'I'm not asking for a wizard's pay!' Tobas retorted quickly.

The captain smiled. 'Good, because you wouldn't get it. You haven't even earned the boots we gave you or the food you've eaten. I'm a kind man, though, so if you want to stay aboard, you may; our next port is Ethshar of the Spices, if you care to leave us there; after that, it depends on what cargo we can get – probably we'll head back west.'

Tobas nodded. 'Thank you, sir.' He glanced down at the boots just mentioned, which had been donated by a lad in the crew who had outgrown them. The captain was right; he hadn't really done enough work yet to earn them.

He sighed; he was a long way from the rich, easy life he wanted.

They were two days in port, unloading roughly half the cargo of furs, oils, and other goods and replacing it with freshly slaughtered beef – and a warlock, whose magic would keep the meat cool and prevent spoilage. There was enough lifting, hauling on ropes, and general hard labor involved that, by the time the ship was loaded full again, Tobas felt he had earned a cobbler's entire shop. Once or twice he gave serious thought to deserting – or rather, since he had never formally signed on, leaving – but the sight and sound and smell of the crowded streets were still enough to deter him. Ethshar of the Sands was terrifying in its immensity and alienness; Ethshar of the Spices might not be.

He also remained on board in hopes of getting to know the warlock and perhaps even learning a little of this strange new school of magic that required none of the rituals and paraphernalia of wizardry. After all, a career in any sort of magic might well be profitable; simply because he had been initiated into the Wizards' Guild, he saw no reason not to pursue studies in the other varieties of arcane skill.

Of course, the ship had had another magician aboard all along; the white-robed woman who had stood beside the captain when Tobas first came aboard was a priestess, an expert theurgist, Tobas had learned, and was the magician charged with defending the vessel against pirates or other perils.

Theurgy, however, was not a form of magic that appealed to Tobas, since he understood it to call for a great deal of hard study and abstinence from many of life's little pleasures, while still being less than perfectly reliable and predictable in its effects. Besides, the priestess refused to associate with anyone aboard other than the captain.

Tobas thought warlockry sounded far more appealing.

However, one sight of the warlock's dark and forbidding face convinced him not to press the issue. This was obviously not a person eager to make friends.

No one else seemed to know the warlock any better than Tobas did; even Captain Istram, who treated the theurgist as just another crew member, seemed slightly wary of him. As with the priestess, no one spoke of him by name; he was simply the warlock. Tobas was not entirely sure he *had* a name; for all he knew, warlocks were not even human.

This warlock slept in a hammock slung down in the hold, close to the meat he was there to preserve; he had his meals brought to him there. As the cook's assistant, Tobas was responsible for their delivery.

Once settled in his place, the warlock spoke to no one; he accepted his meals in silence and never emerged from the hold for any reason. Tobas guessed that maintaining the spell – for the hold was always very definitely chilly, despite the summer sun glaring on the sea on every side – took all his concentration and energy.

The journey passed uneventfully, for the most part, and Tobas was reasonably content with his lot. He was fed and housed. His clothing left something to be desired, as he still had only the one outfit, but he was able to wash it twice a sixnight in the communal tub.

Still, shipboard life, with its crowding, hard work, and poor food, was far from his idea of the ideal life, and *Golden Gull* would never be home.

On the last night of the voyage, after the ship had rounded the great peninsula and begun beating its way northwestward up the Gulf of the East, the entire crew was awakened by the warlock screaming as if he were being gruesomely murdered, perhaps skinned alive, or, one imaginative crewman suggested, eaten by rats. Tobas, as the one who had the most contact with him and the purported magician in their midst, was selected by acclamation to go and investigate.

The screams had stopped by the time he made his way down into the hold. He stood at the foot of the ladder for a moment, his lantern flickering, before he found the nerve to go on.

The candle in the lantern had not been very well lit or

was perhaps clogged with wax; he considered using Thrindle's Combustion to brighten it, but, upon remembering the explosion in Roggit's cottage, decided against it. Using the spell on something already burning was dangerous, and he had no intention of blowing even this feeble flame out while he stood surrounded by unknown horrors.

When he finally gathered his courage and made his way back to the meat storage area, he found the warlock sitting up in his hammock, leaning back against the bulkhead with his head in his hands. His long, thin legs thrust up pale bare knees that gleamed white as bone in the lantern light; his elbows rested upon his knees, and his face upon trembling fingers.

'Sir?' Tobas ventured, trying to keep his voice and hands steady despite his terror and the unnatural chill in the air.

The warlock looked up. 'My apologies if I disturbed you, child. I had an unpleasant dream.' His voice was deep and mellow, and he spoke with an accent very slightly different from the Ethsharitic of the crew.

Tobas could not believe he had heard the warlock's words correctly. 'A dream? Just a dream?'

The warlock smiled bitterly. 'Yes, just a dream. A drawback of my craft, child – warlocks are prone to nightmares of a very special variety. They arrive when we attempt to overextend our abilities, as I have on this journey, and they can lead to . . . well, we do not know what they lead to, but warlocks for whom the nightmares have become a regular occurrence tend to disappear. I may well have doomed myself for the sake of fresh meat for the aristocrats of Ethshar of the Spices. Don't let it concern you – it's not your problem. Go back to sleep. I promise that *I* will not sleep, and that you need fear no further disturbance.'

44

This was by far the longest speech anyone on board had ever heard the warlock make and Tobas was almost overwhelmed by it, but curiosity stirred; after a few seconds' hesitation he asked, 'Do they always come again, these nightmares, if you've had them once?'

'I wish I knew,' the warlock replied. 'This is the first time I have had them in any strength since the Night of Madness in 5202, when warlockry first came to the World – before you were born, I'm sure.' His smile twisted. 'I never needed an apprenticeship, child; the gods, or demons, or whatever power it was that brought us our craft gave it to me whole, when I was a boy. Had you been born, you might have received it yourself, even in the cradle – you might well have been carried away by the dreams yourself by now. You were born too late, fortunately. I was not. Go, now – dream your own harmless little dreams and leave me to mine.'

Tobas obeyed, backing out to the ladder and departing the hold, glad to get away from the cool air, the smell of the hanging meat, and the warlock's pale, haggard face.

There were no further disturbances, as the warlock had promised, but Tobas was quite convinced now, as he settled back in his hammock, that he would not be pursuing warlockry as a career, whatever happened. He would stick to wizardry; it seemed much safer, despite the occasional risk of spells backfiring or getting out of hand, as the combination of the protective rune and Thrindle's Combustion had. He was, after all, already an initiate into the art, with his ritual dagger prepared and charged – a member, however minor, of the mighty Wizards' Guild. All he had to do was learn more spells in order to be a real wizard; becoming a warlock apparently involved a good many mysteries and dangers of its own that he had never heard of before, and he did not care to investigate them further.

He was also now convinced that he was having a real, genuine adventure, of the sort stories are told about. Telven had had no excitement to compare to screaming warlocks or cities like Ethshar of the Sands, and the busy, crowded life of the ship was far more interesting than life on the village farms. Not *better*, but more interesting.

Not, he reminded himself, that he wanted to spend his whole life at sea or go about having adventures; that was not the way to become rich and reach a comfortable old age. Storytellers' heroes notwithstanding, adventures were dangerous things that could easily get a person killed. At Ethshar of the Spices, he promised himself, he would go ashore and look for an easier, safer, and more promising career. He knew he would not be able to get another wizard to take him on as an apprentice, but perhaps he could somehow pay one to teach him a few more spells. That would be all he needed to begin a quiet career in wizardry. Once he had earned a little money, he would find himself a home somewhere.

With that thought, he fell asleep.

In the morning, when he came up on deck after cleaning the breakfast dishes, he almost changed his mind.

Ethshar of the Spices was, if anything, even bigger than Ethshar of the Sands. The coastline here was fairly clear-cut and rocky, and the land comfortably hilly and broken, rather than an eerie dead-flat expanse of sand jutting out into a maze of sandbars, as the land around Ethshar of the Sands had been, but once again the city covered at least a league of the shore. And although no Great Lighthouse towered above everything else, no palace dome soared to incredible heights, and no towers guarded the harbor, the city was, in general, built taller than

Ethshar of the Sands. There, save for the great civic structures, nothing had been higher than three stories, at most; here, four and even five stories were commonplace. Instead of a single immense lighthouse, there were two smaller ones; instead of harbor towers, Tobas glimpsed immense guard towers in the city wall; instead of a palace dome, he saw warehouses, tenements, and shops jammed together in truly unbelievable numbers. The waterfront in Ethshar of the Sands had been awesome, but almost two-dimensional; the mere length of it had been daunting. Here the length was just as great, and the slope of the land allowed him to see depth as well; the city reached well inland, covering hills and ridges as well as the waterfront.

And the smell that reached his nose was even less familiar than what he had encountered at Ethshar of the Sands; smoke and crowded streets mingled here with spices and a strange mustiness, as if the entire city were perfumed to hide underlying mildew.

Still, he told himself, he had to get off the ship eventually. And the captain had said the next journey would probably be back around the peninsula and westward again; this was, therefore, probably as far east as he could get on this vessel. If he stayed aboard, he would merely be retracing his steps and he had no desire to do that.

The Small Kingdoms, the sailors had told him, were just the other side of the Gulf, and beyond them lay the eastern and southern edges of the World; surely he would find no better spot to make his fortune out there than he would here in this city of wonders, on its reassuringly familiar, hilly terrain. A city of this size would certainly be fraught with wizards, and he needed only to find one who would part with a few spells. Once he knew a reasonable amount of magic, he was sure he could establish himself in business and make himself a new home – perhaps not in Ethshar of the Spices, but somewhere.

With that in mind, once the ship was securely tied up at Long Wharf – which the sailors told him was in the Shiphaven district of the city, for whatever that might signify – he wrote a quick note to the captain explaining that he had stolen his boat and describing as best he could its proper owners, so that the captain might, if the whim took him, return it. That done, he gathered up his belongings, took a deep breath, and walked down the gangplank, leaving Istram's *Golden Gull* behind forever.

Chapter 6

Long Wharf, Tobas discovered, was indeed very long; it wound its way in from the deep waters of the Gulf, across the shallows and rocks around the western lighthouse, and split into two diverging causeways just short of the high-water mark. He chose the more traveled route and turned left, toward the southeast.

The smell of the sea and the constant splashing of wavelets against the stone piers were quickly buried beneath the thick odor and steady clatter of the city. Ethshar's smell was compounded of fish cooking over charcoal in a thousand kitchens, the wood of a thousand homes slowly decaying in the harbor's damp air, and a myriad of other human activities, leavened with spices and the perfumes that gave it a strange and exotic tang, and blessedly free of the outhouse aroma that clung to most human settlements; the city boasted an efficient sewer system.

The causeway Tobas followed curved to the east and quickly became a street along the water's edge, lined with shops and taverns and brothels on the right and open to the sea on the left, with an occasional dock or wharf jutting out into the water; he wandered along aimlessly at first, taking in the sights, sounds, and smells.

The brothels caught his eye immediately; where the shops and taverns relied on signboards and window displays to attract customers, the handful of brothels, although they also had signboards, were distinguished by balconies above the doors, where comely young women –

49

and sometimes young men as well – leaned over railings, occasionally calling suggestions to potential customers. They wore attire not quite like anything Tobas had seen before – tunics cut low across the breast, skirts that clung to the hip enticingly, hems cut at a slant to display one ankle – all of expensive-looking fabrics, soft and shiny, or filmy, or glittering with golden threads.

Telven had no brothels. Although Tobas had heard that Shan on the Sea had half a dozen, he had never come across them in his few brief visits there. He had never given such establishments much thought before, but here they were hard for a newcomer like himself to ignore. Some of the women were very tempting – but of course he had no money.

He noticed, also, that some of the women were older than they had appeared at first glance and that no customers were to be seen going in or out; business was obviously not good.

By the time Tobas paused to consider his destination, he had lost sight of everyone he knew from aboard ship. Overawed as he was by the city's unfamiliarity, he could not bring himself to ask passing strangers for advice. Even strangers were in fairly short supply; this was obviously not a thriving neighborhood. Most of the spaces at the docks were unoccupied, and maintenance of the port facilities was clearly not what it should be. He wondered whether the actions of privateers back in the Free Lands had anything to do with the empty slips and shuttered shops – had trade suffered that much from their depredations?

He shivered. If the pirates were to blame and anyone here recognized him as a Freelander, his life would probably be short and unpleasant.

He considered going back to the last brothel and asking

the women on the balcony for directions, but could not quite get up the nerve. Instead, when he came to a particularly large wharf that did not seem as badly decayed as the others, he turned right, on to the street leading directly inland from the docks. He did not care to stay on the waterfront, under the circumstances; sailors would be far more likely to recognize his accent, if they heard it, and to do something about it, than would people who remained safely ashore.

He walked silently along two long blocks lined with warehouses and shipfitters' shops, marveling at the size and splendor – and age! – of the buildings and at how very straight the street was, then found himself emerging into a market square.

Unlike the waterfront shops, the market was far from deserted; shipping might be poor but the difficulties did not appear to have reached two blocks inland as yet. Knots of men – and a sprinkling of women and children – were scattered thickly across the hard-packed ground, and the air around him was awash in their conversation, as loud and constant as a heavy sea breaking on rocks. A good many wore the blue kilts of sailors, and most of the others had on tunics and breeches no different from the everyday garb in Shan on the Sea, but a few were clad in strange and fantastical gowns, robes, jewels, furs, odd caps, or leather harness. Tobas was not sure what to make of these.

A strong smell of spices hung over everything, more heavily than in the streets he had previously traveled, though he could find no source for it; he guessed it came from the surrounding warehouses.

He saw relatively few booths or carts displaying goods, and those which he did see held not grains and produce, as he was accustomed to finding in markets, but rope samples, ironmongery, candles, or other hard goods, generally of varieties that would be useful aboard ship.

Most of the market, however, was taken up with people clustered about individuals with no visible goods at all. Some of these stood on boxes or stools; others made do with the ground.

Curious, Tobas stepped up to the back of one group, composed mostly of sailors, and listened.

'. . . further, you need have no fear of passing the Pirate Towns!' the man was saying, 'because we will have aboard not one, but two magicians of the first order – the incomparable Kolgar of Yolder, wizard, and Artalda the Fair, warlock! Either one of these mighty enchanters can easily defend the ship against the best the pirates can throw against us, and they will be sleeping in alternate shifts, so that at no time can our vessel be caught by surprise! A minimum of risk for a maximum of gain – all the wealth of Tintallion there for the taking! Who among you will sign aboard the *Crimson Star* for this voyage?'

'Where's her old crew?' one aging sailor demanded.

'Ah, my friend,' the recruiter replied, 'you haven't been listening! The *Crimson Star* is a new vessel, fresh from the shipyards!' He waved a hand toward the west, which Tobas assumed to be the direction wherein lay the shipyards. 'Who will sign?'

The old sailor turned away and saw Tobas at the outside of the crowd. 'Don't listen to him, lad,' he said. 'Tintallion's a cold and miserable place and no richer than we are here.' He stalked off.

Tobas had had no intention of signing up for a journey to Tintallion; he, too, turned away, but only to move on to the next group.

That group was listening to a similar harangue; this recruiter claimed he needed only three skilled sailors to replace men lost in a storm. The third was different – a soldier in a yellow tunic and red kilt was announcing, in a loud but bored and monotonous voice, various recent decisions of the city's overlord, Azrad VII, that would affect the shipping industry.

The fourth group centered around a young woman in a flowing gown of white velvet, the hem spattered with mud; her hair was bound up in a manner Tobas had never seen before, held in place with jeweled clasps. She claimed to be a princess, apparently, and sought brave young men to restore her to her rightful inheritance in some place called Mezgalon, whence she had been driven by treachery and violence. Tobas stared in fascination; he had never seen a princess before. Her story sounded much like some of the more lurid tales he and Peretta had heard as children at her mother's knee; he found it hard to take the woman seriously.

For one thing, quite aside from the difference he had always assumed to exist between fiction and reality, this princess did not quite fit the mental image he had always had of princesses; despite her finery, she was plain-faced and flat-chested, with an unpleasantly nasal voice and a singularly ugly accent. Some of the whores on the waterfront had looked more like the traditional storytellers' description of a princess.

Well, Tobas told himself, not *all* princesses can be beautiful, can they?

It seemed very odd to be in a place where anyone could even *claim* to be a princess; he wondered if perhaps some of the old stories he had taken for mere tales were truer than he had thought and seemed like fantasy to a Telvener only because Telven was an exceptionally dull part of the World.

Tobas moved on, intrigued by the idea that there might

53

be far more to the World than he had realized. Perhaps, he thought, he would find an opportunity here that would be better than trying to make a living off wizardry. It seemed unlikely, but it might be possible.

The next group was again recruiting for a ship, and the one after that hiring miners to work in the diamond mines of Tazmor; Tobas began to lose interest. This was all very well, but none of it was getting him anywhere. These job opportunities were not what he wanted, and he berated himself for his momentary foolishness in thinking he might find anything worthwhile here. He had no money, no food, no place to sleep, and the afternoon was already on the wane; he had done nothing about learning more spells. If he really wanted to, he could come back here later; right now, though, he had more urgent matters to attend to.

What could he do, though? He had not thought this out in advance. He cursed himself for wasting all the time aboard ship that he could have spent thinking and planning for every eventuality.

He had no money, so he could get no food or shelter save by stealing or by selling something. He had nothing to sell save himself and his single spell, and he was not yet desperate enough to sell himself into slavery – nowhere *near* it! – and could not imagine why anyone in this vast and wealthy city would want fires lit by magic. He might find work of some sort – would have to, he supposed – but all the recruiters in this particular market appeared to be hiring for work outside the city, usually dangerous or unpleasant, and he was not yet ready to leave the city, nor desperate enough to sign up for anything that might get him killed. He would prefer to learn more spells, somehow, and become a proper wizard. To learn more spells he needed a teacher, and surely, if there were wizards anywhere in the world, there would be wizards in Ethshar of the Spices!

And that brought him to his one feeble hope of establishing himself without immediately having to undertake any hazardous or strenuous work. He could appeal to his Guild brothers, tell them his tragic tale, and hope that they could spare him enough to keep him alive until he could find a worthwhile position.

They might even teach him more spells at no charge.

First, though, he had to find them. Gathering up all his nerve, he tugged at the sleeve of a man listening in amusement to a particularly incoherent speaker.

'Excuse me, sir,' Tobas said when the Ethsharite turned, 'but I'm newly arrived . . . ah, from Tintallion. Could you tell me where I might find a wizard?'

'Wizard Street, I suppose.' The man stared at Tobas' rather worn and dirty clothes with obvious disdain.

'Of course, sir, I should have realized. Ah . . . how do I get there from here?'

The Ethsharite smiled unpleasantly. 'I'll be damned if I know,' he said. 'That's not my part of town. The Wizards' Quarter is all the way across the city, down by Southgate.' He pointed in a vaguely southeasterly direction.

Tobas thanked him and looked about.

Seven streets radiated from the marketplace: three to the north, one each east and west, one to the southwest, and one to the southeast. He chose the last and began walking.

After half a dozen long blocks of shops, tenements, and warehouses, he found himself in another market, this one a long, narrow triangle pointing to the south, with its eastern side open to a canal. This market was more traditional than the other; piles of goods were on display on all sides, and no one in the milling throng was making speeches, though a raised wooden platform stood empty on one side. The goods were obviously freshly arrived by ship – furs, fabrics, jewelry, carvings of stone and wood, and boxes, jars, and bottles of herbs and spices.

That meant, Tobas realized with a shock, that he was still in the waterfront district – Shiphaven, the sailors had called it – when he had walked a distance as great as the entire width of Shan on the Sea. The depth of the city, as seen from the ship, had been no illusion. He marched on, deeper into the metropolis.

The streets leading out the south end of the second market were a confusing tangle, and Tobas found himself doubling back and going in directions he did not care to go before he finally emerged on to a broad avenue running due south. He followed this for a few blocks, then paused when it crossed another avenue just as broad and busy, full of the clatter of cartwheels and the acrid smell of hot metal from somewhere farther on.

By this time the shadows were beginning to lengthen; where the buildings topped four floors, their shade reached clear across the avenue and partway up the faces of the structures on the east side. Tobas was hopelessly lost and knew it. Reluctantly, he tugged the sleeve of a strolling passerby and again asked for directions to Wizard Street.

The Ethsharite, richly clad in black velvet, smiled at the ignorant foreigner and explained, 'Follow High Street through the New City, then turn southeast on Arena Street, and about a quarter of a mile past the Arena you'll see the signboards.' He pointed east along the cross avenue to indicate High Street.

Tobas thanked him profusely and set about following the directions.

By the time he arrived at his destination, he was tired,

hungry, footsore, and convinced that he could not be surprised by anything else the city might have to show him; he had walked past mansions and collapsing slums, past the huge arena, among people of every description, for a greater distance than he had imagined could be enclosed in a city's walls. The sun was invisible behind the buildings on the west side of the street, and the sky above them dimmed to red, when he finally reached Wizard Street, just in time to see torches and lanterns being lit to illuminate signboards and storefronts.

He knew Wizard Street immediately, beyond question; he had passed any number of signboards that afternoon, but none like these.

At a corner a broad green board announced, 'TANNA the Great, Wizardry for Every Need, Love Charms a Speciality.' The next shop proclaimed in red letters on peeling gold leaf, 'Alderamon of Tintallion, EXPERT WIZARD'; a third was labeled 'THORUM the MAGE, Love Charms, Curses, Sundry Other Spells.' Similar advertisements hung on every shop on both sides of the street for as far as he could make out the writing. Strange sounds, thumps, and flutterings, trickled from the surrounding shops; colored lights flickered eerily in one nearby window, and a smell resembling fresh lye soap, but somehow not exactly right, reached him.

Tanna the Great sounded slightly intimidating, so Tobas skipped by that door and knocked at the next, beneath the board announcing Alderamon of Tintallion. He hoped, also, that a fellow foreigner might not be upset by a Freelander accent.

The door opened to reveal a large, middle-aged man wearing a black tunic, brown suede breeches, and a carefully trimmed reddish beard. An odd, squarish black cap adorned his head and, Tobas guessed from the visible expanse of gleaming brow, hid a sizable bald spot.

'May I help you?' he asked.

'I hope so,' Tobas replied. 'I'm a wizard myself – sort of – and I'd like to ask a favor.' He looked hopefully up at the red-bearded wizard.

Alderamon stared at the stranger for a moment, seeing a ragged and exhausted youth plainly on the brink of despair. He stood aside. 'Come in,' he said, 'and tell me about it.'

The interior of the shop was draped in red velvet and gold brocade and furnished with three low black tables and six velvet-upholstered chairs. Tobas noticed, even in his weary state, that the upholstery looked somewhat worn; he could not decide if that was good because it meant the man had a lot of customers and was therefore presumably a success, or bad, because it meant that he was too poor or too lazy to pay for new fabric.

It was clean, at any rate.

At Alderamon's invitation, he sank into one of the chairs, infinitely relieved to be off his feet; the wizard sat across the table from him.

'A little wine?' he offered.

'Yes, please,' Tobas agreed.

The wizard rose again and vanished through a draped doorway at the back of the shop, to emerge again a moment later with a tray bearing a decanter, two glasses, and a few small cakes.

'I'm afraid the cakes are a bit stale,' he apologized.

Tobas saw no need for the apology as he wolfed down all but one of the cakes and drained a glass of thin golden wine.

When he had recovered himself somewhat, he sat back,

a little shamefaced at his display of ill manners, and tried to think of the best way to begin.

'You said you're a wizard?' Alderamon prompted.

'In a way; I was apprentice to Roggit of Telven, but he . . . he died, before the apprenticeship had gone very far.'

'Oh? How far had it gone?'

Tobas was too tired and desperate to lie. 'A single spell; he taught me one spell.'

'Which one?'

'Thrindle's Combustion.'

'Hmmm.' Alderamon stared at him thoughtfully for a moment, then asked, 'May I see your dagger, please?'

Puzzled, Tobas drew his athame and handed it to the wizard.

Alderamon drew his own knife and very carefully touched the two blades together, point to point.

A sharp crack split the air; multicolored sparks showered the table, and an odd smell that reminded Tobas of the air after a heavy thunderstorm filled the room. 'I didn't know it would do that!' he exclaimed.

'Now you know,' Alderamon said, as he handed back the knife. 'You are indeed a wizard, beyond question, since you own a true athame. An athame has many special properties, including that sensitivity to others of its kind; even the experts don't know everything an athame will do.'

'Roggit never told me that; he just said that I would need it for most of my spells and that it was the mark and sign of a true wizard.'

'It is that and rather more; did you know that so long as you touch its hilt, you cannot be bound? No rope or chain can hold a wizard so long as he has his athame. Touching the points, as I have just demonstrated, will tell you whether another knife is an athame or just a dagger, and thereby whether its owner is a wizard or a fraud; the intensity of the reaction varies with the proximity of the rightful owner, so that, had you stolen the knife from him who made it, the noise and sparks would have scarcely been noticeable.'

Tobas was fascinated. 'Really?'

'Really.'

Tobas stared at the dagger in his hand for a long moment, then recalled himself and returned the blade to its sheath.

'Now, you say your master died after teaching you only one combustion spell?'

'Yes.'

'When was this?'

'He died about three sixnights ago.'

'How old are you?'

'Seventeen,' Tobas admitted reluctantly.

'And in five years he taught you just one spell?'

'Ah . . . I was older than twelve when he took me on, and he was a very old man, slow to teach me.' He stared at the worn floorboards, wondering what Alderamon would do about this confession of unforgivable irregularities in his apprenticeship.

'Oh, well, it's none of my concern,' Alderamon said. 'What's done is done, and you're a wizard now, however it happened. What do you want of me?'

'Well, I'm alone in the world now – my parents are dead, my master is dead, my cousins have thrown me out. I was hoping that the Wizards' Guild would take care of one of its own and help me out. I have no money, no place to stay, and no prospects as a wizard with a single spell. Could it be arranged that I be taught more spells, so that I can earn a living?'

60

Alderamon stared at him for a moment. 'Why did you come to *me*?' he said at last.

'You were the first wizard I found,' Tobas replied.

Alderamon shook his head. 'Boy, I am no Guildmaster, no member of the inner circles – if there truly are any inner circles.'

'But you're a wizard, a member of the Guild!'

'Well, yes . . .'

'Can't you help out a fellow wizard, then?'

'It's not my problem, lad; why should I burden myself? The Guild has done little enough for me over the years, and you've done nothing for me at all.'

'I'd do anything I can for you, in exchange for being taught more spells, but what is there that I can do?'

'Nothing – that's just the problem. I have an apprentice of my own coming next month, when she turns twelve, so I have no need for a student – particularly as you can't be apprenticed at your age in any case. You have no way to pay me for food or shelter, let alone teaching you spells. We don't *do* that, you know; a wizard's spells are his stock in trade, and he's not likely to give them out to the competition. I'll trade spells on occasion – teach a fellow one of mine in exchange for learning one of his – but I don't sell them and I certainly don't teach them for free.' Seeing Tobas' look of utter desolation, he tried to soften the blow by adding, 'But you can stay here tonight; I can do that much for you, keep a roof over your head for one night and give you breakfast in the morning. When you've rested and had a good meal, the world will look better. Perhaps you can find *someone* on Wizard Street who will take pity on you.'

Tobas nodded in mute acceptance.

'All right, then. I'll show you where you'll sleep; I have

an extra bed upstairs that my apprentice uses, when I have an apprentice. You're probably weary from your travels and ready to sleep, aren't you?'

Tobas nodded again and followed.

Chapter 7

Tobas spent the entire day after his arrival talking to wizard after wizard, up and down Wizard Street and all through the Wizards' Quarter – which, despite the name, also included an incredible variety of other magicians, from warlocks to witches and priests to prestidigitators, seers, sorcerers, and soothsayers, demonologists and necromancers, scientists and ritual dancers.

It was one of the most frustrating and depressing days of his life. Every single wizard acknowledged that Tobas was indeed a true compatriot and member of the Guild, and that he had had amazingly bad luck in having Roggit die when he did – and every single wizard refused to consider teaching him anything at all. His age, obviously well over thirteen, immediately ruled out the possibility of an actual apprenticeship, and his complete lack of money or negotiable skills ruled out any possibility of buying lessons.

And no wizard in all of Ethshar of the Spices gave away trade secrets for free, not even to acknowledged compatriots and fellow Guild members.

Alderamon had been exactly right.

'Listen,' one very sincere young woman had told him after rejecting his desperate offer of a month's servitude for a single useful spell – since she could get apprentices, why bother with a bondsman? 'Why don't you just forget about being a wizard for now? Go out and make your fortune at something else, then come back and *buy* spells. All of us can use money, despite what some of these hypocrites may have told you; if we didn't need money, we wouldn't be running shops here, would we? You won't see any really powerful wizards around the Wizards' Quarter, you know – they can afford better. So go and get rich and you can come back and laugh at us all. Don't tell anyone you're a wizard; keep the Combustion a secret, for emergencies. *Any* spell can be useful if used cleverly, and there are plenty of opportunities for a brave young man.'

'I don't think I'm particularly brave,' Tobas answered doubtfully.

'Well, a clever young man, then; brains are better than brawn, anyway.'

'But I don't know *how* to make my fortune at anything else! I've never learned to fight, or farm, or sail, or anything!'

'Well, you'll have to find something; because, Tobas, you are simply not going to get anywhere as a wizard here in Ethshar. Go up to Shiphaven Market and sign up with one of the recruiters there – that'll get you started.'

'If it doesn't get me killed,' Tobas replied under his breath. More audibly, he thanked the wizard for her advice and politely took his leave.

That had been midafternoon; by dusk he was convinced he would need to find some sort of work immediately, even if it meant leaving the city. When the torches and lanterns in front of the shops began to be extinguished or allowed to die, around midnight, he could see no alternative but Shiphaven Market. He had not eaten since Alderamon's generous breakfast; his feet were tired, and his knuckles sore from rapping on so many doors.

The thing that amazed him, however, was that he had covered less than half the wizards in the area. The competition for magical business here, he decided, would be much too fierce for him, even if he *did* pick up a few more spells.

He remembered the shipmasters and the dethroned princess and shuddered slightly at the thought of signing up with someone like that, with no clear guarantees of just what might be involved.

He had little choice, however. Reluctantly, he turned north on Arena Street and set out for Shiphaven Market.

Not surprisingly, given his unfamiliarity with the city, he got lost no fewer than three times on the way and in the hours between midnight and dawn there were very few passersby he could ask for directions.

Eventually, however, he arrived at his destination, only to find it empty and deserted – hardly surprising, as dawn was still more than two hours off. He settled down in a doorway to wait.

He was shaken roughly awake and sat up, blinking.

'What in Hell are you doing sleeping there? Don't you know that's against the law? If you haven't got any place of your own, you go sleep on Wall Street with the other beggars, you don't sleep here! We don't allow vagrants on the city streets.' The red-kilted soldier glared down at him, his left hand on his hip and his right on the hilt of his sword.

'Oh . . .' Tobas managed, 'I must have dozed off.' Thinking as best he could under the circumstances, he added, 'I'm meeting a recruiter here.'

'What kind of a recruiter?' the soldier asked suspiciously. 'For the Guards?'

'Ah, no,' Tobas said, hoping desperately that the soldier would not be offended by a lack of interest in a military career. 'From the Small Kingdoms.' He was not actually sure what sort of recruiter he would choose, but that seemed reasonable.

'One of those, ha? That's trouble enough, I'd say, without my adding to it. Suit yourself, boy. But if I catch you sleeping in the streets of Shiphaven again, I'll flog you half to death and then turn you over to the slavers – this is a respectable neighborhood.'

'Yes, sir,' Tobas agreed immediately.

'I *should* turn you over to the slavers now, you know; that's the penalty for vagrancy. Even a foreigner should know that.'

'But I just dozed off! I wasn't really sleeping here!' Tobas spoke before the significance of that 'foreigner' could sink in.

'All right, boy, I said I *should*, not that I will. You can go – but I'll keep an eye on you, and you better be telling the truth about waiting for a recruiter.'

Tobas nodded desperately, praying that the man hadn't recognized his Pirate Town accent. The soldier seemed satisfied. He stepped back and allowed the Freelander to get to his feet.

Beyond the soldier, Tobas could see that the sky was gray with the approaching dawn and that already a few men – and one woman, the princess he had seen almost two days before – were standing here and there about the square, waiting for potential customers. Eager to be rid of the soldier, Tobas headed directly for the nearest, a middle-aged man in green-dyed deerskin.

'Ho, there, boy,' the man said at Tobas' approach. 'Are you looking for a quick and easy road to wealth and glory? I'm looking for a few brave souls who are willing to help my homeland of Dwomor in its hour of need.'

'What sort of hour of need?' Tobas asked warily. 'A war?'

'Oh, no, my lad! Not a war at all! Merely a minor

nuisance that's been harrying a few of our far-flung mountain outposts.'

'Bandits?'

Before the recruiter could answer, the soldier was at Tobas' shoulder.

'Is this the one?' he demanded.

Terrified at the prospect of being caught in a lie and sold into slavery, as either vagrant or enemy alien, Tobas nodded. 'This is he, sir.'

'You're signing this boy up?' the soldier asked the recruiter.

The recruiter was not about to pass up an opportunity like this. 'Yes, indeed, sir, it's all agreed!'

'All right, then; get on with it.' He turned and stalked away.

Tobas watched him go, then turned back to the recruiter and asked, 'Now, what's this nuisance of yours, bandits?'

'First, lad, I'll ask you to sign here.' He pulled a document from his sleeve.

'Oh, no!' Tobas protested. 'Not until I know what's going on!'

'Oh, indeed? Shall I call back that fine soldier and tell him I made a mistake and that I never saw you before this morning?'

Tobas glanced at the soldier's retreating back and reluctantly accepted the proffered pen. He signed his name neatly, 'Tobas of Telven,' then handed back the pen and demanded, 'All right, what's this nuisance?'

'It's not bandits, it's a dragon. It's been eating people up in the mountains – and when it doesn't eat people, it eats sheep, which is almost as bad.'

'A dragon?' Tobas stared for a moment, then looked

after the soldier again, wondering how bad slavery could be.

'Oh, it's not that bad,' the recruiter said. 'And the reward is really something worth having – the hand of a princess in marriage, a respected position for life at Dwomor Keep, and best of all, one thousand gold pieces!'

Tobas gaped stupidly for several seconds. 'A hundred-weight of gold?' he squeaked at last.

'That's right.'

After all, he thought, how dangerous could a dragon be? Every well-stocked wizard had a jar of dragon's blood on his shelves, and the legends said that during the Great War dragons had been tamed and trained. A reward of that magnitude was worth a little risk – with that much money he could, as his advisor had suggested, come back and buy a few spells. Not that he'd need to; he could live quite comfortably for the rest of his life on that much! And all that without even considering the position or the princess.

The princess – he was not at all sure he wanted to marry anyone as yet, princess or otherwise. If one of the prettier young women in Telven had shown an interest, he might well have married, but they had never really taken him seriously after he apprenticed himself to old Roggit, and he was not eager to wed a stranger, someone from an entirely different background. Well, if by some miracle he somehow did kill the dragon, surely he need not accept *all* the reward; let some worthy prince marry her. Tobas would settle for the money.

Of course, he thought, he mustn't count the money before he had it; he had no idea how to kill a dragon. He knew almost nothing about dragons. He had never seen any, but they had figured in various stories he had heard as a child; they reportedly came in various sizes and shapes and colors. Some were said to breathe fire; some were said to speak in various languages and to be as dangerous with their clever tongues as with their claws and teeth. During the Great War, both sides had reportedly trained them to kill the enemy. A dragon could be almost anything. He would need to look the situation over carefully and see just what the story was, what sort of a dragon this Dwomor had roaming the hills. If the odds looked too bad – and realism told him that dragon slaying couldn't be easy, if these people had sent a recruiter all the way to Ethshar to find volunteers – he would simply leave. At least he would be somewhere new; Dwomor, whatever and wherever it might be, might well have more opportunities available to him than Ethshar. He would not be an enemy there simply by virtue of his homeland, either; he had never heard of anyone sinking or capturing ships from any place called Dwomor.

He could not possibly be much worse off wandering in Dwomor than wandering in Ethshar, he told himself, and at least, as a recruited dragon slayer, he wouldn't have to worry about being sold into slavery as a vagrant.

'All right,' he said. 'You've got a recruit. When do we leave?'

The recruiter smiled. 'Oh, not for some time yet; I'm hoping to bring back a dozen young adventurers like yourself.' He raised his voice and began calling to the handful of Ethsharites entering the market square. 'Here's your chance for riches and glory! A chance to travel and see the world! Come over here, folks, and let me tell you all about it!'

Tobas' stomach growled, and he sighed. He was committed now; he would either have to face a dragon of unknown size and ferocity or break his signed agreement and desert somewhere in the Small Kingdoms. He could not stay in Ethshar.

At the very least, if the recruiter wanted Tobas to reach Dwomor well enough to go dragon hunting, the blackmailing scoundrel would have to feed him sometime soon.

Chapter 8

When they finally boarded the ship, there were nine of them in all; the recruiter seemed well pleased with his catch.

Tobas was not well pleased with anything. His companions seemed to be either fools or blackguards, which made him wonder which category he belonged in. The ship was small, crowded, and stank of fish, and Tobas had doubts about its seaworthiness. Worst of all, the meals were sparse and unappetizing, consisting largely of stale bread and ill-flavored cheese served with cheap, warm beer.

Even this food, however, was better than nothing, and his narrow, scratchy hammock was better than sleeping in the streets.

He could not quite bring himself to complain to the recruiter about the conditions; but by the second night at sea, he could no longer resist complaining to *someone* and unburdened himself to the rather plump, baby-faced young man – roughly his own age – in the adjoining hammock.

'Oh, but it's an *adventure*!' Tillis Tagath's son burbled happily. 'Hardship and sorrow toughen a man for battle!'

Tillis, in Tobas' opinion, was very definitely one of the fools among the recruits.

'I don't think they're toughening us for battle,' Tobas replied. 'I think they're just too cheap to do better. It makes me suspicious about that reward of a hundred pounds of gold.'

'Oh? Do you think they're lying?' Tillis turned and stared at him with wide, worried eyes.

Tobas sighed. 'Not exactly *lying*, perhaps,' he said. 'But exaggerating a little.'

'Oh, but they wouldn't *dare* refuse anything to the man who slays the dragon! What would the people think? Surely the peasants would rise up against any king so treacherous as to refuse the kingdom's saviour what might be due him!'

Tillis, Tobas thought, talked like a storyteller and was undoubtedly aboard the foul-smelling and nameless little ship as a result of listening to too many storytellers. 'I wouldn't put much trust in peasants,' he said. 'Nor in kings, either. Do you know anything about this place we're going to – Dwomor I think it's called?'

'It's in the mountains in the Small Kingdoms, and they say it was the original capital of Old Ethshar.'

Startled, Tobas asked, '*Who* says so?'

'The Dwomorites, of course!'

'Oh, of course.' He settled back in his hammock again. From what he had always heard, virtually every one of the Small Kingdoms claimed to be the original capital – or else its government claimed to be the rightful government of all Ethshar. Or both. If any capital had ever actually existed, its location was long since forgotten. 'Tillis,' he asked, 'how do you expect to kill a dragon?'

'I don't know,' Tillis confessed. 'I hadn't really thought about it. How big a dragon do you suppose it is?'

'I don't know,' Tobas replied. 'But it's big enough to eat people.'

'That's pretty big,' Tillis said, his voice hushed and uncertain. Then, more confidently, 'But a good sword and a stout heart should serve!'

'Tillis,' Tobas said in exasperation, 'unless you've been hiding it somewhere in the hold, you haven't got a sword.'

'No, I don't, but I can get one from the castle armory, I'm sure.'

Tobas sighed again. 'What in the world made you decide to sign up to be a dragon slayer, anyway?'

Tillis was silent for a long moment before replying, 'Sixteen siblings.'

'What?'

'I have sixteen older siblings. Every single inheritance or apprenticeship or wealthy marriage – or *any* sort of arranged marriage – my parents could possibly claim was spoken for before they got to me. Nine brothers and seven sisters can use up a lot of property, and my parents were never rich.'

Tobas whistled. 'If they were raising seventeen children, it's no wonder! They wouldn't have *time* to get rich, and that crowd would eat it as fast as they brought it in!'

Tillis nodded silently.

Tobas lay for a moment, trying to imagine what it would be like to live in such a large family. He had sometimes pretended Peretta and Détha and Garander were his siblings instead of his cousins, but he had never considered what a really large family would be like.

He didn't think he would like it. 'How old's the oldest?' he asked.

Before Tillis could answer, a voice came from another hammock. 'Aren't you two ever going to shut up?'

'Sorry,' Tobas said. He rolled over to face the wall. The speaker was one of those he had classified as blackguards or scoundrels, a small man with a scarred face, at least ten years older than himself, who carried no fewer than three knives. Tobas had not caught his entire name – Arnen of something.

He was not someone Tobas cared to argue with.

He lay silently awake for some time after that, reassured that there were others, like Tillis, at least as ill prepared as himself, but more worried than ever about facing the dragon. He had assumed that the crew would include a genuine dragon fighter or two, so that, if a mere unskilled nobody like himself were to hang back or simply vanish, nobody would much care, and the dragon would eventually be disposed of just the same.

Now that he had met the other recruits, he was not at all sure that as a wizard, even a wizard with a single spell, he might not be the best chance the kingdom of Dwomor had. Dragons were usually said to breathe fire and were therefore presumably fire-resistant, but some way of using Thrindle's Combustion against a dragon might still exist.

He dozed at last, as the ship sailed on into the east.

At dawn the next day, the lookout sighted land ahead; they had crossed the Gulf of the East, leaving the Hegemony of Ethshar for the Small Kingdoms. Tobas and the other adventurers came on deck to see the jagged, rocky coastline for themselves.

'Is that Dwomor?' someone asked a crewwoman, pointing at the cliffs.

'No, of course not,' she replied in heavily accented Ethsharitic. 'Unless the captain's gotten us off course again, that's Morria; we should be able to see the castle in an hour or so.'

Tobas had never actually seen a castle, though he had heard numerous descriptions, some of them going into elaborate detail; the only castles were in the Small Kingdoms, the other nations of the World being either too advanced and peaceful or too barbaric and primitive to have any. He resolved to watch carefully, so as not to miss it. One story he had heard as a child had described a

74

castle as a great pile of stone, leading him to believe that some were camouflaged, and he was afraid that he might mistake this one for a natural outcropping.

He need not have worried; Morria Castle towered up quite unmistakably atop a low cliff, with no fewer than six turrets jutting above its battlements.

'Will we be putting in there?' he asked, noticing the small harbor below the cliff.

'No,' a sailor replied briefly.

'What's our course, then?'

The crewman looked him over. 'You've been to sea before?' He spoke with the accent of Ethshar of the Spices.

'My father was a captain, and I worked my passage to Ethshar,' Tobas replied.

The sailor nodded. 'Well, we'll be cruising down the length of Morria here, and on past Stralya, and then up the river at Londa to Ekeroa, where we'll put your party ashore. No stops; I think your leader is afraid he'd lose some of you if we put in anywhere before that. I wouldn't be surprised if he's right – in fact, he'll probably lose a couple during the overland trip. It's a good seven leagues of rough travel from Ekeroa to Dwomor Keep.'

'You've been there?'

'Not I!' The sailor laughed, though Tobas saw nothing humorous in the question. 'No, I've never been there, but all the traffic from Dwomor comes along the same route. There isn't any other way, I suppose.'

'Oh. Ah . . . have you heard anything about this dragon?'

'A little. Rumours say it's a fifty-footer – that's a bad size, big enough to be smart and strong, small enough to be fast and vicious. It breathes fire, they say, but that might be an exaggeration. Some people seem to think *all* dragons do.'

Tobas shivered, 'You're not very encouraging.'

'Oh, don't worry,' the sailor said. 'It's not all *your* problem. Look at all these other heroes coming to kill it. And this is just the group from Ethshar of the Spices; there are bound to be others as well. Chances are the old king will be sending an entire army of volunteers against the poor beast, and you'll be lucky to get a few whacks at its tail.' He paused. 'Assuming they don't all back out, anyway. It's a mystery to me why he didn't just hire a real expert; there must be some. Maybe he couldn't find any.'

Tobas, who had wondered the same thing, glanced at his comrades – those who were on deck, at any rate. Tillis was staring eagerly ahead, holding on to a foremast shroud and staggering every time the ship rolled. Arnen was talking to a knot of off-watch sailors by the mainmast; Tobas thought he saw the flash of coins and suspected that the group was involved in some sort of wager. Three others – Peren the White, Arden Adar's son, and a fifteen-year-old orphan girl named Azraya of Ethshar whom Tobas suspected of being not merely a fool but actually insane – were in various places on deck.

The other three were presumably below somewhere, still being seasick. Peren, whose cognomen came from his bone-white hair and pale skin, had been sick the first day, but recovered quickly; the others had not been bothered.

None of them looked much like dragon slayers to Tobas. He was, so far as he knew, the only magician in the bunch; Peren had the only real sword, and Arden, between them in age, was the only particularly large, strong one. It was confusing, having both an Arnen and an Arden – at least they had no two with exactly the same name, and no one named Kelder. Practically every village

76

in the Free Lands, and presumably every street in Eth-shar, held a Kelder or two.

Tobas classed Arnen and two of the trio struck down by seasickness as scoundrels and the other five as various sorts of fool. Peren, a tall, thin, frail fellow two or three years older than Tobas, seemed determined to prove he was stronger than anyone else, which he obviously wasn't, though he might well outclass Tobas; Arden, a big man in his twenties, was simply stupid; Azraya, fifteen and wild, was perpetually angry about something and would will-fully misinterpret anything said to her as an insult; Tillis was lost in ancient legends of heroism; and the seasick Elner seemed to honestly believe he could single-hand-edly slay the dragon and, in his lucid moments before succumbing to the ship's motion, had already been brag-ging about how he would spend his reward money.

The scoundrels talked less and appeared far more dangerous, but Tobas thought it far more likely that they would kill their comrades than that they would kill a dragon. Knives, lies, and stealth would not be much use against dragons.

He hoped that Dwomor did have other recruits, because he did not believe this bunch could kill even a small dragon.

Of course, that meant that he wasn't going to get rich.

Oh, well, he thought, perhaps there would be other opportunities in Dwomor. He took a last look at Morria Castle, then turned and went below.

Dusk of that third day found the ship approaching the mouth of the river – not the Great River, someone explained, but another, the largest in the Small King-doms, which had half a dozen names. The Londa River seemed to be the most popular label. It flowed south from the mountains, then hooked to the west to reach the sea;

they would be following it north to the lake that was more or less its source.

It seemed odd to Tobas that there was no castle guarding the mouth; he mentioned it to one of the sailors.

'I think there was a castle, once,' he replied. 'But we're on the border between Stralya and Londa here, and it probably got destroyed in a border war. Or maybe it fell into the sea – the river's wearing down those cliffs, you know.'

Tobas nodded. He was about to ask another question when a roar from the bow answered him before the words left his mouth; the anchor had just been dropped. No attempt would be made to navigate the river by night.

The crew lifted anchor at dawn. By the time Tobas had eaten his meager breakfast, they were in sight of Kala Keep.

The name was misleading, as the keep itself was part of a large castle that stood within a walled town. Boats of every sort lined the riverfront.

One boat, bearing a large red and gold banner, pulled up beside the ship. Tobas noticed that it could move far faster by means of four oars than the ship moved beneath full sail; the wind, which had never in the course of the voyage been particularly strong, was dying, cut off by the surrounding hilly land.

A long discussion ensued between the ship's captain and someone in the boat, but Tobas could hear none of it and resisted the temptation to move closer. Finally the captain came away and gave an order in a language Tobas did not understand – he had discovered within hours of boarding that this ship's crew was of mixed nationality and that all of them understood and spoke several tongues.

A moment later a green and black flag was hoisted.

'Dwomoritic colors,' someone explained. 'Kala must be at war with someone, if they're demanding colors be flown.'

'Oh.' The sailor seemed very casual about it; Tobas wondered how anyone could be casual about war.

They sailed on past the town; but before noon, the wind had died away completely, leaving them still within the kingdom of Kala, drifting back downstream with the current. After a careful study of the sky, the captain ordered sweeps.

Tobas had never seen sweeps before – long oars that took three men apiece to haul, three sweeps to each side. He watched in fascination as the ship picked up speed again.

They anchored in a wide, slow stretch of river that night, with orchards and fields lining either shore; this, the passengers were told, was a spot somewhere in southern Danua. The next day should take them past Danua Castle and into Ekeroa; if the wind were to pick up in the right direction, they might reach Ekeroa Lake.

The wind did not pick up. Danua Castle was very much like Kala Keep in appearance, and the farms of southern Ekeroa were indistinguishable from those of Danua or Kala. Tobas wondered why these tiny realms were separate kingdoms, when they had no natural boundaries or apparent cultural differences, but decided it would not be tactful to ask any of the natives of the Small Kingdoms on board, and none of the Ethsharites seemed likely to know.

That night they anchored in the mouth of an unnavigable tributary that poured in from the east; by midmorning of the following day, the river had widened out into Ekeroa Lake. The sun was only a few degrees past its zenith when they sailed up to the docks below Ekeroa Castle.

When they had all disembarked, Tobas took a long look around. He saw the castle looming above him, dark and ominous and alien; the town clustered tightly around it – tall, dark, narrow wooden houses, and scattered among them seemed to be an inordinate number of trees. The people were mostly short and pale, clad in oddly styled clothes and speaking a strange, liquid tongue. Behind him lay the dark, smooth, still water of Ekeroa Lake and the odd, stubby fishing boats the natives used; on all other sides, the town appeared to be ringed by forest, a forest that was mostly made up of the peculiar needle-leafed trees he had heard called 'pines'. Off to the east he could see misty gray shapes rising jaggedly above the trees on the far side of the lake – those, he realized, must be mountains, the first he had ever seen.

Not a single feature of the landscape, either natural or man-made, resembled the familiar rolling grasslands, sprawling villages, and gravelly beaches around Telven. The calm black-shadowed green of the lake was utterly different from the never-still blue and white of the ocean he had always known, while the alien pine forest filled the air with its curious scent.

He realized for the first time just how far from home he had come.

Chapter 9

'All right, heroes!' the recruiter bellowed. 'Line up here and we'll get you aboard the wagons!'

Reluctantly, Tobas joined the other adventurers in gathering at the spot indicated. The wagons did not look particularly inviting – simple unpainted wooden boxes on mud-spattered, spoked wheels, each with a wide sheet of brown canvas draped over a sagging ridgepole to provide a modicum of shelter. They were drawn by mules, rather than the usual horses or oxen. Five wagons had been provided, each drawn by two mules, which seemed more than necessary, since their only cargo appeared to be the party from Ethshar.

The caravan master seemed to agree. 'Is this all of them?' he demanded.

The recruiter nodded. '*You* try signing up Ethsharites! They just aren't an adventurous people.'

'Well, get them aboard, then, and let's go!'

The recruiter began herding his charges in, two to a wagon; Tobas, in the second wagon, found himself paired with Tillis, as he had been aboard ship. Before he could decide whether that was good or bad, the wagon started with a jerk, and they were off again.

Only after they had been rolling for twenty minutes did Tobas realize he had seen almost nothing of Ekeroa, which had looked like an interesting place, despite its strangeness.

At first the caravan headed almost due north, through dense forest along the lakeshore and then, when they were past the lake, beside the river; about two leagues from town, however, they abruptly turned east and forded the stream, which had shrunk to a manageable size.

From then on their course remained east by southeast, climbing steadily into the mountains, for almost three days, save for a bad stretch late in the second day when the road wound back and forth so much that Tobas was never entirely sure of the direction.

Three days alone in a wagon with no one to talk to but Tillis sent Tobas into a deep depression. His luck was obviously still bad, after all, he told himself; he should never have stolen that boat, as that wicked deed had probably cursed him. He should have stayed in the Free Lands, waited until he could board a vessel honestly, or even have walked to Ethshar.

And once in Ethshar, he should have known better than to fall asleep in the street. That carelessness might be the true font of his misfortune. If he had stayed awake, he would not now be on his way to be killed by a maneating dragon somewhere in the middle of nowhere.

Looking out past the edge of the canvas as the wagon jolted along, he wondered why anyone would live in country like this, rocky and steep – but after a time, he realized that almost no one did. The caravan passed no villages and few homes. Dwomor, if this was the only way to reach it, must be unbearably isolated.

For a bad moment, he wondered whether any dragon really existed. Perhaps they were on their way to be sold as slaves in some barbarian realm, the story of the dragon being merely an explanation to cover their failure to return. Perhaps they would be sacrificed to demons. Perhaps they would be cooked and eaten.

Tillis babbled on maddeningly about how strange and

beautiful the countryside was; Tobas did his best to ignore him.

The first night they reached an inn in the forested hills just as dusk was beginning to fade. There they received the best food Tobas had eaten since Roggit had died; he eagerly wolfed down everything put before him, then fell pleasantly asleep in a corner before the evening was well begun.

The next morning he awoke stiff and sore and foul-tempered and spoke to no one at breakfast. He refused to help with preparations for the next leg of the journey.

Only when he climbed aboard the second wagon, as directed, did he realize he was being put in with Tillis again. He turned to protest, but it was too late; the caravan master had given the mules the signal, and the wagon was moving.

The second night they were out of the thickest part of the forest and well into the lightly treed foothills; the inn was rougher, and the food less appealing. This time Tobas stayed awake, but contributed little to the after-dinner conversation, as it seemed to be made up almost entirely of boasting about prior exploits.

Tobas did not consider any of his prior exploits anything to boast about. He could not even resort to family, as Tillis did, since his ancestors had all been quiet farmers save for his father – and bragging about a pirate captain among Ethsharites did not seem a wise thing to do.

In the morning he tried to put himself in a different wagon, the fourth; its previous occupants, seeing him there, shrugged and boarded the second.

A moment later Tillis climbed into the fourth wagon. Tobas closed his eyes and pretended Tillis wasn't there.

At times during the long day it almost worked.

The third inn was a ramshackle structure clinging to a

rocky mountainside, but included an enthusiastic staff that made up for the physical shortcomings. Tobas took a particular interest in one of the proprietor's daughters, a dark-haired beauty who appeared to be roughly his own age, but she was fascinated with Peren's strange coloring and laughingly brushed aside Tobas' tentative advances in order to devote herself to the albino.

Tobas shrugged off his disappointment; he was used to it. His successes with women had been few and far between.

But then, he was still young, he told himself.

For the last day he finally managed to pair himself with someone other than Tillis; he waited until the young Ethsharite had boarded the fourth wagon, then jumped into the fifth.

He found himself sharing the vehicle with Arnen and one of the other scoundrels, Korl Korl's son. They stared at him for a long moment when he climbed in; then Arnen drew one of his knives, a long, narrow dagger, and began cleaning his nails with it. Korl simply leaned back against the side of the wagon and stared.

The entire morning passed without any of the three saying a word. Early in the afternoon, however, Korl whispered something to Arnen, who smiled nastily in return.

That was the full extent of conversation in the wagon that day, and Tobas quickly found himself wishing he'd stayed with Tillis.

Late in the afternoon the wagons pulled to a halt. Tobas had dozed off, despite the bumping; he woke with a start, sat up, and peered out the end of the wagon, wondering why they were stopping when day was still bright.

He realized why quickly enough; this was not another inn, but a castle, set in the middle of a small plateau.

This, obviously, was Dwomor Keep, the castle he had come to save from a dragon.

He wondered why anyone would want to bother. If he had lived in such a dismal place and had found it to be threatened by a monster, he would simply have left.

Dwomor Keep was a large, sprawling structure, obviously built piecemeal over a period of centuries; the various towers, turrets, and wings had only one unifying feature, that being that they were all in a sad state of disrepair. The town this miserable fortress guarded was a pitiful huddle of no more than a dozen sagging cottages, though a few scattered farmsteads could be seen here and there on the surrounding plateau; the entire area stank of manure. Any claim to be the rightful capital of Old Ethshar was obviously an unfounded boast. Either that, or the ruins of the capital had been completely buried centuries ago, and this place built on top.

He leaned out for a moment, gazing about at the surrounding countryside.

The castle stood at the approximate center of a more or less level area perhaps half a league in diameter; to the west, in the direction of the setting sun, Tobas could see nothing beyond, as if the World simply ended at the edge of the plateau. In every other direction, however, hills piled up around the little plain, and to much of the north and east mountains rose beyond the hills.

Looking back toward the castle once more, Tobas saw that the wagons had paused to allow a portcullis to be opened; when that had been done, the caravan proceeded on into the castle courtyard, where he remained unimpressed.

The courtyard was unpaved, simply an expanse of bare

dirt that undoubtedly turned to a sea of mud whenever rain came; the castle structures around it were even more ramshackle and mismatched than the portions visible from the outside. The exterior, after all, had to be built of stone in order to be defensible, while the stables, mews, sheds, and other added interior features could be – and were – built of a variety of woods, bricks, and what appeared to be mud and straw.

What, he wondered, did Tillis make of this brave castle? It hardly lived up to the storytellers' images.

The wagons came to a final halt, and the recruiter came marching back along the line, shouting, 'All out! We're here!'

Tobas clambered out of the wagon and dropped to the ground. He glanced at the gate they had entered through and noticed that the portcullis was being cranked back down; presumably the locals did not want any of their hired dragon slayers to escape.

And having thought of the locals, he noticed that there were certainly plenty of them around. He estimated thirty or forty people, mostly women and old men, were standing about the courtyard, studying the new arrivals.

He resisted the temptation to draw his athame and hidden vial of brimstone and set someone's clothes on fire. The gesture would be startling, impressive, and probably very satisfying, but it might make too many enemies. Besides, he didn't *want* to impress anyone; if he did, they might actually expect him to kill their ravening monster, wherever it was.

He wasn't sure just what he wanted to do or where he wanted to be, but he was sure he didn't want to tackle a dragon. Any fantasies he might have had back in Ethshar, brought on by the mention of a thousand pieces of gold, had been jounced out of him in the course of the long and uncomfortable journey from the city to Dwomor.

'All right, you people,' someone, a middle-aged man who was apparently a local official, called in truly barbarous Ethsharitic. 'Do any of you speak Dwomoritic?'

No one answered.

'I was afraid of that. What about Trader's Tongue?'

Two people admitted to that.

'We may need an interpreter, I guess. At least the king speaks Ethsharitic. All right, follow me.'

'Wait a minute!' the recruiter interrupted. 'I want my money!'

'You'll get it,' the official replied testily.

'I want it *now*! You said payment on delivery. Well, here they are, delivered, nine of them. Pay me; I'm not going to risk losing out if you scare some of them away.'

'You couldn't wait five minutes?' He glanced at the nine adventurers, all of whom were listening with interest, then dug in the purse on his gold-trimmed belt and fished out a handful of coins. He counted out eighteen – Tobas could not see their size or metal – and handed them to the recruiter, who immediately, without a further word, headed for the gate. Tobas grinned; someone, he did not see who, laughed aloud, rather unpleasantly.

'All right,' the official said again. 'Follow me. I'll take you to your audience with his Royal Majesty Derneth the Second, King of Dwomor.'

The adventurers obeyed, filing haphazardly through the door. Rather to his surprise, Tobas found himself last in line; looking about, he realized that there were no guards or other restraints to keep him from deserting. The recruiter had departed with his money safely in hand; the caravan master was busy unhitching the mules; nobody else seemed likely to argue if Tobas simply turned and walked out, as the recruiter had, using a small door he saw standing open beside the portcullis that apparently led through the gatehouse.

No, he decided after an instant's hesitation, he would follow along. He had nowhere to go in the surrounding mountains; furthermore, it might not be safe to wander aimlessly about the unfamiliar countryside. There could well be bandits and brigands, or wolves, in the area, not to mention the dragon that might be roaming about somewhere out there. The natives might not be friendly. He couldn't speak the local language; it was, from the little he had heard, similar to Ethsharitic, but not similar enough to be intelligible.

And he was, he realized, curious to learn just what the true situation was, whether the dragon hunt was legitimate, and, if it was, why anyone with a thousand pieces of gold would be hiring nobodies in Shiphaven Market instead of experts to dispose of a dragon as formidable as this one was said to be. Dragons had been around for hundreds of years, after all; somewhere, somebody must have developed methods of dealing with them, other than gathering up a bunch of desperate young men and letting them try their luck. Maybe, by pointing this out, he could earn himself a little something. Not a thousand pieces of gold, of course, but something.

Also, if he hoped to find any wizards around here who might teach him new spells, the castle was the likeliest place to find them – or, for that matter, anything else that might lead to a career of almost any sort.

Besides, he wanted to meet his Royal Majesty Derneth the Second, King of Dwomor. He was curious; he had never seen a king before. The Free Lands didn't have any, and, although the three overlords of the Hegemony of Ethshar might count, he hadn't had a chance to see any of them, and they didn't call themselves kings, anyway. They were triumvirs, not monarchs.

With that much settled, he followed the others into the castle.

Chapter 10

The inside of the castle was far more respectable than the outside, as long as one ignored the smell of dry rot and didn't look closely enough to see the cobwebs and dust that adorned the corners. The ceilings were low, and the corridors not particularly wide, so that it was far from spacious, but the walls were covered with tapestries and hangings, more than Tobas had ever seen before, and most of them only slightly faded, providing an air of moderate luxury.

The party from Ethshar was asked to wait for ten minutes or so in an antechamber that was somewhat crowded with a dozen people in it – the nine adventurers, their guiding official, and two guards – but the velvet-covered chairs that were provided looked comfortable enough, and the room was elegantly furnished through-out, if not particularly well kept.

Of course, the antechamber had not been intended for twelve people at once and was not furnished with a full dozen chairs, but only with eight.

Tobas managed to claim one of the eight and discovered for himself that they were indeed quite comfortable, albeit a trifle threadbare and prone to squeak when he shifted his weight. And the great black wrought-iron candelabra were magnificent beneath the heavy coating of old wax and cobwebs. He wondered idly why only a dozen lit candles were in use, leaving – he made a quick count – sixteen empty sockets. The room had no windows and was rather gloomy; more light would have been welcome.

Were candles in short supply in Dwomor? Surely a court that could afford to pay a thousand pieces of gold as a reward could afford all the candles anyone might want!

This castle simply did not live up to the glorious images in childhood tales – though the tapestries and velvet seemed to indicate that it might once have come close.

After their brief wait the entire party was shown into the audience chamber at once, rather to Tobas' surprise; he had somehow assumed that they would be shown in and introduced individually. Such elaborate pomp seemed appropriate to castles, even so run-down a one as this.

They were allowed to enter together, however, crowding through the heavy double doors with Tobas in the middle of the group.

Once inside, Tobas looked around curiously.

This audience chamber actually came close to being impressive, he decided; the tapestries here were not visibly faded at all, and a few used thread-of-gold that gleamed brightly in the candlelight. Everything obvious was sparkling clean; the only cobwebs in *this* chamber were higher than a tall man could reach with a whisk broom, up among the carved ceiling beams. The room was as big as two or possibly even three of the typical little Ethsharitic wizards' shops, such as he had seen so many of in that long, depressing day of begging for spells, all put together; it was almost as big as the old boathouse in Shan on the Sea. Tobas guessed it, finally, at forty feet long, though he knew that might be generous. Clerestory windows on one side let in the last of the afternoon sunlight, and a dozen candle racks along the walls augmented that nicely, with no empty sockets in any of them and the layers of wax much thinner. The dominant smells were hot wax and perfume.

Most of the room was crowded with people, with the

91

heaviest concentration at the far end; the majority seemed to be dressed in faded sumptuousness – worn velvets, stained silks, tarnished bracelets – reinforcing the impression that Dwomor had seen better days. In the midst of the largest group, Tobas caught glimpses of a man on a throne.

Someone spoke a command in Dwomoritic; Tobas still could not understand a word of the language but he was now able to distinguish it fairly reliably from other unfamiliar tongues by its lilt and the maddening sensation that he could almost make it out if he listened hard enough. The crowd parted, allowing the party of newcomers to approach the king.

Tobas felt a moment's disappointment at his first good close look at indisputable genuine royalty, but he forced it down, telling himself that he knew better than to be disappointed. The king was just a man, like any other, sitting on a large wooden chair on a raised platform. He appeared to be about fifty years old, going slightly to fat, his beard graying at the edges and his temples gray-streaked. He wore scarlet velvet trimmed with an unfamiliar golden fur; given that attire and the temperature in the room, Tobas was not at all surprised to see beads of sweat oozing from beneath his simple silver crown.

Tobas had never before given any thought to the inconvenience of wearing royal robes in the summer. Royalty, it seemed, had its own little drawbacks. Surely, though, the king did not wear such garb all the time?

No, of course not; this was a formal occasion, Tobas reminded himself.

'You may approach,' the king said grandly, addressing the new arrivals. The other people in the room fell silent.

The Ethsharitic party shuffled forward and stood before

the throne, the behavior and expressions of its members ranging from arrogant to curious to abject.

'If you would be so kind as to introduce yourselves . . .' Derneth said, letting his sentence trail off to nothing.

The adventurers looked at one another, none eager to be first. Finally Tillis stepped forward and said, 'I am Tillis Tagath's son, at your Majesty's service.' He bowed deeply, but awkwardly.

'Ah,' the king replied. 'And do you have any experience in dragon slaying?'

Tobas found that a very interesting question; had the king expected his recruiter to bring back expert dragon slayers? If so, he had been swindled, and the recruiter had done well to leave hurriedly.

'Alas, no, your Majesty,' Tillis replied. 'There are no dragons to be found in Ethshar of the Spices, for it is a drab and peaceful place with few opportunities for valor and daring to befit a lad such as myself. Thus I have come to your delightful realm of Dwomor seeking adventure, in the hope that I might, by pluck and good fortune, make a place for myself. May the gods smile upon you for giving me a chance to conquer or perish in your service, and long may you reign!'

The king's smile became somewhat frozen and glassy as he listened to the baby-faced Ethsharite's bizarre little speech. 'Ah,' he said after a moment's hesitation, nodding; that settled, he turned to Peren, whose sword and white hair stood out in the crowd and asked, 'And you?'

'Peren the White, of Ethshar of the Spices.' The Ethsharite bowed with a lithe grace that startled Tobas.

'And have you ever slain a dragon?'

'No.' Peren was neither apologetic nor forceful in his denial, but simply stated the fact.

'Very well,' said the king, moving on. 'What about you?'

Arden introduced himself, then Azraya, and so on through the rest of the little band. When Azraya presented herself, the king seemed somewhat taken aback and whispered something behind his hand to one of the men near the throne; Tobas assumed that this had something to do with Azraya's sex. After all, a female could hardly marry a princess – but she could certainly use the gold.

When Arnen's turn came, he introduced himself as Arnen of Ethshar, which Tobas was quite certain was not the cognomen he had used before; and when asked if he had ever slain a dragon, he replied, 'Not a *dragon*.'

The others confined themselves to their names and a simple no. Tobas was seventh of the nine and did nothing to draw attention to himself.

'Ah,' the king said when the last introduction had been made. 'No experienced dragon slayers, I see, but I suppose I could expect nothing else from Ethshar. You will have questions, I'm sure; but first, let me introduce you to my daughters, my court, and to some of your fellow adventurers from other lands.' He stood and motioned to someone; a handsome, dark-haired young woman stepped out of the little crowd to the right of the throne, wearing an ornate white gown trimmed with pearls. 'My second daughter, Falissa,' he said. 'One of you, if successful, may marry her.' He gestured again, and another young woman appeared to be introduced, also dark-haired and elegant.

It had not occurred to Tobas until this moment that there might be more than one princess available as part of the reward.

In all, five princesses were brought forth, all attractive;

94

in addition to Falissa were, apparently in descending order of age, Sellatha, Tinira, Alorria, and Zerréa. Zerréa appeared to be perhaps fourteen, barely of marriageable age, but her father still commented, as he had with each of her sisters, that she might wed one of the dragon hunters. Tobas had never heard of anyone named Zerréa before; he rather liked the name and wondered if the king had made it up after running out of ordinary ones. Not that Sellatha was common around Telven, either, he realized when he thought about it; it was likely he decided, that both names were in common usage in Dwomor, whether they were found in the more westerly lands or not.

Tobas resolved to stop wondering about trivia and pay attention to more important concerns. The king was making a speech about how these five of his six daughters had willingly promised themselves as wives to anyone who could save the kingdom from the monster that now ravaged the countryside, whether that hero should be noble or commoner, no matter that this might mean giving up their royal birthright, and so on and so forth.

Elner, at Tobas' left, leaned over and whispered, 'Some great sacrifice! They were probably desperate for husbands – or at least their royal father was. Surplus princesses are a major export in the Small Kingdoms.'

This sounded far more informative and interesting than the king's rather tedious speech, so Tobas leaned back and whispered, 'What are you talking about?'

'I'm talking about surplus princesses! Look, the first duty of any royal family is to ensure the succession, right? They need heirs. Or one heir, anyway. That means sons, in most kingdoms; only a few let girls inherit. Daughters are just surplus, to be married off to make alliances with the neighbors. To keep up the dignity of the throne, you can't let them marry commoners – it goes against all the traditions! Royalty marries royalty. And each kingdom only has one throne to pass on, to one prince and the one princess he marries; that means that younger sons and unmarried daughters are all just extras. The sons go off adventuring or soldiering, and a lot of them get killed, and some make love matches with commoners or run off to Ethshar and marry for money, but the daughters just hang around cluttering up the castle. Poor old Derneth here has six of them; I guess he married one off to a neighbor, but that leaves five more he needs to get rid of. He can't just let them marry whom they please, since that's against the rules, and he hasn't got anyone in the kingdom suitable for any ordinary arranged marriages; but by promising them to dragon slayers, he can kill two birds with one stone and get rid of dragons and daughters all at once! Marrying princesses to heroes is traditional and about the only respectable way to use up the extras. Gets new blood into the royal family, as well.'

Tobas looked at Elner with new respect; his explanation made a great deal of sense. Perhaps the fellow was not completely a fool, after all.

'I think I'll take that one, Alorria,' Elner said, pointing behind his hand. 'When I've killed the dragon, I mean.'

That immediately dragged Tobas' opinion of him back to its previous level. He bit back a snide retort.

He had to agree, though, that Elner had picked the beauty of the bunch; Alorria was of medium height, with thick black hair, pale skin, and dark eyes, as were all five, but she stood out, her features a trifle finer, her figure a little lusher than the others. Tobas guessed her to be very close to his own age. If, by some miracle, Tobas did somehow manage to kill the dragon – and he knew that it would take a miracle, despite what Elner might choose to

96

believe – he supposed Alorria would be his choice, too, if he were to marry any of the princesses.

Looking the five of them over, he found the thought of marriage was not particularly unpleasant; he knew that many things were more important than beauty in the long run, but beauty certainly didn't hurt. He wondered if there were any way he could marry a princess without killing the dragon. Might a Dwomorite princess bring enough of a dowry for two people to live on? He had never really seriously considered marrying for money as a way to survive, but it was a possibility he might want to think about. Plenty of handsome young people of both sexes did it. It was not really a career to be proud of, but it could keep him from starvation or slavery.

All the while that Elner had been explaining and Tobas had been admiring the princesses, the king had gone on talking, describing the beauties and accomplishments of each of his daughters – all were said to be skilled at needlework, which left Tobas wondering why the castle tapestries all appeared old, and each played some sort of musical instrument and sang, danced, and otherwise had achieved all the traditional accomplishments of princesses.

'. . . And now,' the king said when he had completed the five-woman roster, 'allow me to introduce your companions in adventure. Perinan of Gellia, step forth and greet your comrades!'

A young man clad in blue finery emerged from the crowd and nodded politely.

'Perinan is a prince of Gellia, second son of good King Kelder.'

Elner whispered, 'What did I tell you about younger sons?'

Tobas made no reply.

The introductions continued through a dozen princes, a few lesser nobles, three witches, a sorcerer, a theurgist priest, and several dozen miscellaneous commoners, all of them male; some did not respond until their names were repeated in their assorted native tongues, and Tobas had the distinct impression very few understood enough Ethsharitic to know what was going on. Except for the king, his daughters, four guards, and a handful of councillors, every member of the crowd that almost filled the huge room had come to slay the dragon. Tobas recalled with a smile what the sailor had said about an army being sent; he had been completely correct.

He was somewhat surprised by the assortment of magicians, though, and that there were so many without a single wizard included. In all of his experience, wizards were by far the most common variety of magician, and witches relatively scarce – not so scarce as sorcerers, but less often encountered than warlocks, priests, demonologists, and the like. He wondered if this was a peculiarity of Dwomor or perhaps of the Small Kingdoms in general, that witches should be more common.

Or perhaps witches didn't like dragons. He dismissed the question as not worth worrying about. Given the presence of magicians, the lack of wizards seemed rather more important; he had hoped, when the first magicians were introduced, that he might somehow pick up a few spells here, but it seemed he would be frustrated.

If he had a few good spells, the right spells, he would not mind tackling the dragon himself, he thought.

But then, if he had a few good spells, he could find easier ways to earn his bread; would a princess and a hundredweight of gold tempt a competent magician? Perhaps not.

The king had completed introducing the would-be

heroes by the time Tobas came to the conclusion that the typical magician would not care to take up dragon slaying; he had gone on to point out his advisors, giving their names and ranks and years of service. Tobas had thought about the situation and had reached a decision. This might be his chance to learn more wizardry.

'. . . And now that you all know one another,' Derneth was saying when Tobas stepped forward. He stopped. 'Yes? Ah . . . Tolnor, was it?'

'Tobas, your Majesty. I hope I am not disturbing anything, but I felt the time had come to mention something about myself.'

'Yes?' the king said.

'Since you did not ask before, I did not care to bring it up, but I think you should know that I am a magician, a wizard.' He made a meaningless gesture in the air, hoping it looked suitably arcane.

The king looked at him for a moment. 'Are you indeed?' he said at last.

'Yes, your Majesty.'

'Well, that's very good, isn't it? That should be very useful against the dragon.'

'I hope so, your Majesty. Ah . . . I have a request, however.'

'Ah. I thought you might.'

'You have introduced me here to several magicians, but no wizards. I had hoped to discuss the dragon with the local members of my Guild, to be better prepared to face it. Could this be arranged?'

'Members of your Guild? You mean wizards?'

'Yes, your Majesty.'

'There *are* no wizards in Dwomor, so far as I know – except, of course, yourself.'

'Oh.' That put an end to that idea. He had revealed his

99

wizardhood to no purpose, then. He had hoped to appeal to the patriotism of any local wizards, asking them to teach him new spells that he could use against the dragon. Even if they did not care to devote their own time to monster-killing, he had thought they might be willing to help him take on the dragon, perhaps for a share of the reward.

Now that he knew there were no such wizards, patriotic or otherwise, he realized that he should have waited and asked around quietly, instead of making a spectacle of himself; he sighed inwardly. He would have to think things through more carefully in the future, he told himself.

'I'm sorry, Wizard,' the king said. He cleared his throat and addressed the entire room again, delivering a speech in Dwomoritic.

Tobas and the Ethsharites waited, fidgeting, through this. Finally, when Tobas was beginning to wonder if a mistake of some sort had been made and the king had not been informed that some of the people present did not understand the language, he finished and switched to Ethsharitic, repeating what was apparently the same speech.

'Now that you have all arrived,' he said, 'and you *have* all arrived, for the Ethsharites are the last, and now that you all know who you are, let us explain that our intention is that you should be organized into parties of five – we do not believe that one man alone would stand much chance against the dragon, be he commoner, prince, or magician. These groups will be sent out to hunt for the dragon, by whatever methods they choose; the reward will be given to whichever party finds and kills the dragon and brings back proof of the deed. We have witnesses to the monster's depredations who will be able to identify

100

the remains and assure that you have killed the right dragon, as there may well be others in the area who do no harm. Each surviving member of the successful party will be given, as promised, the hand of a princess in marriage – we are fortunate in having five unmarried daughters – and with her, a position of honor here in Dwomor Keep. The thousand pieces of gold, all the royal treasury can afford, will be divided amongst these happy bridegrooms as they agree amongst themselves – or, if they cannot reach a peaceful agreement, divided evenly, two hundred to a man, or for those slain by the beast in the killing, to his heirs, if known. No recompense will be made to members of any party save that which actually slays the dragon. The hunt is to begin on the first of Harvest, four days from now, though if any party of five cares to set out before that, we have no objection. These four days will give you a chance to choose your comrades and make your preparations. Some of you appear to have no weapons; the royal armorer may be able to help you. If you have any questions, speak to the royal councillors in the morning; for tonight, we have spoken enough. The sun is down, and the hour for dinner upon us; you are all guests of the castle until the hunt begins!'

That was clearly a signal, and a heavy oaken door in one of the long walls swung open almost the instant the king finished his speech. The thrilling scent of roast beef spilled into the audience chamber. As Tobas joined the mob that pushed its way through into the dining halls, he forgot all about dragons and wizardry and did not worry about them again for the remainder of the evening.

Chapter 11

'Are you really a wizard?' Alorria asked in her oddly lilting Ethsharitic, leaning over the table.

Tobas smiled. 'Yes, I am.'

'Could you show me a magic spell? Please?'

Tobas noticed that he could smell her hair and that he liked the scent very much. She seemed a very agreeable person.

'Oh, I suppose so,' he said, drawing his athame and reaching into his pouch for his vial of brimstone. He looked around for a target and spotted a fat peach sitting atop a convenient bowl of fruit. 'Watch,' he said as he transferred the ripe fruit to an empty pewter plate.

Alorria watched as he made the single simple gesture; the fruit burst into flames with a satisfying sizzle as the dew burned off the fuzz. It was too moist to burn very well; the flames died down quickly, but continued to hiss and smolder until he doused the peach with a sprinkle of rosewater from a finger bowl.

'Ooooh!' Alorria said, and a few seats over Tinira applauded. Tobas smiled and tried to look modest. He had never considered Thrindle's Combustion much of a spell, but to people who had never seen wizardry, it seemed impressive enough. He remembered old Roggit, ancient and feeble as he was, casually drawing glowing runes in the air with a fingertip, or walking calmly up a nonexistent staircase to repair the roof thatch; the Combustion appeared depressingly trivial next to such feats.

'A pretty little trick,' one of the princes nearby

remarked, his words almost incomprehensible with his barbaric accent. 'But the dragon has his own fire; what use will your magics be against that, Ethsharite?'

Tobas, worried about exactly that, dodged the question, replying, 'I am no Ethsharite.' He noted mentally that everyone seemed to agree that the local dragon was a fire breather, which did not bode well.

'You can tell from his accent he's not Ethsharitic,' Arden remarked. 'He speaks the language very well, though.'

'Oh?' The prince looked at Tobas with new interest. 'Did you not arrive with the party from Ethshar of the Spices?'

'Yes, but I was only visiting Ethshar; my home lies farther west.'

'Ah! Tintallion, perhaps?' someone farther up the table asked.

'No. My homeland has no name.' That was more or less the truth. The Free Lands of the Coast was more of a description than a name in the usual sense, and it had become apparent that no one outside the Free Lands used that term. Tobas had no idea what outsiders *did* call the place – Captain Istram had referred to the 'Pirate Towns', but Tobas was not sure what that included.

That answer seemed to satisfy his audience, even to impress them somewhat. Tobas realized he was building up an air of mystery about himself; but, looking into Alorria's fascinated eyes, he could see nothing wrong with that.

He was beginning to think seriously about ways he might manage to get into the successful dragon-slaying party; Alorria was quite a temptation, aside from the money. She looked fifteen, maybe sixteen, he decided, just a little younger than himself.

None of the other princesses was undesirable, either, not even the oldest, Falissa, who was, as best Tobas could judge, in her midtwenties.

The servants were clearing away the dishes; a footman hesitated as he reached out for the plate that held the smoldering peach. 'It's safe,' Tobas assured him.

Someone thoughtfully translated that into Dwomoritic; the footman bowed acknowledgment and removed the unsightly remains.

Tobas turned back to Alorria. 'You speak Ethsharitic very well,' he said.

'Thank you,' she replied. 'Daddy thought it was important that we all learn it. Sellatha refused – she's just not very good with languages – but I thought it was fun.'

'Do you speak any other tonges?'

'Oh, yes! Gellian, Amorite, Vectamonic, and – don't tell Daddy, he thinks it's common – I've picked up a little Trader's Tongue.'

'That's quite impressive.'

'What about you? Is Ethsharitic your native speech?'

'Yes, it is; I'm afraid Ethsharitic is . . . ah . . . the only *human* tongue I know.'

'Oh!' she said.

Tobas felt a little guilty about deceiving the girl by accenting 'human' as he had, but the wave of adulation she poured over him drowned that out quite effectively.

Just then someone at the high table called out something in Dwomoritic, and the buzz of conversation died as everyone's attention turned in that direction.

The king rose and made a short speech in Dwomoritic. Tobas resolved to learn the language as soon as he could – but he would hardly have time, if in four days he was to be out in the mountains hunting dragons.

The speech ended, and Tobas joined in the polite

applause. Immediately, the guests arose, and the dinner party broke up. He was amazed at the speed at which the gathering dissipated and wondered where the princesses, in particular, had vanished to.

He also wondered where he was expected to go. The Ethsharites, he noticed, were similarly confused, lingering in the dining halls.

Just as he was deciding simply to wander off and explore the castle, a robed official appeared, a tall, thin man in late middle age.

'Gentlemen . . . and lady,' he said, belatedly noticing Azraya, 'I am the Lord Chamberlain and I will show you to your rooms, if you will be so kind as to accompany me.' He spoke slowly and stiffly, his phrasing and pronunciation a little old-fashioned, but his accent was very good.

Tobas and the others followed obediently. Four were dropped off as two pairs in tiny, bare stone rooms, and three more were given a slightly larger room. Azraya got a garret to herself and a cot instead of a straw pallet, and, finally, Tobas found himself escorted up a steep, winding staircase to a high-ceilinged, narrow, drafty room atop a tower.

Looking about in the light of the chamberlain's lantern, Tobas spotted an old lamp in a niche on the wall; he lit it with a flick of athame and brimstone, revealing the little chamber to be furnished with a small featherbed, a blanket, and a pile of rusty debris.

'Thank you,' he said as the chamberlain turned to go. 'But why do I have my own room, and why up here?'

The chamberlain turned back. 'It was our understanding that this was customary for a wizard's accommodations,' he said politely. 'If there is any difficulty . . .'

'Oh, no,' Tobas assured him hastily. 'It's fine, thank you.'

The chamberlain bowed and departed, leaving Tobas shivering slightly. The month was still Summersend, but he was chilled nonetheless; the weather seemed to have turned unseasonably cool as the caravan climbed from the hills into the mountains, and the wind that muttered around this tower room felt downright cold.

He looked about, shrugged, and lay down, wrapping himself tightly in the heavy woolen blanket.

This was not how he had pictured himself spending the night; the warmth and luxury of the dinner had misled him, but undoubtedly the castle was jammed to the rafters, with no beds to spare. He knew he had no right to complain, since most of the adventurers had only straw whereas he had a featherbed, but he could not help wondering if the other rooms were as drafty as this one. As a great magician, he supposed he was expected not to mind the cold and to have spells to keep himself warm.

As a matter of fact, he *did* have a spell that would keep him warm, but he was afraid he might burn down the castle if he used it on the rubbish pile and then fell asleep.

He wondered what Alorria's bed was like, then quickly wished he hadn't.

He turned over the evening in his mind, remembering the rich food and the beautiful princesses – and, for that matter, some of the other women at dinner had been comely enough, too.

Women were not a good thing to think about; he forced himself to concentrate on the food and drink, the clever conversation – at least, that part of it which had been in Ethsharitic. Most of the conversation had been pure gibberish to him.

He hoped that whoever he was teamed with for the dragon hunt would speak Ethsharitic.

That turned him to thoughts of the dragon, wondering what it might be like and whether he would actually meet it, which led to reviewing his entire adventure so far, and the next thing he knew, he was awakening to sunlight in his eyes.

The tower had three windows, a fact he had not observed the night before, all of them shuttered and none of them glazed; no wonder it was drafty! He had slept against the western wall; light was seeping in around the edges of the eastern window, and a stray beam had struck his face, waking him.

He sat up and brushed himself off. Doing so, he was reminded how dirty his one tunic and one pair of breeches had become. No one had minded last night, since he had just arrived from a long journey, but he dreaded the thought of facing Alorria and the other inhabitants of the castle in the same garb for another day.

He had no choice, though. He had no other clothes and knew of no way he could wash those he had.

From the angle of the sun he judged it to be about two hours past dawn – breakfast time, if Dwomor Keep followed the same pattern as Telven. He found the door and headed down the stairs.

At the foot of the tower he found himself in a short corridor that debouched into a longer one, and he hesitated for a moment, trying to remember which way led down to the castle's dining area. To the left he thought he saw stairs; he turned left and a moment later was descending an unfamiliar flight of worn stone steps.

At the foot of those stairs, however, he was stymied; he was in a large square hall he did not recognize that was

107

equipped with several doors, all closed, and no other exits but the stairs.

A serving maid emerged from one door and then vanished through another without acknowledging his presence; after a moment's hesitation, he followed her and found himself in the kitchens.

Here, at least, were people, many of them, all busily going about their everyday business, servants of every degree. He tried to ask the nearest person, a lad with a broom, for directions, but got only a blank stare. He shouted and was rewarded with a brief moment of silence, but no answer.

No one in the room spoke Ethsharitic.

Defeated, he returned to the hallway and tried the door the servant had emerged from.

That was better; he was in a small dining chamber, not the one he had eaten in the night before. Half a dozen young men, surely some of his fellow dragon hunters, were arrayed around a table.

'Hello,' he said. 'Am I in the right place?'

No one answered. Again, none of them spoke Ethsharitic.

Baffled, he again retreated to the hallway, where, this time, he found the Lord Chamberlain.

'Ah, the wizard! A pleasure to see you!'

'Lord Chamberlain! Someone I can speak to!' His relief was evident in his tone.

'Have you a problem?' The Lord Chamberlain was all polite solicitousness.

Tobas explained his situation and a moment later found himself in yet another dining hall, taking his place at the table. Four of his companions from the journey from Ethshar were there as well; the others had already eaten and departed. When breakfast had been announced an hour before, no one had cared to disturb the wizard.

Tobas wished more than ever that he had not demonstrated his magical ability – what little he had.

He was relieved to see that the others, save for Peren, were also still dressed in their same travel-worn and dirty clothes.

He settled down and ate quickly, ignoring the fact that the porridge, never particularly tasty, had cooled and congealed, and that the bread had begun to go stale.

The other four had for the most part finished eating and were lingering only to nibble and talk – rounding out the corners, Dabran had called it when Tobas was a child. Elner, Peren, Arden, and Tillis were present, but Elner was doing most of the talking.

When Tobas had eaten enough to hold him for a time, he waited for a lull in the conversation, then asked Elner, 'Tell me, do you speak Dwomoritic?'

'No; I never even heard of it until I signed up to kill this dragon of theirs. I can't tell one of these barbarian tongues from another, anyway.'

'What about you?' Tobas asked Peren.

The albino shook his head.

'Don't bother asking,' Arden said. 'I have enough trouble with Ethsharitic.'

'Tillis?'

'Well, no, not really.'

'What about you, Wizard?' Elner demanded belligerently. 'I suppose you have the gift of tongues and speak it like a native?'

Tobas shook his head. 'Not a word. All I know is fire-magic. If I knew something as useful as the gift of tongues, I wouldn't be here, I'd be safe at home working as an interpreter.'

Somewhat mollified, Elner accepted that and asked, 'Why didn't you ever *tell* us you were a wizard, on the way here?'

Tobas shrugged. 'I didn't think it mattered. As I said, I'm not much of a wizard at all, really.' He saw no point in lying about it – but no point in admitting the sorry truth in detail, either.

'I've heard that mighty wizards will sometimes slay dragons in order to drink their blood,' Tillis said. 'Dragon's blood is said to have great magic in it.'

'You don't just *drink* it!' Tobas said, startled.

'But it does have magic?' Elner said.

'Well, yes, I suppose so,' Tobas admitted, remembering Roggit's precious jar of the stuff. The old wizard had begrudged every drop, but had used it in a wide variety of spells, none of which he had lived to teach Tobas.

'So *that's* why you're here!' Elner exclaimed.

'No, it isn't,' Tobas insisted. 'I'm here for the same reason as the rest of you – I couldn't find anything more secure back in Ethshar.'

'But you're a wizard?' Arden asked.

'A very poor one.'

'But you *are* a wizard?' Peren insisted.

'Yes, I'm a wizard!' He was almost shouting. 'What difference does it make?'

'Before you came in, we were talking about how we would team up,' Arden said. 'Since not everyone here speaks the same language, we can't go with just anyone.'

'*I* shall accompany a prince!' Tillis announced. 'Prince Thed of Mreghon has agreed to permit me to join his noble band in pursuit of the monster!'

'The prince speaks Ethsharitic?'

'Certainly – as well as you or I do!'

'What *I* want to know,' Elner said, 'is where in the

110

World Mreghon is. I never heard of it, and nobody here in the castle seems to know.'

Nobody had an answer to that.

'Have the rest of you made plans?' Tobas asked.

'We were thinking of staying together, the three of us,' Arden said, indicating Elner and Peren.

'You'll need two more,' Tobas pointed out. This seemed as likely a group as any to join.

Elner shrugged. 'Oh, we don't *need* anyone else. I suppose we'll take two more if the king insists.'

Tobas thought about making his request plainer, but his pride rebelled. He had been plain enough. If these fools did not want a wizard along, he would accept that.

He had another three days to find companions; there was no need to hurry.

Chapter 12

Three days passed quickly. Five by five, the adventurers set out for the hills, starting on Tobas' second day in the castle; each night the dining halls were a little less crowded.

The castle armory was also partly emptied, as well as the dining halls, though Tobas noticed that only the second-rate, bent, ill-balanced, or rusted swords were handed out. When he finally decided that he should have a sword, even though he didn't know how to use it, he spent over an hour coaxing a decent blade out of the armorer, using dire threats of magical vengeance and unbreakable curses; and even then, he found a few rust spots and had serious doubts about the metal's temper.

He asked several Dwomorites about the dragon and got a variety of descriptions. It was said to be blue, silver, black, or green and anywhere from forty to a thousand feet long, with the most common estimate fifty or so. One woman claimed it could fly, another that it recited poetry to its victims before devouring them. Everyone agreed that it was scaly and shiny and shaped much like the traditional storytellers' dragon, that it breathed fire, that it ate people, and that it had a very nasty disposition. No one had any useful suggestions on how to go about killing the creature.

Among the various foreigners, no one he spoke to seemed the least bit interested in taking a wizard along with his party while hunting the beast – at least, no one who spoke Ethsharitic. A rather sickly-looking prince from somewhere called Teth-Korun expressed interest through an interpreter, but Tobas reluctantly turned him down; the language barrier would be too much trouble. The prince didn't even speak Dwomoritic; his native tongue, the interpreter said, was Quorulian, and his only other language a variant of Trader's Tongue. He lived in virtual linguistic isolation, since only one other person in the castle, a minor official of some sort, spoke Quorulian; Tobas pitied him, but not enough to join his party.

Although Tobas made it a point to find the other magicians, none of them were any more interested in his company than were the various princes and fortune hunters. The sorceror spoke no Ethsharitic; the theurgist knew only a few words and phrases, most of them religious in nature, and seemed to be generally suspicious of everything about Tobas. The wizard finally concluded that the priest had gotten wizardry and demonology confused, somehow; naturally, no theurgist wanted anything to do with a demonologist.

The witches could all speak to him; only one had actually learned Ethsharitic in the normal way, but the other two had enough magic to pick it up as needed. Witchcraft, Tobas had heard, was very good at that sort of thing; many witches had the gift of tongues. In other schools of magic, it was rare and difficult to achieve.

Ease of communication did not matter, however, as all three wanted nothing to do with him. The three worked as a team and made it plain, politely but unmistakably, that they needed no wizard, with his tools and chanting and ritual, getting in their way. They seemed to consider wizardry somehow old-fashioned and unreliable.

Tobas, for his part, had always considered witchcraft to be a sort of poor relation of true magic, since, in all he had heard as a child, witches tended to be very limited in

113

what they could do and traditionally lived in genteel poverty, unable to compete with the mightier magicians, the wizards and warlocks and sorcerers and the rest, who often became quite wealthy and powerful.

He had to admit, though, that his one pitiful spell was probably of less use than even the feeblest witchcraft. A witch could light a fire without athame or brimstone and with no need of gestures or incantation. Thrindle's Combustion did not require much in the way of ritual or preparation, but it called for more trappings than any witch needed. Disappointed, he gave up on the idea of teaming with a witch and perhaps picking up a little of the craft.

Tobas had also hoped to see more of Alorria, but was disappointed in· that; with several dozen adventurers around, Alorria could spare little time for any one, even the only wizard. Her mother, Queen Alris, was not particularly impressed by claims of magical power and did not allow any of the princesses to show undue favor; after all, any one of them might find herself required to wed any one of the dragon hunters, and any premarital attentions to others might crop up unpleasantly in later years.

He thought that Alorria seemed somewhat disappointed, almost as disappointed as he was, when her mother the queen would come and chase her away from him to take a turn speaking to another adventurer. He hoped that this wasn't just wishful thinking on his part.

He had not even realized that first night in the castle that Dwomor still *had* a queen, but her Majesty Alris of Dwomor certainly made her presence felt during the rest of his stay; it was she who actually ran the household. The king and his courtiers were responsible for the country as a whole; the queen and the Lord Chamberlain were responsible for the castle and everything in it, including the people.

That meant the queen and the Lord Chamberlain were the final authority on who slept where, who ate when, who could see the armorer, who could practice swordplay or magic in the courtyard, and who could speak to whom. Tobas discovered that, as a commoner, he was not allowed any contact with several members of the royal family. The king and queen could do as they pleased, of course, the five princesses had a special dispensation in light of the prospects for marrying one of the adventurers, and not even Queen Alris could control the widowed Queen Mother, but the three young princes – Derneth and Alris had not produced females exclusively – were carefully kept away from the ordinary dragon hunters at the same time that they were encouraged to hang around the foreign princes. Since the foreign princes were often in the company of commoners, making their plans for the hunt, and since a true nobleman is never rude enough to snub someone openly and obviously, this got quite complicated, and Tobas found himself pitying the boys.

There were other princes and princesses around, as well; Derneth had two sisters and a brother who still lived in Dwomor, and the brother had a wife. These four stayed in their own quarters and out of the way. Tobas might not even have known they existed had the attempted robbery not occurred.

The entire theft was bungled from the start.

One of the first parties to equip itself was made up of the three Ethsharites Tobas had considered scoundrels, along with two men from the Small Kingdoms, not of royal blood; Tobas never did get all the names and nationalities straight. He did see the five men together, though, and noticed that they had chosen rapiers from the armory rather than broadswords and carried an assortment of knives, all more practical for use against men than against dragons. No one else seemed to find anything odd about this, so Tobas said nothing.

Although apparently as prepared as they were going to get, this group did not depart, but stayed in the castle, roaming the corridors and making nuisances of themselves, until the final night, the thirtieth of Summersend.

Tobas was in his tower, in that vague state between sleeping and waking, when he heard shouting. The thought gradually penetrated his mind that if he could hear the shouting all the way at the top of a tower, then it must be quite loud indeed, and that in the ordinary course of events nobody had any business making such a racket in the middle of the night.

He sat up and listened. Several voices were yammering at each other.

He rose, pulled on his tunic – he had gotten in the habit of removing it at night, despite the cold, so that it might air out – and descended the stairs to find utter chaos below.

He was unable to make sense of what was going on, but he noticed, with some surprise, unfamiliar faces moving about; he had thought he had at least glimpsed everyone in Dwomor Keep by this time, but here were several he had not previously seen, including a handful with a noticeable resemblance to the king.

After fifteen minutes or so, he gave up trying to make sense of the noise and returned to his bed.

The next morning at breakfast he got the full story pieced together. Arnen and his companions had never had any intention of fighting a dragon; they had planned from the first to steal the reward money and anything else valuable that they happened to come across. Their frequent wanderings about the castle had been attempts to locate the treasury.

They had thought that they had found it when they discovered an entire small wing that no one was allowed to enter and from which no one ever seemed to emerge, directly adjoining the wing occupied by the royal family itself. Accordingly, that night, when they believed everyone to be asleep, they had somehow gained entry to the forbidden rooms; but instead of gold, they had found two middle-aged women who had assumed that rape was intended and had raised a cry.

The five would-be thieves had scattered. The two princesses, Sadra and Shasha, had gone to their nearer brother, Debrel, for aid; it was he whose shouting had first awakened Tobas.

Debrel's wife, Shen, had misunderstood what was happening and thought that her sisters-in-law were somehow conspiring against her; she began her own shouting.

The king and queen and their eight unmarried children had all been awakened, along with a dozen assorted servants, by the noise, each with his or her own interpretation of what was going on, resulting in the incredible confusion Tobas had observed.

The Queen Mother had managed to calm down her family, finally, and the Lord Chamberlain had gotten the commoners in line. Two of the thieves were captured immediately; the third, Korl Korl's son, was found in a larder when the cooks started preparing breakfast. The remaining two, Arnen and one of the ones from the Small Kingdoms, had apparently gotten out of the castle and escaped.

The whole affair struck Tobas as singularly stupid. He had no idea where the thousand pieces of gold might be, but surely they would not take an entire room, let alone

117

an entire wing! One fair-sized chest should do, he estimated. That assumed that the money really existed; at times, he had his doubts. This entire dragon hunt seemed preposterous, and he had wondered whether it might not all be an elaborate fraud of some sort. He had noticed that a few of the adventurers had departed alone or in pairs or threesomes, presumably giving up the quest, and Tobas suspected they might have had the right idea. Azraya had been one of them to his surprise; he had thought she was the sort of person who would stick it out no matter how foolish or dangerous it might become.

He had never quite found the nerve to ask any of the Dwomorite officials why the hunt was being carried out as it was and why no experts or high-order magicians had been called in; that still seemed to him like a far better approach than turning this motley group loose on the countryside.

The attempted theft was the sole topic of conversation throughout breakfast and on into the morning, but Tobas was far more concerned about his own fate than Arnen's. He had signed up to fight a dragon, made a commitment at least to get out in the hills and look, and he intended to make at least a pretense of honoring that commitment, if only because he saw no other way to survive for long in Dwomor and no way to get safely out of the country. He would accompany four others out there and would wander around a little; if they had the monumental bad luck actually to come across the dragon, he would do everything he could to help the others kill it. That, he felt, was as much as anyone could expect from him under the circumstances. As yet, however, he had found no team willing to take him on, and this was the final day, the first day of Harvest.

By the midday meal the population of the castle had

dropped significantly, despite the disturbance of the night before. The king himself made a tour of the dining halls as the adventurers ate, then returned to the chamber where Tobas and the remaining Ethsharites – the trio of Peren, Arden, and Elner – were eating and announced, 'Only nine of you remain. Two groups, then – five in one and four in the other. Have you decided how the division is to be made? There are four in here and five in the Lesser Hall; is that to be the final ordering?'

Tobas and the others looked at one another; this quickly transformed into the other three studying Tobas while he looked warily back.

'I have no plans to the contrary, your Majesty,' Tobas said, breaking the silence.

'We have no objection to the wizard's aid,' Peren said, ignoring distressed glances from Elner and Arden.

'Then that's how it shall be,' Derneth declared. 'We would not send even a wizard against this dragon alone.'

'Your Majesty is very considerate,' Tobas said.

The others said nothing, and Tobas looked at them with some misgivings as the king departed. For the most part, they avoided looking at him at all.

Three hours later the four found themselves in the castle courtyard, their supplies heaped at their feet and the sky thick with clouds above their heads.

'I guess we can't put it off any longer,' Arden said.

'There's no reason to; we're all here. Let's go kill a dragon,' Elner said, hoisting his pack.

'You make it sound easy,' Tobas replied as he picked up his own.

'It will *be* easy,' Elner answered. 'With your magic and Arden's strength and my cunning, that dragon's as good as dead. I just hope someone else didn't get to it first; some of those princes and other foreigners had horses, where we're on foot. We better hurry if we want that reward.'

'Oh, really?' Tobas demanded. 'You're sure it'll be easy, are you? Who do you think you are, Valder of the Magic Sword?'

Startled, Elner stared at Tobas.

'Valder didn't kill any dragons that I ever heard of,' Arden commented.

'He killed demons, though, and if he could kill demons he could presumably kill dragons,' Peren pointed out.

'It doesn't matter what Valder killed; *I'm* the one who's going to kill this dragon,' Elner insisted. 'It's not as hard as you think.'

'What do you know about dragons?' Tobas demanded.

'More than you, anyway!'

'Ha!'

That ended the discussion for the moment; when he judged that it was safe to speak, Peren asked, 'Can you provide transportation, Wizard?'

'No,' Tobas said. 'All I know is fire-magic.'

Peren shrugged. 'It was worth asking.' He shouldered his pack and started toward the gate.

The other three followed, and together the four marched out beneath the raised portcullis.

On the road outside they paused, looking about at the drab scenery and leaden skies.

'Which way?' Arden asked.

'North,' Peren answered. 'All the sightings and killings have been north of the castle.'

'Which way is north?' Elner asked.

Tobas thought he remembered the castle's orientation, but to be sure he looked for the sun, which he hoped would be visible as a bright spot in the deepening overcast. Before he could locate it and reply to Elner's question, Peren pointed off to the right. 'That way.'

Tobas nodded agreement.

'There's a road up ahead that branches off that way,' Arden pointed out.

'The dragon won't follow the roads,' Elner said. 'Why should we?'

This received general agreement, and the four headed off cross-country, around two of the village's houses and past the castle midden.

Tobas tried to ignore the stench of the refuse heap by studying the land and sky around him; the mountains were fascinating, a little like gigantic frozen whitecaps. He looked them over, wondering how much climbing he would be doing in the next few days, then glanced up in time to catch the first raindrops in his face.

By dusk they were past the first ridge, out of sight of the castle, lost in the forests, and soaked through. They stopped for the night in the first clearing they found, which had once been the dooryard of a small cottage. The cottage was now a burned-out, roofless ruin, and after a brief debate about making some use of its charred and crumbling walls, they chose instead to stay well clear and set up their two small tents in the yard in miserable silence.

When the tents were up, Arden and Elner immediately crawled into one. Tobas glared at them through the flap for a moment, then said, 'Hey! What about dinner?'

'What about it?' Elner demanded.

'Someone's got to gather firewood.'

'What for? We can't light a fire in this rain! We'll just eat dinner cold.'

Tobas drew his dagger and stuck his other thumb into his pouch for a little brimstone. 'I,' he declared, 'intend to have a hot dinner, even if it means roasting one of *you*.' He worked his spell, and a small shrub near Elner's elbow burst into flame. 'After slogging up these hills I think we deserve something warm, don't you? *I* can light a fire, rain or no rain!'

Elner stared at the burning shrub, even as the rain doused the flames. Peren announced, 'I'll get the wood.'

Even as the albino vanished in the surrounding trees, Tobas regretted his actions. He had driven a wedge between himself and the others, he knew, by showing off his magic and ordering them around; that might be a serious error. He had no way of knowing how long he would be with these people.

He was not at all sure just what he and they would do. Elner seemed certain that they would quickly find and dispatch the marauding dragon; Tobas was just as sure they would not. Elner probably assumed that this cottage had been burned out by the dragon, Tobas thought, but more likely someone had simply been careless with a cookfire.

Of course, if he was right and the monster was not anywhere near them, what would become of them when the dragon failed to materialize was uncertain.

The hospitality of Dwomor Keep was intended for dragon hunters; if they returned there empty-handed, they would not be welcome. That left two choices – stay in the mountains looking for the dragon indefinitely or go somewhere else. Tobas was all in favor of going somewhere else, but had not yet broached the subject to the others. Elner, convinced that he was destined to kill the dragon, would surely refuse to consider the idea. Arden would go along with the majority.

And Tobas was not sure of Peren. The albino did not usually talk much and did not seem inclined to volunteer opinions or information. However, he was here, so he presumably intended to tackle the dragon.

Maybe a few days of sore feet and wet clothes would change their minds, Tobas thought as he waited for Peren to return.

Chapter 13

'Which way?' Arden asked, staring up at the cliff.

Tobas looked up at the sheer rock face that blocked their path through the trees. They would not be climbing up that, obviously. He glanced both ways, then made his decision. 'Right,' he said, pointing. 'It doesn't look as far around in that direction.'

Arden nodded agreement. Tobas looked at Elner and Peren, but neither seemed inclined to argue; they had let Tobas make the decisions about route, campsite, and so forth since the first night. The entire party turned right and marched on, up the slope through the trees and brush.

Three days had passed since their departure from Dwomor Keep, three days they had spent climbing ever steeper slopes, both up and down, as they zigzagged back and forth and worked their way gradually northeastward into the mountains. The rain, fortunately, had stopped after the first night.

The eastward trend to their travels was Peren's idea; he had pointed out that the mountains in this direction were more rugged, providing more places for a dragon to hide and probably discouraging dragon hunters. Tobas had had some misgivings about the idea of intentionally taking a harder route, but had secretly thought the increased difficulty might convince the others to abandon the quest all the sooner and look for some safer way to make their fortunes. He could, of course, have struck out on his own, but he had no confidence in his ability to survive alone in such unfamiliar and unfriendly terrain; he preferred to stay with the others.

He was particularly worried because every house, hut, or cottage they had come across so far had been a burned-out ruin, far too many for coincidence. The dragon had certainly been in this area at some time and did, indeed, breathe fire; no other explanation made sense. Tobas had no intention of taking a chance on meeting the monster single-handed, and for that reason alone he was determined to stay with the group.

Two days earlier they had caught sight of another party wandering about, five people on foot atop the next ridge over; that had, they all agreed, almost certainly been another group of dragon hunters. Tobas had hoped someone would suggest that the two groups join forces, but no one had; he had been on the verge of saying something himself, when he realized that the other party was moving almost directly away and was already out of sight, making it unlikely that any attempts to catch them would succeed.

That had been their only encounter with other people since losing sight of Dwomor Keep.

'I doubt we're in Dwomor anymore,' Peren remarked as they clambered onward across the slope beneath the cliff, out of the sheltering pines on to an expanse of bare rock.

Elner demanded, 'What are you talking about?' He stopped climbing, forcing Peren, behind him, to stop as well.

'I don't think we're in Dwomor anymore,' Peren repeated. 'The Lord Chamberlain said that most of the higher peaks are across the border in Aigoa, and we're pretty far up now. We haven't seen any ruins since this morning.'

'But the *dragon* is in Dwomor!' Elner said.

'Who says it is?' Peren replied. 'It's been attacking people in Dwomor, but that doesn't mean it lives there!'

Tobas, who had paused and turned back to listen, added, 'Dragons aren't much on boundaries, as I understand it.'

'What do *you* know about dragons?' Elner demanded. 'I thought you only knew fire-magic! That's what you keep saying!'

'That's the only *magic* I know,' Tobas retorted. 'But I do have a little common sense, which you obviously don't! Just how would you know any more about dragons than I do?'

'I know enough. Listen, Wizard, if you know so much, why don't you tell us some of it? Who are you really, anyway, and what are you doing here?'

'I told you who I am – Tobas Dabran's son, of Telven. I'm here for the same reason we all are, to make my fortune.'

'I never *heard* of Telven,' Elner shouted. '*I* say you're some old wizard in disguise here to trick us somehow. Maybe this dragon's a pet of yours, and you're going to feed us all to it!'

'I'm not in disguise,' Tobas said, startled out of his annoyance by the accusation.

'Well, I never saw any wizard who looked like *you* before, with those grubby peasant clothes and that stupid face!'

'And I never saw an idiot who looked like you, but it's pretty plain you're an idiot of the first order! Who do you think I am, then, if I'm not what I say I am?'

'I told you, you're some famous, powerful wizard playing games with us.'

'If I were a famous, powerful wizard, why in the world would I be climbing over these damned rocks and cutting

126

my hands up? I'd fly over them! A wizard needs his hands to work his spells, you know; if I had any choice, I'd take better care of mine!'

'Oh, your poor hands! How do we know you're not healing them as you go and just casting an illusion of the cuts and bruises?'

'I can't *do* that!'

'How do we know that? All we have is your word!'

'What more do you want? Why won't you believe what you see?'

'Because I can't imagine what a young wizard is doing hunting dragons, instead of sitting at home selling love potions!'

'Because I don't *know* any love potions, you idiot! My master died before he taught me anything useful!'

This outburst of honesty was answered by a long moment of silence, broken at last by Arden, who had come back to hear the argument, asking, 'Really?'

'Really!' Tobas said, relieved to have the whole truth out at last. 'His heart gave out before he'd taught me anything but some simple fire-magic.'

'Oh,' Elner said. He sat down on a stone to consider this. 'That's all you know?'

'That's all I know.'

'We never thought of that,' Arden said. 'I know you said you weren't much of a wizard, but we figured that anyone who finished an apprenticeship would be able to make a living without hunting dragons like this, so we didn't believe you. We thought you were some old man in disguise, playing tricks on us. That's why we didn't want you along at first.'

Elner nodded. 'And we thought you enchanted the king into sending you with us. We did what you wanted so as not to anger you.'

'Oh,' Tobas said, too dumbfounded to say more. He, too, sat down.

'I wasn't sure,' Peren said as he joined Tobas and Elner in sitting. 'But it seemed safer to cooperate.'

'Oh,' Tobas said again.

Another moment of silence ensued. 'But I let Peren choose the route,' Tobas said at last.

Elner shrugged. 'We thought either it didn't matter, or he had happened to pick the direction you wanted to go.'

'No,' Tobas said. 'I didn't care.'

'So you don't know if the dragon is anywhere around here?' Arden asked, still standing.

'No, I don't,' Tobas said.

Arden accepted this with mild disappointment and, having said his piece, wandered off ahead. The other three remained sitting, by mutual consent, resting for a moment.

Elner sighed. 'I was hoping you were leading us to it.'

'*I* was hoping you'd forget about it – I don't think we could handle it,' Tobas answered.

'Really?' Peren asked interestedly. 'Even with your fire-magic?'

Tobas shrugged. 'I'd just as soon not try,' he said. 'Dragons are dangerous.'

'But – ' Before Peren could finish his question, a yell from Arden interrupted him.

Elner jumped to his feet; Tobas rose more slowly. 'What is it?' he called.

Arden had vanished around the rocky shoulder at the end of the cliff; now he reappeared, scrambling desperately across the rocks.

'I found it!' he shouted.

'Found *what*?' Tobas asked, but no one bothered to answer as a yard-long blast of flame followed Arden,

128

narrowly missing the top of his head. Obviously, the dragon really did breathe fire.

'At last!' Elner cried, drawing his rusty sword. 'We found it!'

Tobas spared one wondering glance at the madman before he turned and ran for the limited shelter of the forest. Peren was right beside him, and Arden close on his heels.

When they were under the trees, Tobas paused long enough to glance back and got a good, clear look at the dragon.

The creature was fifty or sixty feet long, just as most of the reports had said, and it stood at least fifteen feet at the shoulder, its monstrous head raised up even higher on a long, arching neck. Four huge claws dug cream-coloured talons into the solid rock of the hillside, and an immense pair of wings lay folded on its back; the scales that covered its entire body were a glossy blue-green. Its eyes were red and bright, its nostrils flared and edged with crimson; the fangs that gleamed from its upper jaw were at least a foot long, Tobas was certain. Smoke trailed upward from its mouth, but, after that first gout of fire, it had not spat flame. It gave no sign of speaking, let alone reciting poetry. It looked utterly bestial, with no trace of intelligence beyond what it needed to stalk its prey.

Elner was standing frozen, staring at it as it walked toward him at a leisurely pace; the sword was shaking wildly with his trembling as he finally realized that slaying this dragon would *not* be easy.

The dragon bent its head down for a closer look.

'*Do* something!' Arden shouted in Tobas' ear. 'It's going to eat him!'

'Either that or roast him,' Peren said.

Tobas simply stared in horrified fascination.

'Wizard! Do something!' Arden repeated, pointing. 'Use your magic!'

The dragon was reaching out with one of its great foreclaws, about to snatch Elner up and devour him, and Tobas had no more time to think; he snatched his athame from his belt, dipped a finger in brimstone, and flung Thrindle's Combustion at the dragon's face.

Flame erupted with a roar, pouring out of the dragon's mouth and nostrils, not projected forward, but simply rushing up around the monster's muzzle, across its eyes. Startled, the creature reared back, forgetting about Elner and batting at its mouth with its armored foreclaws.

Tobas could smell the smoke, sour and oily, as he stared out at the frantic monster.

Peren, in a display of phenomenal courage, rushed out and grabbed Elner, dragging him back toward the trees before the dragon could regain its composure.

It had managed to extinguish most of the flame by simply closing its mouth and smothering the fire, but smoke and flame were still streaming from its nostrils. It dropped back to all fours and shook its head back and forth, trying to put out the remaining fire, but without effect. Finally, it snorted with a sound like a windstorm, blowing out the last flickers.

By then, however, Peren had dragged Elner into the forest, out of the monster's sight.

Elner was still shaking, still incapable of moving without guidance; he cowered behind a tree, whimpering softly.

Arden stood behind another tree, staring wide-eyed at the dragon. 'I didn't realize it would be so *big*!' he whispered.

Tobas was also watching the dragon, trying to decide

130

what to do next – run, stay hidden, or use the Combustion again.

'Good work, Tobas,' Peren said, the albino suddenly close at his side. 'Can you do anything else, anything that might kill it?'

'No,' Tobas admitted. 'I only have that one spell with me.'

'Try it again – maybe you can set the beast on fire.'

Tobas shook his head. 'I don't think so. I've heard that dragons are fireproof, especially fire-breathing ones. They have to be. If I hadn't caught it off guard and ignited its own fuel, I don't think my spell would have done anything at all.'

'Try it anyway,' Peren insisted.

'All right.' Tobas raised his athame, fished out another pinch of brimstone, and threw his spell.

Sparks spattered harmlessly from the dragon's flank for a moment, but nothing more. The monster did not even seem to feel anything. Tobas tried again, aiming for the dragon's face, but with its mouth held tightly closed, the creature was protected; sparks showered ineffectually from its jaw.

'No,' Tobas said. 'I didn't think so. I can't do anything more to harm it.'

'What do we do, then?' Arden asked.

'We wait,' Peren replied. 'If it comes toward us, we run.'

The dragon was not coming toward them. It was pawing at its mouth again, apparently in some discomfort, even though the fire was out. The pawing did not seem to be doing any good; after a moment, it reared back and roared, spitting out a tongue of flame half the length of its own body, then spread its wings, flapping vigorously. Tobas suppressed a gasp at the sight of its wingspan, which he guessed to be over a hundred feet. It fluttered clumsily off the ground, wings beating wildly and managed to get twenty or thirty feet up before making a crazy sideways swoop down the hillside.

Tobas watched it go with inexpressible relief. Until the moment it took off, he had not believed it could fly at all, even in the awkward fashion it had just displayed; that aerial ability added to its terribleness.

He guessed, from the direction it took, that it was heading for a small lake that the four young men had passed that morning; the unexpected mouthful of flame must have given the monster a sore throat. He was inexpressibly grateful that the creature had not been angry enough to set the forest ablaze out of spite.

When the dragon had flapped off down the hill and was safely out of sight, he turned and said, 'Let's get out of here; when it's feeling better it's likely to come looking for us.'

Arden and Peren immediately nodded agreement; Arden helped the still-dazed Elner to his feet, and together the four of them set out into the forest with no goal in mind save to put as much distance as possible between the dragon and themselves.

Chapter 14

When the four youths were all satisfied that the dragon was safely behind them, they settled on the banks of a small, gurgling stream almost a league northwest of the site of their confrontation with the beast. By mutual consent, they collapsed to the ground and for several long minutes they simply rested, drinking from the stream and gnawing on dried apples from Peren's pack.

When he felt himself able to breathe without effort again, Tobas raised himself up on one elbow and said admiringly, 'That was a brave thing you did, Peren, dragging Elner away from the dragon.'

Peren shrugged, his face pink – though whether with embarrassment or exertion Tobas could not be sure.

'Thank you,' Elner said. 'You saved my life.'

Peren still said nothing.

'I didn't know dragons got so big!' Arden said. 'I saw one once in the Arena, during Festival, and it wasn't anywhere near that size.'

'My father told me they come in all sizes,' Tobas said, thinking in particular of one of Dabran's visits during his childhood, when he had asked whether pirates ever met dragons or sea monsters. His cousins had told him more about dragons over the years than his father ever had, but it was his father's words he remembered.

'I wish my father had told *me* that,' Elner said. 'I didn't have any idea; I just thought that all the stories must be exaggerated. My mother used to say that half of every good story is exaggeration. I saw a twelve-foot dragon once, in the Arena – I guess it was the same one you saw, Arden – and I was pretty sure I could handle something that big. I didn't know they got any bigger. The dragon's handler said it was an adult; he claimed it had laid eggs. My father took me around to talk to him after the show, and the handler told me that his dragon was full-grown. I believed him, so I was sure I could handle a dragon and that all the stories were exaggerated.'

'I wondered why you seemed so sure of yourself,' Tobas said.

'Maybe that one you saw in Ethshar *was* full-grown,' Peren suggested. 'If it laid eggs, it was a female; the males might be much larger.'

'Was that one we just saw a male?' Arden asked.

'Who knows? How does one tell with dragons?' Peren answered.

'Or maybe they come in all sizes, like dogs or fish,' Tobas suggested again.

Elner listened, blushing. 'I guess I made a fool of myself, didn't I?' he said.

Tobas had enough tact to not answer that directly. Instead, he asked, 'Why did you want to be a dragon slayer in the first place?'

'Oh, I don't know . . . no, that's not true. I wanted to show my parents that I could make it on my own. They're rich, you know – my mother's father was the Lord Magistrate of Westwark, and my father owns three ships and a warehouse. I lived comfortably, if you know what I mean – didn't go out of my way looking for an apprentice-ship or a rich marriage or anything, didn't join the Guard or anything stupid like that, and my father kept asking when I was going to make something of myself, and my mother kept worrying that I'd get in trouble somehow if I didn't do something with my time. I got fed up with their

134

nagging, finally, and decided to do something to impress them. Killing this dragon seemed easy enough; I didn't know it would be so big, and I thought the fire-breathing part was a myth.' He shook his head. 'I guess it didn't work.'

Tobas said thoughtfully, 'Oh, I don't know; you tried, anyway. You don't need to tell them all the details. Just tell them that you stood your ground and faced the dragon alone when all the others fled, but that it was too big for you actually to kill by yourself.'

'But I froze! I was too *scared* to run!'

'Why tell them that?'

Arden chimed in, '*I* won't tell anyone.'

Something occurred to Tobas suddenly. 'Arden,' he asked, 'what did you see around the rocks there before the dragon came after you?'

Arden shrugged. 'Not much. There's a little flat area – not a plateau, really, it's too small for that – and it looks as if there was a village there once, but it's just cellar holes and loose stones now. And there's a cave back in the other side of that cliff, and that's where the dragon was.'

'That's probably its lair,' Tobas said.

'I don't know,' Arden said. 'It's just a cave, I think.'

'You couldn't have seen much of it, though.'

'Well, no . . .'

'And what does a dragon's lair look like, anyway?'

'I don't know,' Arden admitted.

'I think that's the dragon's lair, then,' Tobas declared.

Nobody argued the point further.

After a long moment of silence, Elner asked, 'Well, what do we do now?'

Tobas hesitated, but finally asked, 'Do you still want to go after the dragon?'

135

'By all the gods in Heaven and the demons of Hell, of course not!' Elner declared. 'Do you think I'm crazy?'

'I was just asking,' Tobas said mildly, trying not to smile at Elner's vehemence. 'We know what it's like now and where its lair probably is. We know what we'd be up against if we went after it.' He had no intention of going after the dragon, but he wanted to know where his companions stood on the matter.

'I don't think that cave is its lair,' Arden insisted.

'Whether that's it's lair or not, I'm not going back there and I'm not going to try and kill it,' Elner said. 'I'm going back to Dwomor and buy passage back to Ethshar. If they ask me at the castle, I'll tell them as much as I can about the dragon, but I'm going home; I've had enough of this. Let my parents nag me if they want to.'

'You won't try to seduce Alorria?' Tobas asked, teasing. 'I'm sure marrying a princess would impress your family.'

Elner snorted. 'There are plenty of pretty girls at home, and *they* don't care that I'm a commoner. Alorria can marry a dragon slayer or a prince, with my blessing.'

'What about you, Arden?' Tobas asked.

Arden looked uneasy. 'I guess I'll go back,' he said. 'I don't want to see that dragon again, and I don't much like Dwomor from what I've seen of it. I don't have any money to buy my way home, but maybe I can find work and earn enough to pay for my passage.'

'I'll pay your fare,' Elner volunteered. 'I'd be glad of the company, and you can pay me back later. Maybe my father can give you a job, if you want, aboard one of his ships.'

'All right,' Arden said, obviously relieved. 'I'd be grateful. I'm no sailor, though; maybe he could find a job for me on shore.'

'Whatever,' Elner said, dismissing the matter.

'Peren?' Tobas asked. 'What are your plans?'

The albino did not answer for a long moment. Finally, he said, 'What about you, Tobas? Aren't you going back?'

Tobas hesitated for a few seconds before answering. He had been asking the others at least partly to help him make up his own mind. He had arrived at a decision, but was not yet entirely sure of it. 'No,' he said slowly. 'I don't think I am – at least, not unless all three of you go back. There's nothing for me in Dwomor or Ethshar, and I'm not welcome in Telven anymore. I was never very welcome in Ethshar, for that matter. I think I'd rather go on over the mountains into Aigoa, or whatever it is that's on the other side, and see if I can find something profitable to do there. I'm not going to try and go alone, though; if all three of you want to go back to Dwomor, I'll come with you and see about finding some way to make a living there – or to get somewhere else.'

'I'll come with you,' Peren said. 'I don't have anything in Dwomor or Ethshar, either.'

'Thank you,' Tobas said sincerely. He turned to the others. 'Arden? Elner? Would you reconsider?'

Elner shook his head. 'I'm going home,' he said emphatically.

Arden wavered, but then likewise shook his head. 'No. I'm going with Elner. These mountains, and trees, and dragons and castles, and princesses – they're all strange. I'm going back to Ethshar. I grew up on the streets there and I guess that's where I belong.'

Tobas nodded understandingly; his own home was gone, but he did not begrudge the others theirs. 'I guess this is good-bye, then. Peren and I will be heading on to the east, over the mountains, and you'll be heading south, to the castle. We'll probably never see each other again.'

He paused, then said, 'Good luck; may the gods watch over you.'

'Don't be in such a hurry to get rid of us!' Elner said peevishly. 'It's almost sunset; I figure we'll camp here tonight, the four of us, and split up in the morning.'

Tobas glanced at the western sky and realized Elner was right. 'Well, then, let's get the tents set up,' he said, reaching for his pack.

The four of them spent a pleasant evening together, talking about their lives, discussing wild schemes for disposing of the dragon – though they all knew none of them would be implemented – and enjoying one another's company. The tensions that had previously kept them at arm's length had faded with Tobas' revelation of the extent of his wizardry and with the greater understanding that had resulted from the confrontation with the dragon.

In the morning they packed up the camp, divided the supplies, and headed off in their separate directions.

As Elner and Arden were about to vanish from sight among the trees, though, Tobas called after them, 'Hey! What will you do if you meet the dragon?'

Elner turned back, drew his sword, flourished it over his head, took a heroic pose, and called back, 'Run for our lives!'

Tobas and Peren laughed, then turned and hiked on up the slope.

Chapter 15

They came upon the ruined town on the morning of the second day after leaving their companions. Peren was the first to see it; he pointed it out to Tobas.

Although the ruins looked quite old, they were well up into the mountains by now, and Tobas wondered whether looters would have gotten this far. Even if they had, they might have missed a few items; the town looked fairly large. He could not imagine why a community of any size would have been built up among these empty mountains in the first place. Curiosity, combined with the possibility of finding abandoned valuables, compelled him to suggest they investigate more closely.

Peren had no objection, and together they headed across the forested valley that separated them from the ruins.

The town had been built into the stony slopes of a fair-sized mountain peak. Tobas estimated that it had once been home for three or four hundred people, but that seemed incredible up here in the barren middle of nowhere.

They reached the outskirts just after noon and paused to rest and eat before continuing.

When they had brushed away the last crumbs, they cautiously approached the nearest ruins and looked them over. Tobas guessed that the building had been a house, but a very peculiar house; the few windows were narrow slits, so that the interior would have been very dim and gloomy had the roof been present.

The rooms inside were arranged oddly. Tobas could not locate a kitchen at all; he found no oven and no chimney.

As Tobas poked through the scattered stones in a back room, Peren exclaimed in surprise. Tobas turned and peered back through the door; the albino was holding up something small and black.

'What is it?' Tobas asked.

'Sorcery!' Peren announced.

'Really?' Tobas came back to look at Peren's find.

It was a convenient size and shape to fit in the palm of a man's hand, partly corroded metal and partly something black that had a texture resembling shell or ivory.

'What is it?' Tobas asked again, when he had studied it closely.

'I don't know,' Peren admitted. 'But doesn't it look like a talisman? You're the magician; don't you know what it is?'

'I'm a wizard, not a sorcerer. I've never seen sorcery in my life. It looks like a lady's jewel case to me, not a talisman.'

Offended, Peren took it back, saying, 'Well, it looks sorcerous to me!'

'All right, maybe it is,' Tobas agreed.

They found nothing else of interest in that first building, and moved on to other ruins.

They turned up nothing of value. In one roofless and crumbling ruin Tobas found a sword lying atop a heap of rubble, thick with rust; When he picked it up the blade fell to powder, leaving him clutching the lead-wrapped hilt and sneezing uncontrollably, a long reddish rust streak down his arm.

'This place must have been built during the Great War,'

he remarked. 'Maybe they came up here to get away from the Northerners.'

'Or from the press gangs,' Peren suggested. 'I can't believe the Northerners ever got anywhere near this far into the Small Kingdoms.'

'How long would it take a sword to rust away like that, anyway?' Tobas asked. 'The air up here is pretty dry, isn't it?'

Peren nodded. 'Yes, it is. I'd say that must have been lying there . . . oh, three or four hundred years, anyway. The war's been over for two hundred, after all.'

Tobas looked at the hilt with increased respect for a moment before tossing it away. 'Three hundred years ago, Telven was empty grassland.'

'Ethshar was about half the size it is now, I guess,' Peren said.

Tobas looked at his companion. 'I suppose you're used to old things, then, but in Telven . . . well, if my grandfather made it, it was old. We didn't have anything from the war; Telven wasn't built until long after it was over.'

'Where is Telven, then? You've never said.'

'Oh, it's near the coast, west of Ethshar of the Sands,' Tobas said, trying to sound casual. His reply was truthful enough, if not quite complete. He was unsure how Peren might react to learning that his companion was a pirate's son.

'Near the Pirate Towns?'

'Near there,' Tobas agreed uncomfortably.

They moved on, spending the rest of the day exploring the town. They found nothing of any value, but accumulated considerable evidence that led them to surmise that the place had been abandoned roughly three hundred years earlier, after only a century or so of occupation.

Several of the buildings were cut directly into the living

rock of the mountain; Tobas judged that most of the work had been done by magic. He had heard that the ancients used much more magic than modern people, and this town seemed to bear that out quite emphatically. They found traces of a demonologist's pentagram carved into the stone floor in one house, shattered jars and broken shelves reminiscent of wizards' workrooms in several others, and any number of mysterious objects that Peren thought might be sorcerous. Witchcraft and theurgy left no traces, of course, and warlockry had not been known until the start of the fifty-third century, so they came across no evidence of those, but they encountered what Tobas thought might be wholly unfamiliar magics, perhaps entire schools now lost – strange etchings in floors and walls, substances neither of them could identify, and shards of oddly shaped vessels of glass and porcelain.

They made camp in one of the larger, cleaner ruins that night and made a very peculiar discovery when Tobas tried to light their campfire. Thrindle's Combustion would not work. He tried it several times, with no success.

Finally, he gave up and let Peren light the fire by means of slow, laborious work with flint, steel, and tinder.

When the fire was going and two strips of dried beef were soaking in a tin of hot water, Tobas shook his head. 'I don't understand why the spell didn't work,' he said for the hundredth time. 'I know I did it right. It's been months since I made any error in it. It *always* works.'

'Maybe you're just tired,' Peren said.

'No, that's not it; I've done it plenty of times before when I was tired.'

'Maybe it's something about the ruins, then.'

'Maybe. Maybe so much magic was used here that some of it still lingers, and that's messing up my spell somehow.'

'That sounds reasonable.'

'I suppose it does.' Tobas was still not fully convinced, even though the theory was his own. Finally he shrugged.

'I'll just have to try again in the morning.'

In the morning he tried the spell again, several times, still without success.

'I'm going to go back down and see if it works outside the ruins,' he announced.

'I have a better idea,' Peren said. 'Why don't we go the rest of the way up to the peak and take a look around? From there we may be able to see the far side of the mountains and see how much farther we have to go to reach Aigoa – or someplace, anyway. And you can try your spell up there; the ruins stop before the top.'

Tobas had to admit that sounded reasonable; he followed as Peren led the way through a broken wall on to the open slope.

Fortunately, the mountainside above the town was not particularly steep. It was, however, the highest peak in the area, and the winds were ferocious and unpredictable, whipping Tobas' tunic about like a flag. He climbed with his arms wrapped about himself, keeping the garment from ballooning out with each gust.

A few feet from the top Peren stopped abruptly and fell to his knees, then crawled forward, first on all fours and then on his belly. Tobas stopped in his tracks and watched this performance with surprise.

Then he looked on ahead of his companion and saw the reason for it. Squinting against the wind and concentrating on his own garments and feet, he had not really watched the terrain ahead. They had reached the peak, and, rather than the symmetrical slope down the other side he had expected, Tobas saw that it ended in a cliff. Peren had not dared to approach that sheer drop while standing upright in a high wind.

Tobas realized he didn't care to, either, and dropped to his belly before inching up to Peren's side.

The view looking over the cliff was incredible – and distressing. The mountains continued for as far as they could see, row after row of them, some wooded all the way to the top, others with bare gray rock peaks that reached above the timberline or lacked sufficient soil for trees to grow in.

Tobas glanced back the way they had come and noticed a determined patch of lichen clinging to the rocks. Remembering what he had come up here for, he fumbled at his belt, found his dagger and brimstone, and tried Thrindle's Combustion on the lichen.

Nothing happened.

Annoyed, he sheathed the blade and looked out over the cliff again.

Peren was staring off into the distance, studying the mountains, and Tobas saw little point in that. Instead he looked down toward the bottom of the drop.

Something very odd stood almost directly below them. He inched up farther toward the edge and stared down, shading his eyes with one hand.

'Peren,' he said, 'do you see that?' He tugged at the albino's sleeve and pointed.

Peren looked. 'What is it?' he said at last.

'I think,' Tobas said, 'it's a castle.'

'That's ridiculous,' Peren said. 'Why would anyone build a castle down there, where an enemy could drop things on them, instead of up on a mountaintop, where they could see farther? And besides, I can see the sides as well as the roofs; it's all crooked.'

Tobas studied the structure for another long moment. It was undeniable that whatever it was, it was at a very

144

strange angle. 'I don't think it was built there,' he said. 'I think it *fell* there.'

Peren looked at him in surprise, then ran a hand along the edge of the cliff. 'You mean from here?'

Tobas nodded. 'Maybe,' he said.

Peren looked down at it again, then back toward the ruins. 'You can't be right,' he said. 'I mean, it would make sense, a castle up here would have guarded the town behind us, I suppose, but the fall would have smashed it to pieces!'

'Not if it had strong magic holding it together,' Tobas suggested.

'But magic won't *work* here, will it? Your spell didn't.'

'Wizardry doesn't work here *now*, but maybe it did once; after all, weren't there ruins back there that looked as if they were wizards' laboratories once? Besides, I don't know about other kinds of magic; maybe it was sorcery that held it together.'

Peren stared down at the red roof and white walls of the mysterious structure. 'Maybe you're right,' he admitted grudgingly.

Tobas said, 'I want to go look at it.'

Peren looked at him, then back down the cliff. 'That must be a thousand-foot drop,' he said. 'We can't climb down that.'

'No, of course not!' Tobas said. 'But we can go around.' He pointed off to their right, to the south, where the cliff dropped down to meet another slope.

'Besides,' he added 'that's no thousand feet. Three or four hundred, if you ask me.' He started backing away from the edge.

Reluctantly, Peren followed him.

When they were both upright and walking back down through the ruins, Tobas remarked, 'That castle looked intact, not very ruined at all; I mean, not only did it survive the fall, but it hasn't weathered away since. I guess it's pretty well sheltered there, with the mountain on one side and trees on the other. And hidden, too. There might still be some valuables.'

Peren nodded. 'Maybe. I wonder what it's doing there, though. Why would anyone build a town and a castle up here? A town of draft dodgers or refugees I suppose I can understand, but a castle? And on a precipice where it fell off eventually? Who would build such a thing?'

'I don't know,' Tobas said. 'But maybe we can find out.'

As they worked their way down the mountainside, Tobas insisted on stopping every few hundred yards to try his spell. As he had expected, it failed completely all the way down through the ruined town and at the first two stops beyond the ruins as well.

After that, however, it worked, feebly at first, and then more reliably. He successfully ignited several small shrubs and a patch of moss. Peren grew annoyed at the frequent stops and the need to put out the various fires Tobas started, but made no protest.

As they circled around to the southeast, the spell's power faded again, so that it elicited only a few sparks by the time they reached the south end of the cliff face, and ceased to work at all as they turned northward again, toward the fallen castle.

Trees blocked their view for almost the entire way, even when they had rounded the mountain, but at last they caught glimpses of their goal through the leaves. As they drew near, it became quite clear that it was, indeed, a fallen castle.

It stood upon a great slab of stone, tilted at what Tobas estimated as a third of a square angle from the natural horizontal and vertical; one tower had apparently crumbled upon impact and lay stretched out across the edge of the slab and into the forest. It was a fair-sized but compact castle, several stories tall but with no outbuildings, no extraneous wings or walls, and no moat or outer defenses at all. It had once had six towers; five still stood.

The central structure was rectangular, with a tower at each corner and one at the center of each of the long sides; the main roof was steeply sloped so that the ridgepole was almost even with the tops of the surviving towers. Almost all of the red-tiled roofs were intact, though several were streaked with moss or bird droppings, and dead leaves were packed into corners. The walls were of some unfamiliar smooth, pale stone.

It looked nothing at all like the crudely constructed castles Tobas had seen in the Small Kingdoms, at Morria, Stralya, Kala, Danua, Ekeroa and Dwomor. The walls were flat and straight, the corners sharp; even in its fallen and filthy state, the roof showed no sag at all.

As they drew nearer, Tobas studied the slab on which the castle stood, growing ever more perplexed. It was immediately obvious from the color of the stone that it was not the same as the cliff from which it had presumably fallen; the slab, like the stone of the castle walls, was almost white, while the cliff had been dark gray granite. Furthermore, the slab seemed to be perfectly circular. The castle was tilted toward them, more or less, allowing them to see the upper surface of the stone, and Tobas could see no sign of where it might have broken loose from the cliff.

When they reached the edge of the stone, Peren quickly circled to the lowest part of the rim and started to climb up on to it, but Tobas reached out and grabbed his arm. 'Wait a minute,' he said. 'I want to look underneath first.'

Peren looked down in surprise. 'How?' he asked. 'Do you plan to lift the entire castle?'

'No, I mean I want to look at the other side of this chunk of mountain it's sitting on.'

'Oh. Well, I'll wait here if you like.'

'All right.' Tobas let go, leaving Peren sitting on the edge of the white stone surface, three feet above the floor of the surrounding forest, his legs dangling down over the side.

Unsure what he expected to see, Tobas worked his way slowly around the rim, which gradually rose up well out of reach as he moved along. He looked up at the great tilted stone, studied the widening gap between the rim and the ground beneath, peered into the shadows under the castle, and finally became absolutely convinced of his theory. The slab was shaped like a slice off the side of a globe; it had never been attached to this cliff or any other.

He made his way back to where Peren sat whistling.

'Well?' Peren said.

'This castle didn't fall off that cliff,' Tobas said.

'I know it doesn't look like it, with the different stone, but where else could it have come from?' Peren demanded.

'I think it flew; it flew here and then crashed – maybe because magic doesn't work here.'

Peren was openly skeptical. 'A flying castle? Are you serious? I know that magicians did some amazing things during the war, but a flying castle?'

'You come and take a look at this thing and tell me how it could have gotten here any other way.'

Peren turned and looked thoughtfully up the slope behind him. 'You *are* serious, aren't you? And I can see why, really. I don't need to look; I believe you, I guess. But Tobas . . . a flying castle?'

Tobas nodded. 'I've heard of them before, though I admit I didn't really believe in them until now. Roggit – my master – told me about them. He used to brag a lot about how wonderful wizards were, to keep me from asking him to teach me more spells more quickly. He said I had to know all about wizards before I could be one. According to Roggit, the wizards during the war knew how to build flying castles and move them around anywhere they pleased – at least, some of them did, for a while. Roggit said that most of the really big magic got lost long before the war was over, so that people now don't believe half of it ever existed.'

'So you think this castle flew and then crashed here because wizardry doesn't work here?'

Tobas nodded. 'That would be my guess, yes. Maybe it was a weapon of some kind that was responsible. What if the castle had been attacking that town up there, and they had used some secret emergency weapon that stopped magic from working? After they used it, the enemy castle would be down, but who would want to live in a town where magic doesn't work? So they left, and that's why those ruins are the way they are.'

Peren studied the castle thoughtfully. 'Maybe,' he agreed. 'We don't know about *all* magic, though, just wizardry. Something like this castle, and all those wizards who lived up there, maybe they just used up all the wizard-magic around here.'

It was Tobas' turn to be thoughtful. 'Maybe,' he said, 'but I didn't think it worked that way. I don't think you *can* use up all the magic in a place. If you could, would magic still work in Ethshar?' Before Peren could reply, he added hastily, 'Maybe it would; I don't know for sure, I'm just guessing.'

'If it was attacking the town,' Peren said uneasily, 'then

149

wouldn't it have been a Northerner castle? I don't think I like the idea of messing around with anything Northern.'

'It might have been,' Tobas conceded. 'But I think it's more likely that it was a local dispute of some kind, if there was any fighting at all. After all, Old Ethshar broke apart into the Small Kingdoms while the war was still going on. And I never heard of the Northerners getting this far; you said yourself that it doesn't seem possible.'

'That's true enough,' Peren admitted.

'We'll never find out anything by standing out here,' Tobas said. 'Do you want to go in?'

Hesitantly, Peren nodded.

Tobas was both frightened and eager. The castle did not look safe, perched on a sliver of stone and tipped at so uncomfortable an angle, and he suspected there was a very real possibility that any disturbance might bring the whole thing crashing down, but this was a wizard's castle; it could be nothing else. And not just any wizard; this had been the airborne stronghold of a wartime wizard, one of the really powerful ones. No ordinary wizard would have a flying castle. In its prime, the place would have been fraught with wizardry of every sort.

And some of those spells might still be here, in books or scrolls or charms, all of them harmless, their protective spells inoperative in this strange place of no wizardry, but ready to function when he took them back to the normal, everyday world.

Here he might at last find magic that would not only make him a wizard but might make him truly great! What reward would be too great for the Wizards' Guild to pay the member who rediscovered the lost arts of the ancients? He could be set for life if this castle held such spells!

He was quite literally trembling with fear and anticipation as they crawled up the sloping stone slab toward the castle gate.

Chapter 16

The heaped debris in the old gateway puzzled Tobas at first; but as they got close enough to see it properly, he realized that the gates had been solid iron and had rusted away like the sword in the ruined town, but, unprotected by even a ruin, they had collapsed beneath their own weight, or perhaps caved in before a storm.

Whatever the exact events had been, Peren and Tobas were able simply to crawl through the open gate on hands and knees. Had it been at a different angle, they could have walked in, but neither felt secure standing upright on the steep slope of cool, slippery white stone.

The castle had no courtyard – not even a garden, so far as they could make out. Neither Tobas nor Peren had ever heard of such a thing. But then, neither one had ever encountered an ancient wizard's stronghold before; the ordinary rules of castle building would not apply to an airborne fortress.

Instead of a court, the gate opened directly into a large hall, dimly illuminated by dirt-encrusted windows in the upper part of the wall at the far end. Arcades ran along either side on three different levels, while below the windows the first floor ended in a wooden screen topped by a broad balcony.

The room was tilted so that the near left corner was the lowest point; the slope from side to side was pitched roughly twice as steeply as from one end to the other. Tobas half climbed, half slid down into the lowermost arcade and got cautiously to his feet.

A layer of dirt and debris had accumulated along the seam of wall and floor where he stood, providing fairly solid, secure footing. He was able to walk easily along the side of the hall, under the arcade, save where doorways opened off into other chambers. At each doorway he was forced to brace himself with his hands and step carefully across to avoid slipping down into the side room or corridor.

Behind him, as he reached the first such opening, he heard Peren sliding down from the doorway to follow him.

The walls of the great hall were polished stone, white up to shoulder height and black above that. Tobas guessed that the change in color was to prevent smoke stains from showing. The wires and brackets that had once held tapestries were still hanging, but the tapestries themselves had rotted and crumbled, for the most part. A few recognizable fragments were tangled in the layer of rubble on which he stood.

Rusting fragments of candelabra still clung here and there as well, both on the walls and on the pillars of the arcades. However, there was no evidence that the hall had ever held any considerable amount of furniture; neither Tobas nor Peren could find any trace of tables or chairs. Peren found something he believed to be the remains of a fur rug, but Tobas was not sure that the foul, black, stiffened thing wasn't the remains of some small animal that had wandered into the castle and died there.

One small comfort was that whatever decay there might be had mostly taken place already, and the only smell was of dry, ancient dust.

When they reached the innermost end of the arcade, Tobas studied the wooden screen and balcony with misgivings. As he understood it from stories he had heard as a child, the lord of a castle would traditionally have his own apartments on an upper floor, leading off the inner end of the Great Hall, but he had no way of knowing whether this long-dead wizard had followed that tradition. Dwomor Keep had not, since it had no proper Great Hall, but this castle had no such lack. If the lord's apartment were indeed reached by way of the balcony, that would be where they would be most likely to find valuables – gold and silver do not rust or rot, so they presumably would have survived, though the silver would be badly tarnished.

The wood looked solid, but Tobas found it hard to believe that no ants or termites had gotten at it and that damp breezes through the rusted-out gate had not rotted it. He tapped at the screen.

It *sounded* solid. Perhaps it had been painted or stained with some powerful preservative, Tobas thought. He motioned for Peren to come closer.

Neither one of them had spoken since entering the building; both of them felt, without knowing why, that speech would be somehow inappropriate. Now, though, Tobas broke the silence, saying, 'Catch me if I fall.'

Peren nodded, and Tobas threw his weight against the screen, testing it.

It creaked, and dust whirled up from somewhere above; he felt a very slight give, but the wood held firmly enough to satisfy him. 'Wait here until I call,' he said. 'I want you to be able to come after me if something breaks.'

Peren nodded again, and Tobas began inching his way along the sloping floor in front of the screen, toward the stairs that led up to the balcony. He used the elaborate carvings that decorated the screen as handholds.

There were two staircases, one from either side; they met in a small landing at the center of the balcony's forward edge. The nearer one, however, Tobas did not care to climb; its slope was added to the castle's tilt, making it virtually unnavigable.

The further staircase, however, had the castle's tilt *subtracted* from its own rise, so that it was now very gentle indeed, so long as one could avoid falling forward from the angle of the treads.

Tobas reached and climbed the second stair without incident and found himself on the broad balcony that had obviously been where the head table stood.

The table itself lay upended and broken against the lower side wall, but Tobas could make out the gleam of gold amid the dust and wreckage surrounding it. He made his way cautiously down the sloping floor to investigate; since the wood here, blackened and splintering as it was, was far less slippery that the stone floors below, he stayed upright.

A moment later Tobas leaned out over the balcony's rail and cried, 'Hey, Peren! Catch!'

Peren reached up and caught the object Tobas flung to him, and a smile spread across his face as he looked at it and felt its weight. It was a dented golden goblet, and from the weight it was plain that, unless someone had been foolish enough to use poisonous lead in a drinking vessel, it was not just gold-plated.

Tobas rummaged through the remains of the head table for several minutes, but turned up no more goblets. He did find two small golden bowls.

Nothing else seemed worth digging out, and he turned away at last to see what else he could find.

What he actually hoped for, more than anything, was to find the wizard's Book of Spells. With wizardry inactive, of course, it would be no more than an ordinary book and could easily have rotted away decades ago, but he still hoped.

The wizard-lord would presumably have kept the book tucked away safely somewhere in his own inner chambers – either that, or in a laboratory in one of the towers. If it had been in the tower that had shattered, then the Book was gone, but the odds, Tobas told himself, were against that.

As for the lord's inner chambers, from this public balcony Tobas expected to find access to a smaller audience chamber, which should in turn lead to a sitting room, and that to a bedchamber, and that, finally, to a study. At least, that was what he understood the tradition to be, and, in modified form, that was how Dwomor Keep had apparently been arranged originally, before overcrowding had forced changes to be made. Of course, Dwomor had no Great Hall at all, so he could not use it as a model – but perhaps the Great Hall was what they now used for an audience chamber, or had been broken up into smaller rooms. In any case, the royal apartment had been described to him as following the pattern of audience chamber, sitting room, bedchamber, and study, though the study was off to one side rather than in a straight line and the original audience chamber now served as a dining hall.

This, however, was obviously not Dwomor, and might well not be traditional. He looked around the balcony.

The wall across the back of the hall looked like solid stone, and in fact the windows led Tobas to take it to be the back wall of the castle's main structure, which would mean that the Great Hall stretched the castle's entire length. He looked back along it, trying to judge it, and decided that that was about right. There would be no concealed doors in that wall.

At each end of the balcony, however, were two ordinary, unconcealed doors – one on the level of the balcony, the other reached by way of a narrow staircase. Seeing no grounds for a decision, he simply picked the nearest, the one at balcony level on the lower end, a few feet from the remains of the broken table.

Brief investigation in the semidarkness led him to conclude that the room beyond was a service area of some sort. He found no traces of tapestries or rugs, but a great deal of broken crockery, lit only by narrow, stingy window slits. A staircase at one side led down. He guessed that it led to the kitchens, and this room was where meals were readied for final presentation to the high table.

He did not yet feel up to tackling the stairs to the upper level, so he climbed up the balcony to the far end.

The room at that end also appeared to have been intended for ignoble use; the most recognizable item he found there was unmistakably a chamber pot, and the walls were lined with the rusted remains of coat hooks, indicating a wardrobe or cloakroom.

With those two exits yielding nothing of value, he gathered his nerve and tried the stairs at the high end.

This was more promising. The chamber he found at the top appeared to be a sitting room rather than an audience hall, but it was, at any rate, part of someone's apartment. Furthermore, the furnishings were fairly intact; apparently the rain, wind, and insects had not often penetrated this far. Several chairs were recognizably chairs, and two small tables were completely undamaged.

And, although they contributed nothing to his search for more magic, there were several small items of obvious value – golden candlesticks, a jeweled box, and miscellaneous trinkets. Leaving them for the moment, he moved on through the only door.

This next room was unmistakably a bedchamber; the canopy and mattress were a mass of dry, black corruption, but the frame was still complete, though Tobas was fairly certain that it had not originally been wedged into the lowest corner. Drawers were spilled and tumbled on all sides, and enough of their contents was still recognizable to make it evident that this had been a woman's bedroom.

That did not signify very much, though; there was no reason that the castle could not have been built and flown by a female wizard.

Tobas gathered up several odd bits of jewelry; if all the gems in them were authentic, he knew he had just pocketed enough to live on for four or five years, if he were careful.

He doubted, however, that most of them were genuine.

This chamber had three doors in addition to the one he had entered through; one let out on to the uppermost level of the arcade. Tobas leaned out through that one and waved to Peren, just to reassure him that no accidents had occurred.

The next door he tried led to a privy, and the third to what had apparently been a dressing room. Here he found a few more bits of jewelry, which, again, he gathered up quickly.

Seeing nothing more worthy of investigation in this suite, he climbed back down to the balcony and began working his way toward the other staircase.

Before he had gone halfway, though, Peren called up to him, 'Wait a minute, Tobas.'

He paused. 'What is it?'

'How is it that you're doing all the exploring?'

Tobas had no good answer for that.

'It seems safe enough,' Peren insisted.

'All right, then,' Tobas agreed. 'Come on up. On that

157

side is the lady's apartment; this side should be the lord's then, and I think it was he who was the wizard.'

Peren nodded. 'We'll see,' he said as he headed for the stairs.

As he drew near, Tobas remembered the jewelry. He held out a handful of gold and glittering gems – though much of the gold was probably plate, and the larger jewels glass. 'I found these up there,' he said. 'We'll divide them up later.'

'All right,' Peren said.

'Now, let's see what's up here.' Tobas led the way up the remaining staircase.

As he had expected, it led to an audience chamber roughly the size of the lady's sitting room and bedroom put together. A heavy wooden throne still stood in its accustomed place, obviously bolted to the floor, but the other furnishings had largely been reduced to a layer of dust, sticks, and tatters along the lower edges. The draperies behind the throne that had once shielded the inner chambers had been eaten away by insects, leaving a sort of ragged lacework thick with dust; when Tobas poked at them, they collapsed completely.

He and Peren moved on into the sitting room; here, protected by solid walls, unbroken windows, and the stubborn drapes, time had done little damage. Tables and chairs were heaped along the lower edges, but only a few were broken; boxes lay scattered, their contents spilled and lost for the most part. Some still held powders; Tobas looked at these carefully, sniffing cautiously at some.

He could not identify any with certainty, but he thought several of the powders resembled ones he had seen Roggit use in his spells. Perhaps the wizard-lord had kept ready supplies of some of his ingredients close at hand, in case magic was called for during audiences.

A few of the empty boxes were trimmed with gold, jewels, or time-blackened silver, but those which held powders were unadorned.

Tobas did not bother to pick up any of the valuables here; he had enough from the lady's chambers. Peren, however, still had an empty pouch or two on his belt and gathered up the most obviously precious items.

A door led out to the upper arcade of the Great Hall, and another led farther into the apartment.

The next chamber was not, as Tobas had expected, the bedchamber, but appeared to be a small guardroom or antechamber. Four chairs, their upholstery crumbled to dust but otherwise still sound, were piled in one corner, and several spears and swords lay nearby, blades blackened but still solid.

Beyond that was the lord's bedchamber. Under the thick coating of dust that lay everywhere, the mattress and draperies were still intact – brittle, faded, incredibly dry and fragile, but intact. The bed itself had slid down against the lower wall, but had not tipped over or broken. Two wardrobes had been less fortunate, as had an immense chest of drawers. Something heavy had struck the formal railing below the foot of the bed and reduced it to kindling, a few of the scattered pieces still shiny with gilding.

Their footsteps stirred up the dust, and both youths sneezed a few times in response.

Three doors led onward, one to a privy, one to the arcade, and the third, at last, to the wizard's private study.

The furniture here had been simple enough – no tapestries, no carvings, just a simple unadorned table and walls completely lined with shelves. About half of the shelves had remained in place, though their contents had not; everything else lay in a great heap of rotting books, broken glass, and scrap wood.

Tobas immediately began pulling out the books, looking for a Book of Spells, ignoring the clouds of dust that rose around him and ignoring Peren.

Peren, for his part, went back to exploring the rest of the castle, gathering up anything that looked even remotely valuable in a sack improvised from the most intact of the wizard's bedroom tapestries.

The sack shredded under the weight of the loot fairly quickly, and Peren switched to collecting as much as he could carry and heaping it on the balcony.

He had been at this for perhaps an hour when the fading of the light became unmistakable. He made himself a torch out of tapestry fragments and an old table leg, spent fifteen minutes getting it lit – the fabric might be dry, but igniting it with flint and steel was still no easy task – and then returned to the wizard's study.

He found Tobas squinting in the thickening gloom, trying to make out the contents of yet another book.

'Tobas,' he said, 'it's getting dark.'

'I know,' the young wizard replied. 'Could you make me a torch like that?'

'Have you found anything?'

'Histories, love poems, and even cookbooks, but no books of magic. I thought this was one, but it's not; it's a text on the curative properties of herbs – useful, I suppose, but not wizardry.'

'Have you noticed that there isn't a single fireplace or chimney in this entire castle?'

'Hm? No, I hadn't; I suppose it was heated by magic originally. Could you get me something for more light?'

'Can't the rest of these books wait until morning?'

'What?' Tobas looked about himself absentmindedly;

in his hopeful fascination with the books he had become somewhat distracted. 'Oh, I guess they can, really. I found something else, though – look here, behind these boards.' He rose and crossed to the lower end of the sloping floor, where he pushed aside a pile of fallen shelving and pointed to empty darkness beyond.

The study was not the final room in the wizard's apartment; Tobas had found a door leading on still farther into the depths of the suite.

'What's in there?' Peren asked.

'I haven't looked,' Tobas replied. 'There's no light. I don't think there are any windows, just solid stone walls. I was waiting for you to come back before I decided what to do about it.'

Peren held up his torch and peered in. 'It's a passage-way, I think, not a room.'

'It would have to be; we've come the full length of the castle already. This must run across the front, directly above the gate, inside the thickness of the downstairs wall.'

Peren nodded agreement and held the torch out before him. The flame did not flicker; the air in the passageway was dead and still. 'I'll go first,' he said.

'All right,' Tobas agreed. 'I'll be right behind you.'

Chapter 17

The passageway sloped up across the full width of the front of the castle, Tobas judged, and was unbroken by any windows or ornamentation at all. It consisted of bare stone walls and floor, a simple barrel-vaulted ceiling, and nothing more. It had originally been level, of course, and the angle was not particularly steep even now. The pitch from side to side was greater than along its length, so that Peren and Tobas hung close to the right-hand side, walking along the bottom edge.

Despite the absolute simplicity of the corridor, or perhaps because of it, Tobas was certain that the entrance from the wizard's study had once been concealed, though whether by shelves, draperies, or some other device he could not be sure amid the general ruin. Perhaps there had once been an illusion spell that had been dispersed when the castle's magic ceased to function.

The corridor was narrow; Tobas had to keep his elbows close to his sides to avoid bumping the walls. Peren, who was thinner, had an easier time of it.

They were about two-thirds of the way along, Tobas judged from his memory of the Great Hall's width, when Peren stopped so abruptly that Tobas ran into him; both staggered on the sloping floor, and Peren had to fall to one knee to keep from losing his torch.

'What is it?' Tobas whispered – speaking aloud in such a place was unthinkable.

'Look for yourself!' Peren said, pointing.

With the albino down on one knee, Tobas was able to

see over his shoulder; he took a good look at the end of the corridor.

The right-hand wall continued unbroken for another forty or fifty feet, while the left-hand wall ended after thirty or so; from where they stood, Tobas could not see any details of the wider area, or room, or whatever it was they were approaching.

He could, however, see what Peren had seen, lying on the floor. He had never actually encountered one before, but there could be no mistaking it.

It was a human skeleton, the bones of the legs and feet protruding out into the corridor, the rest still invisible around the corner – or at any rate, Tobas assumed that the rest was there, just around the corner. The tattered remnants of velvet slippers were tangled with the bones of the feet.

A moment of unreasoning dread came and went, and he quickly recovered his calm. 'What of it?' he said, doing his best to sound as if he had come across skeletons dozens of times before. 'He's dead. I want to see what's up there. Let's go on.'

'What killed him?' Peren whispered, horror-stricken.

'How should I know?' Tobas was quite uneasy enough without Peren adding to it; he was determined to move on before he lost his nerve, and was annoyed at the albino's reluctance. 'Probably he fell and hit his head when the castle crashed,' he guessed wildly.

Peren glanced back at Tobas, then ahead again, gathered his nerve, and nodded. 'You're probably right. Or maybe he was a burglar, and the wizard caught him there, and the castle crashed before the body could be removed.' He rose to his feet and started forward again.

Tobas followed, certain that something was wrong with Peren's suggestion and trying to figure out what it was; as they reached the corner, he realized that the crash would not have prevented the survivors from removing bodies. There had undoubtedly been survivors, or else the castle would have been littered with corpses – or rather, by now, skeletons. If anyone had known this body was here, it would have been removed despite the castle's fall.

He liked his own theory better, that the man – or woman – had died here in the crash, and none of the survivors had known this passage existed. Or if they *had* known about it, no one had thought to check it in the confusion and panic that must have ensued.

When he passed the end of the left-hand wall into the room, he paused and looked down at the skeleton first, while Peren held the torch close.

It had been a man, plainly. He had worn leather breeches and a dark tunic with gold embroidery; the golden threads still gleamed in the desiccated and decayed remnants. An assortment of rings mingled with the outstretched finger bones, ranging from a simple gold band to an ornate tangle of gems and metals that must have covered an entire joint from knuckle to knuckle. A wide leather belt was now reduced to a few blackened strands and a tarnished silver buckle, and the purse that had hung from it had rotted and spilled forth an assortment of blackened silver and corroded green bronze. No gold coins, though; the two youths were disappointed in that.

Beside the purse was a dagger, its sheath rotted; Tobas picked it up cautiously while Peren collected the coins.

Hilt and blade were black, black as chimney soot; there was no trace of the brown of rust. Fine detail work was still sharp in places where iron or steel would have lost its shape as it corroded.

Tobas rubbed at the pommel with his tunic, and although he could not work down to a clean shine, he wiped off enough of the black to convince himself, by both look and feel, that the dagger was silver.

Who would carry a silver dagger? Only a wizard. Steel held a better edge, barring enchantment, and was far cheaper.

Forgetting for a moment that he was in a place where wizardry could not work, he drew his own athame and touched the points of the two blades together. Peren watched with interest.

Nothing happened.

Even as he completed the experiment, Tobas cursed himself for a fool. The dagger's owner was long dead, and magic did not work here. He could not test his belief that this skeleton had belonged to the castle's master. He sheathed his own blade and stood up.

'I think that this was the wizard,' he said. 'Or at any rate *a* wizard.'

Peren nodded. 'The rings – they look magical.'

Tobas had hardly noticed the rings, but he nodded agreement all the same. He had almost forgotten that the athame's nature was a closely guarded secret and that ordinary people had no idea a wizard's dagger was anything especially important, until Peren had reminded him with his remark; he had been assuming that Peren would have recognized the knife's peculiarities for himself.

Peren raised the torch, which he had been holding down near the skeleton to aid Tobas' investigation, and said, 'I wonder what he was reaching for.'

'Probably just trying to regain his balance,' Tobas said. The skeleton did appear to be reaching out into the darkness; the left arm was bent as if supporting the shoulders, while the right was stretched out to its fullest extension, fingers spread.

'I guess you were right,' Peren said as he leaned down

near the skull. 'The fall killed him. See? The bone is cracked.' He pointed to where the forehead had been split and almost caved in. 'He must have hit hard; I think he was running.'

The torch lit the domed skull an eerie orange-red, the cavities black with shadows that moved as the flame flickered. Tobas did not care to look at the dead man's remains any longer; instead, he looked around at the space they were in.

The corridor opened out at this end into a room, almost twenty feet square, utterly bare and empty, save for one wall. The floor was blank stone; there was no furniture or debris. One side, to the right of the skeleton, was an extension of the right-hand wall of the corridor; on the wall opposite that hung the only adornment, a broad, dark tapestry.

Tobas stared at it, unable to make out details in the gloom, but certain that there was something odd about it. 'Bring that light here,' he said.

Peren lifted the torch and rose from where he crouched by the broken skull. He took a few steps closer to the tapestry so that the torch lit the entire scene, and together the two adventurers stared at the hanging.

It was unlike any tapestry either of them had ever seen; it was all a single scene, depicted in incredible detail and absolutely flawless perspective, showing a pathway leading across a narrow band of rough stone toward the gates of a castle.

Above the pathway towered the castle itself, shown almost in its entirety, a very strange and forbidding castle built of gray and black stone, its every available feature carved into a leering, demonic face. The main entryway was a gaping, spike-toothed mouth, and two windows above it served as eyes, so that the castle itself seemed to

166

have a malignant face as well. A gargoyle perched atop each merlon in the battlements; each corner was decorated with fiends standing upon one another's shoulders for the full height of the structure. Towers hung out at odd angles, cantilevered without any signs of buttressing, topped with battlements of jagged spikes or conical roofs made to resemble furled bat wings. Inhuman, grinning faces, carved in black stone, peered over the tops of some of these, seeming to look straight out of the tapestry at the viewer.

The base of the castle stood on a rounded mass of rock, like a weathered mountaintop, with a few feet of clearance on each side and then cliffs dropping away out of sight or even seeming to curl back under. It was separated from the pathway by a narrow bridge of ropes and planking that was stretched across a yawning chasm.

To all sides of the castle and pathway, beyond a yard or so of stone, was simply space, limitless space, lit eerily from somewhere unseen with purple and crimson.

Tobas stared at it, studying it. It had none of the fuzziness or texture of an ordinary tapestry, no single underlying background color; it looked almost like a painting, or even a window, rather than mere cloth. Furthermore, it showed no trace of decay at all. At the very least, it was a truly fabulous work of art; he had never seen a tapestry so finely crafted and detailed.

Peren turned away, a trifle unsteadily. 'I don't like it,' he said. 'That thing is hideous! No place like that could possibly exist, with those cliffs, that empty sky, and that foul light.'

Tobas glanced at him, then back at the tapestry, still fascinated. 'It's beautifully done, though. Look at the detail! You can see a red highlight there on that gargoyle's fang and another here – that must be a spider web, that shiny line there. I've never seen anything like that. And the colors would probably be better in daylight; you know torches make everything look reddish and bring out the shadows.'

'I don't like it,' Peren repeated, unswayed.

Tobas ignored this complaint and said, 'Bring that light closer. Notice how it isn't faded or worn? It looks brand new.' Hesitantly, he reached out a finger and touched the cloth. It was cool and slick to the touch, a little like fine silk, with none of the warmth and give of the wool used in ordinary hangings.

Peren reluctantly brought the torch nearer so that Tobas could study the tapestry's fabric more closely.

'Look at this,' Tobas said. 'The fabric's partly made out of metallic threads – gold, I'd guess. And the colors – I think that red is some sort of powdered gemstone. It looks like ruby.'

'That's ridiculous,' Peren said. 'Why would anyone make a tapestry out of gold and jewels? And if they did, why would they hide it up here?'

'It must be magic of some sort,' Tobas said, studying the demonic figures.

Peren took an involuntary step backward. '*What* sort?'

'Oh, I don't know; wizardry, probably, given where we are, but it could be something used in demonology, too, I suppose. If it's wizardry, I can't say what it was for; Roggit never mentioned anything like this. It might be something oracular, or maybe the wizard could use the tapestry to conjure up monsters. *I* don't know; Roggit certainly didn't have any magic of this sort.' He looked up to see how the tapestry was supported; it hung from loops around a metal bar. Tobas took the torch from Peren and held it up.

The bar was gold-plated, which explained why it was

168

intact; even the brackets set into the stone wall gleamed golden. 'Here,' Tobas said, 'I'll take this end; you take the other. We ought to be able to get it down.'

'Why do we *want* to?' Peren asked. 'We should leave it where it is.'

'I want it, that's why we should take it down. This is the only thing we've found in this wizard's castle that's obviously magic and looks as if it might still work, and I'm a wizard in need of more magic. Even if I can't figure out how to use it myself, if I can get it back to Ethshar I can trade it to a wizard there for a few spells. If this wartime wizard thought it was important enough to be hidden away like this, to use up all this gold, and for him to be trying to reach it when he died, then it's *got* to be something really powerful. It *looks* powerful. Even if no one knows what it's for, it would look impressive enough in a wizard's shop to please anybody. And if somebody *can* use it, and it's as powerful as I think it is, this could set me up for life!'

His enthusiasm was not contagious. 'I don't like it,' Peren insisted. 'It scares me.'

Tobas sighed. How could a man who had dashed out in a dragon's face to rescue a companion be terrified by a mere picture? 'Listen, Peren, it's harmless here; no wizardry works, remember? Help me get it down; if you help me get it out of here, you can have first pick of all the other loot, everything you can carry. I'll take this tapestry for my share.'

'You will?'

'I will.'

'It might be a demonological thing, you said.'

'It might be, but it probably isn't, and maybe demonology doesn't work here either. Besides, if it's wartime demonology, it might not work anymore *anywhere*, since

169

the gods closed the old openings into Hell. The rules are different now.'

'But . . .'

'If it were dangerous, wouldn't it already have done something? Come on and help me.'

'All right,' Peren said after another few seconds of hesitation. Reluctantly, he propped his torch up against a wall and crossed to the far end of the tapestry.

The brackets were above their heads, but by standing on tiptoe and stretching Tobas was able to push his end of the bar up and away from the wall. Peren, being taller and at least as strong, had an easier time of it.

Nothing terrible happened; it collapsed like any ordinary hanging. Once it was down, Tobas insisted that Peren help him roll it up around the bar, and together they reduced it to a compact bundle. It was surprisingly thin and light for its size; the rod was roughly an inch in diameter, the tapestry a good seven feet high, but the entire roll was only four inches thick.

It was so light, in fact, that Tobas had second thoughts about his conclusion that thread-of-gold had been used. The bundle was eight or ten feet long, but weighed no more than a hundred and fifty pounds, at most. With effort, Tobas could carry it single-handed.

He hoisted it on his shoulder, staggering slightly on the sloping floor, while Peren recovered the torch and headed for the passageway.

'Wait a minute,' Tobas called. 'What about the wizard's rings? And that dagger of his is good silver.'

Peren stopped and looked down at the skeleton, then back at Tobas. 'Are they enchanted?'

'Who knows? The rings might be. The dagger – well, I think I know that spell, and with the wizard dead it would be broken, permanently. But I can't be sure; after all,

there's so much here I don't know. For all I can say, this
no-magic area may have a permanent effect – I'm not sure
my own magic will come back, even when we're out of it
and back in someplace normal. I'm just guessing.'

This was true, but he did somehow feel that his athame,
at least, would still be enchanted when he left the area.
After all, the dagger held a part of his soul, and he
couldn't imagine that it could have died permanently
without his feeling something.

On that basis, he thought that any sort of magical
imprinting, such as a major enchantment, would be
effective again when removed from this eerie dead area.
He certainly hoped so; he was counting on the tapestry to
be powerful magic. He thought of the deadening effect as
if spells were paintings, and magic the light that made
them visible; the paintings could be taken into a dark
room, and there they would be invisible, no more wonderful than blank board; but when returned to the light,
the colors would be as bright as ever.

At least, he hoped that that was how it worked and that
wizardry was more like color than fire, which, once
extinguished, had to be rekindled.

Peren still hesitated over the skeleton, but at last, with
a sudden grab, picked up the dagger and tucked it into his
own belt. The rings he decided to leave, which Tobas had
to admit was probably a wise decision.

Together, the two youths made their way back down
the sloping corridor; Tobas needed Peren's assistance to
maneuver the long, heavy, awkward roll of tapestry
around the corner and through the door into the study.
Once it was safely through, he lowered it with a gasp of
relief, letting it rest atop a pile of crumbling books.

'Are you really planning to haul that all the way back
to Ethshar?' Peren asked, working the muscles of his back

171

to relax them after the strain of helping Tobas with the ponderous roll of fabric.

Tobas, who had never been fond of strenuous lifting, was still trying to catch his breath; he nodded. He gulped air and, when he felt he could spare a little breath, said, 'Yes, I am. I'll carry it as far as Dwomor, then see about hiring a wagon or something. I think it's worth it, I really do. But right now all I plan to do is eat dinner and then sleep in a wizard's bed. What about you?'

Peren grinned in agreement.

Chapter 18

They spent all the following day exploring the castle more thoroughly. Tobas needed the entire morning to maneuver his prize tapestry step by step out through the wizard-lord's apartment, down the two flights of stairs, and back across the Great Hall to the gate, while Peren gathered a good-sized pile of booty from throughout the castle. In the afternoon it was Tobas' turn to explore, while Peren settled down in the Great Hall to pick through his booty and decide what was worth carrying away and what could be left. By the time the sun set again the wizard had gone through every nook and cranny, while the albino had put together in one pile his final selections – roughly thirty pounds of gold, silver, and jewelry in various forms.

'You know,' Peren remarked to Tobas as they ate dinner at a table they had righted in one of the lower rooms, 'we'll both be rich when we get home. Even if that tapestry isn't good for anything but melting down, that rod it's on must have ten pounds of gold on it, maybe more. Figure ten per cent for the smith's fee, and that's ninety pieces of gold. They say a man can live on one copper a day if he's not picky; ninety of gold are nine thousand of copper. Say four hundred and fifty a year, that's twenty years you can live just on that.'

Tobas nodded. 'And with it all in that tapestry I don't need to worry about sneak thieves picking my pocket or burgling my room at the inn, the way you do!'

Peren laughed. 'Ah, but *I* have far more than ten pounds here!'

'Counting the jewels and silver, maybe, and they're probably half fake, too.'

Peren laughed again. 'What if they are? *Pounds* of gold, and silver, and handfuls of gems! If nine out of ten are just cut glass, I'll still be able to call myself a rich man! How could this one wizard have had so much wealth! It astounds me, it truly does. And Tobas – I think half the castle had already been looted, too. I didn't find anything worth taking anywhere but the two main apartments. The butler's vault had been broken open and all the plate cleared out; the armory had all of three swords left, two of them bent and the other one broken. The towers were empty – at least, the five I climbed. I didn't care to see what was left in the fallen one.'

Tobas nodded. 'I think the castle servants probably carried off everything in sight when they fled after the crash, but most of them wouldn't have had the nerve to go into the private apartments. The wizard died; we saw that. As far as the servants were concerned, he had probably just vanished into thin air – they didn't know about the secret passage. They probably didn't dare steal from his suite, lest he reappear suddenly. What puzzles me is what happened to the lady; her jewels were still there, at least some of them, and I would have thought that she and her maids would have taken them all. There's no sign that she, too, died – and it would have been quite an odd coincidence if she had, don't you think?'

Peren shrugged. 'Maybe she wasn't home.'

'Maybe.' They ate in silence for a moment.

'Tobas,' Peren said at last, 'are you sure you want to go back to Ethshar?'

Surprised, Tobas replied, 'Well, I thought so; why?'

'I don't think I do. I grew up there and I've seen all of it I care to. It's true that I have my own money now, but my hair's still white and my eyes still red, and the children in the street will probably still call me a ghost or a demon, even if I'm wearing velvet instead of homespun. This sword I carry didn't make any difference; I don't think the gold will either.'

'Well, what of it?' Tobas demanded. 'The gods played a nasty trick on you when you were born that way, but what can you do about it? Where else would you go?' He was not comfortable with the subject; he had never paid much attention to Peren's coloration, nor thought about how he might deal with those who did think it important.

'I don't know, not for certain,' Peren replied. 'I think I want to go on across the mountains and see what's on the other side, in Aigoa or whatever land lies to the east.'

Tobas remembered the rows of mountains, marching off into the distance, that they had seen from the peak above the castle. He shuddered at the thought of trying to cross them all, let alone drag the massive tapestry over them. 'It'll just be more miserable little kingdoms like Dwomor,' he said, hoping to discourage Peren. 'The Small Kingdoms extend as far as the Great Eastern Desert, don't they? And that goes right to the edge of the World. There's nothing out there worth seeing. If you don't want to come back to Ethshar, if you think the Small Kingdoms are better, you can stay in Dwomor.'

Peren shook his head. 'I don't think so. We didn't kill their dragon. I don't think they'd appreciate having us come back rich while the dragon's still out there somewhere.'

Tobas had no answer for that at first, but finally managed, 'Well, not *everyone* can kill their stupid dragon. We've been gone more than a sixnight now; probably one of the other teams found it and killed it.'

Peren shook his head. 'You saw that dragon, Tobas,

and you saw the hunters; do you really think anyone's killed it?'

'Uh . . . maybe the witches?' he suggested hopefully.

'Maybe the witches,' Peren conceded. 'I don't know much about witchcraft.'

'Neither do I,' Tobas admitted.

'You just know fire-magic, isn't that right?'

Tobas smiled. 'That's right,' he agreed.

Peren smiled back, then turned serious again. 'No, Tobas, I don't want to come back to Dwomor. Would you want to stay there? It's a pretty dreary little kingdom, even without the dragon rampaging about.'

'What about Ekeroa, then?'

'It's better,' Peren admitted, 'but I really don't want to go back. We might run into the dragon, for one thing, and we'd have to go by way of Dwomor. I simply don't want to see that ramshackle castle again. I want to go on to the east, over the mountains.'

Tobas could avoid it no longer. 'I don't,' he said. 'I'm sorry, but I just don't. It's too far, too lonely, and too hard a journey. I'm a lazy person, Peren; that's how I got into this mess in the first place; I was too lazy to work when I thought I had an inheritance coming. I got this far to keep from starving. But now that I have this tapestry, I don't need to go any further and I'm not going to. We don't have enough food to get over the mountains – hell, I'm not sure we have enough to get back! What will you eat?'

'I'll hunt; I have a sling, a sword, and two good knives.'

Startled, Tobas asked, 'You do? Can you use a sling?'

Peren nodded.

'Oh,' Tobas said. 'Well, maybe you can do that, then, and catch what you need, but *I* can't hunt. And I don't want to depend on you for food like that. I'm going back.

I'm going back to Ethshar, where I'll sell this tapestry to a wizard, trade it for spells, or melt down its metal, and then I'm going to take the money and settle down quietly somewhere and make a home for myself. That's all I want, a home; I don't want any adventures. I'm going back.'

'I'm going on,' Peren said quietly.

'You're sure?'

He nodded.

Tobas nodded acceptance. 'All right. We'll go in the morning, then, you to the east and I to the west.'

That settled, the conversation died away, and they retired early, Tobas sleeping in the wizard's bed, Peren sleeping on a blanket in the Great Hall.

Chapter 19

Hauling the tapestry was more work than he had anticipated; he had forgotten how much up and down there was to the road back to Dwomor Keep. He was also unsure of the best route; until the foursome had split up on the fourth of Harvest they had been zigzagging about almost at random, looking for the dragon. He had estimated that he would have been able to get back to the castle in four days, unburdened, but the tapestry cut the distance he covered each day by at least half.

The first night found him scarcely to the edge of the magically dead area; he worked Thrindle's Combustion three times before he got a campfire lit.

The second day he covered slightly more ground, but watched with concern as the sky clouded over. He hoped that the tapestry would not be harmed by rain; when he settled for the night, he slept uncovered, using his blanket to protect his prize instead of himself, draping his pack over the end the blanket could not reach.

As he had expected, rain began falling around midnight, building from a slow sprinkle to a steady drizzle.

The third day he struggled onward, desperately trying to keep the tapestry dry and out of the mud, and far more concerned with finding shelter than with traveling any great distance. At last, around midafternoon, he found a broad overhanging rock ledge protruding from a steep hillside. He crawled under it, pushing the tapestry as far in as he could.

He remained there that night and all through the next

day, waiting out the rain; his supply of dried beef gave out, leaving him nothing but raisins and one very stale biscuit.

The thirteenth of Harvest dawned gray and dim, but without rain, and Tobas decided to risk moving on. The skies cleared as the day wore on, and he made good time; he was fairly sure when he made camp that night that he had passed the point where he and the others had encountered the dragon. He judged that to be half a mile or so north or northeast of where he finally stopped.

He finished off his last provisions and awoke ravenously hungry on the morning of the fourteenth. Water was easily found in the wake of the rain, in pools on rocks as well as in streams, but food was not so readily come by.

He did find some nuts, which he cooked with Thrindle's Combustion and ate from the shell; that helped slightly. He considered hiding the tapestry somewhere and coming back for it later, so as to conserve his strength, but decided against it; he was fairly sure he was nearing civilization, if Dwomor could be considered civilized, and was afraid some wanderer – such as a dragon hunter – might discover it.

He had not yet dared to unroll it and see whether its magic might manifest itself; he did not want to try that alone and unprotected in the mountains, out in the open air.

Around midafternoon he came across a ruined cottage; something had smashed in the door, the windows were gone, and there were scorch marks on the slate roof, but it was basically intact. Tobas wondered at the slate roof, but a look around at the stony ground helped explain that; thatch would not be readily found here. He wondered, then, why the cottage's builder had wanted his domicile in so barren a spot.

He had no good explanation for that, but he could and did guess at why it was broken and empty; the dragon had undoubtedly eaten the inhabitants, or at any rate had tried to. That heavy, fireproof slate roof might have saved their lives.

And whether it had or not, they might have left some food; he hauled the tapestry inside, dropped it on the floor of the main room, and began exploring the kitchen cupboards.

They were all distressingly empty – in fact, they gave every sign of having been intentionally and systematically stripped bare. Tobas guessed that the cottage's owners had been besieged for a time and had then gathered up supplies and fled. He wondered whether they had made it to the castle safely.

Then he wondered whether the castle was really safe.

That was silly, he told himself; if the dragon had been unable to smash this little cottage to the ground, what could it do against a fortress like Dwomor Keep?

He sat down in a convenient straight-back chair and stared at the tapestry, his stomach growling. He did not feel up to hauling the heavy thing any farther before nightfall, and this cottage seemed comfortable enough; he decided to stay until morning.

As he was leaning back, wondering what sort of spells he should trade the tapestry for, he heard a noise outside, as of something large moving about. He sat up.

Could that be dragon hunters, he asked himself, or perhaps the cottage's owners coming back. He peered out a window.

It was neither; the dragon itself was perched on the top of a nearby hill, gazing out across the surrounding countryside. Tobas stepped back quickly.

He hadn't expected that. The beast had not seen him,

180

he was certain, but it was now quite definite that he would not be leaving this cottage for at least a few hours. If the dragon noticed him, he might never leave it alive at all. Worried and distracted, he started back for his chair and tripped over the rolled-up tapestry.

He caught himself before he fell, then turned and looked at his prize.

Was there, he asked himself, a chance that he could carry out the task he had originally signed up for and somehow kill the dragon? Might there be some way he could use the tapestry's magic – if it had any?

Well, he told himself, he obviously wouldn't be doing anything else for a while, so he might as well look the thing over. He glanced up at the cottage wall and found a likely spot.

The place had not been designed for tapestries, of course; but with a little effort, he managed to wedge the tapestry rod diagonally across one corner, supported on one end by a step-back in the chimney and on the other by a gap betwixt a rafter and the wooden plate that topped the stone wall and anchored the tie beams.

Once he was satisfied that it was securely in place, he began unfurling the tapestry; the rod was wedged too tightly to turn freely, so instead he was forced to drag the fabric up over the top time after time and let it drop back behind.

Finally it hung down freely, brightly lit by the rays of the setting sun pouring in through one of the western windows, and Tobas looked at it with renewed interest – the scene it depicted was so very weird! That ghastly lighting, the strange rocks, the empty areas beyond the castle – whoever had designed it had quite an imagination, Tobas thought, even without considering the castle itself, with its bizarre architecture and hideous carvings.

He reached out to brush the cloth smooth. To his astonishment, he saw his hand go right through, into the picture. The baleful red-purple seemed to leap up around him.

The magic was obviously working; he knew that instantly. This was no oracle or conjuring device, but a magical portal.

He pulled his hand back, shaken, but then realized with a shock that red-purple light still colored his fingertips.

A hot wind blew across his face from somewhere, hot and dry and like nothing that he had felt in the hills of Dwomor; when he raised his eyes to the castle, he saw an indisputably solid and three-dimensional castle, not a mere picture.

He knew then that, without meaning to, he had stepped through the tapestry.

But by all the gods, to *where*?

He had not realized when he reached out his hand that he might be doing something dangerous, but he cursed himself now for not seeing the obvious perils of touching the picture; he had had no idea what lay beyond. Perhaps the wizard had created the tapestry as somewhere to send his enemies or somewhere to keep demons and monsters.

Well, maybe even now it was not too late. He had not taken a single step inside, but only put his hand through; surely that couldn't hurt. He could simply turn around and step back out. The moment he saw that he was, beyond question, inside the scene in the tapestry, actually standing on that barren stony pathway, he lost his nerve. He gave up any thought he might have had of exploring further and stepped back, expecting to find himself again in the abandoned cottage.

Nothing happened; he was still standing on the narrow path across the rocks. He turned around, looking for the little cottage in the hills of Dwomor, but it was gone. All that he could see behind him was empty space.

He turned in a full circle, slowly, taking in his surroundings.

The only things in sight were the castle, the luridly colored void, and the path on which he stood; the path started out of nothing just a few feet from where he had entered and led nowhere but up to the castle. The rocks that supported both path and castle ended a yard or so out in every direction.

He got down on his belly and crawled to the nearest edge; leaning out cautiously he peered over, expecting to see something, a valley of some sort, far below.

He saw nothing at all, nothing but infinite empty space lit an eerie red. The rocks supporting the path were themselves hanging unsupported in midair. As far as he could discern, they extended down about six feet and across about eight feet in all.

Looking over toward that ornate and frightening castle, he saw more of the same; the rocks on which it stood were not parts of a mountaintop, but of a boulder, perhaps fifty or sixty yards in diameter, hanging in nothingness. Nor were they simply flying; below them were no distant fields or forests or even clouds – not even stars – but only endless emptiness. A wave of vertigo overcame him, and he closed his eyes.

Hot, dry wind, curiously odorless, ruffled his hair as he lay there, his eyes held tightly shut.

This place, he realized as he lay motionless, was not a part of the World he knew at all; that much was quite obvious. He inched himself back on to the path and got slowly to his feet, trying to suppress his trembling.

Quite plainly, he had only one place to go, and there could be no point in putting off going there. He walked slowly and cautiously toward the castle, taking it one small step at a time.

The rope bridge across the chasm, the chasm that was actually ten feet of nothing at all, was the worst part, but he managed it and stood at last on the lower lip of that fanged, grinning mouth that served the castle as a gate.

He was utterly terrified.

He peered in; torches blazed on either side of the gateway, which led to a huge pair of iron-bound wooden doors. He forced himself to step forward.

The doors were closed; he reached for the huge iron rings that would haul them open, then drew his hands back. He was trembling too hard to grip anything. He gritted his teeth and put his hands down at his sides, forcing them to stop shaking.

When he was as calm as he thought he was going to get, he reached out again and tugged at the iron rings.

Nothing happened; the doors were locked from the inside. At first a wave of relief swept over him, but that was quickly followed by renewed terror; whatever might lurk within this grotesque structure, it could not possibly be worse than being trapped outside it forever, with nowhere to go, no food, no water, nothing but a few feet of bare rock. He dropped the rings with a loud double clunk and began hammering on the doors with his fists.

When his initial panic had spent itself, his hands dropped, and he turned around, looking out at the void and trying to think what he could do next.

A voice came from inside the castle, an uncertain female voice asking, in a very strange and old-fashioned accent,

'Derry? Is that you? Where have you *been*?'

Tobas froze for a minute; he had not really expected an

answer, certainly not an ordinary human voice mistaking him for someone else.

At last, however, he gathered his wits sufficiently to reply, 'It's not Derry; it's me, Tobas.'

'Who?' The voice was almost plaintive.

'Let me in and I'll explain.' He had no intention of giving up anything that might get him inside, away from all that empty nothingness, out of the ghastly colored light and the desiccating wind.

Tobas could almost hear the hesitation on the other side; although the pause could not actually have been more than five or ten seconds, it seemed like an eternity before the woman said, 'Well, I suppose it'll be all right. You feel harmless enough.' Almost immediately, Tobas heard a heavy bar being drawn back. Then a chain fell, a lock scraped, and finally the heavy doors swung outward, revealing a broad, torchlit hallway. Another equally massive pair of doors, some ten feet in, stood open; beyond that lay some thirty feet of passageway, the walls broken by side passages, and then yet another set of doors, this pair closed. The corridor was completely unfurnished save for elaborate wrought-iron brackets on the walls, holding torches, but demonic faces were carved in the stone at each corner of the ceiling, leering down at him.

Standing in the middle of the hallway was a lovely young woman, tall, slender, and dark-skinned, clad in an elegant crimson gown, her waist-length black hair spilling down across her shoulders. She watched Tobas warily.

'Hello,' he said, trying desperately to look harmless. 'I'm Tobas of Telven, a wizard of sorts.'

'I am called Karanissa of the Mountains; I'm a witch. Did Derry – I mean, Derithon – send you?'

'No, he didn't. Ah . . . if you'll let me come in for a moment, I'll try to explain.'

Karanissa hesitated. Tobas' stomach unexpectedly emitted a loud growl, and he added, 'And could you spare anything to eat?'

The self-proclaimed witch smiled, then nodded. 'This way.'

She led him down a side corridor and through a small open door into the first place he'd seen on this side of the tapestry that seemed fit for humans rather than demons, a quiet, windowless, torchlit little chamber carpeted with furs, with banners on the walls, and furnished with several folding wooden chairs with fabric seats. Karanissa took one chair and motioned for Tobas to take another. When he had settled warily, she clapped her hands.

The air stirred, and Tobas shifted uneasily in his seat.

'Bring us food and drink,' Karanissa ordered, though Tobas saw no one else in the room. 'Is there anything in particular you'd like?' she asked him.

'No,' he said. 'Whatever is convenient. I'm hungry enough to eat almost anything.'

'Some sharp cheese, then, and the new bread, and the best red wine we have left – oh, and apples.'

The air stirred again, then stilled.

'Go on,' Karanissa said, her attention fully on Tobas now.

'Ah . . .' he said, 'I don't know where to begin.'

'Start with how you got here,' she suggested.

'Through a tapestry,' Tobas said. 'I just tried to smooth it out, but I must have taken a step in and I couldn't find my way back.'

'I know *that* story well enough! Derry left me here while he went to check on something, and I haven't been able to get out since.'

Tobas' spirits, which had begun to rise, quickly sank

186

once more; did that mean he, too, was stranded here indefinitely?

Perhaps not; the mysterious Derry, or Derithon, had gotten out. 'If you don't mind my asking, who is this Derithon?'

'You don't know?' The witch's startlement seemed quite genuine and not just a sort of boast. 'You never heard of the wizard Derithon the Mage?'

'I'm afraid not,' Tobas admitted.

'Well, this is his castle – he conjured it himself. And he made the tapestry I came here through, which I would assume is the one you came through, as well. Unless something terrible has happened, it should be hanging in a private room of his *other* castle, which was flying over the mountains of central Ethshar last I knew. That was some time ago, though.'

A strange realization dawned on Tobas as the witch said this. For an instant he refused to believe it, but by the time she had finished speaking, he was almost sure of it. He had assumed that she and Derithon were adventurers who had somehow stumbled upon – or rather, through – the tapestry, but now he thought otherwise. An adventurer would not consider either castle his own.

And the flying castle had been fallen and empty for centuries.

'Lady Karanissa, excuse me, but how long have you been here?' he asked.

'Oh, I don't know!' she replied, annoyed. 'Ages, it seems – it can't really be as long as it's felt like, locked up here all alone, and there aren't any days or nights here, so I just don't know. Why? Do *you* know how long it's been?'

'You said that when you came here, Derithon's other castle was still flying?'

'Yes, of course!' Tobas had startled her again. 'You mean it isn't anymore?'

'No, no, it isn't, and it hasn't been for a long time – and I'm afraid that Derithon was killed when it fell. At least, I think he must have been; my companion and I found a body near the tapestry that must have been his.'

'Derry's dead?' She stared at him, open mouthed with shock.

'I think so; I can't be sure it was he.' Tobas was apologetic.

'What did he look like, this dead person? No, don't tell me. You said that the castle hadn't flown in a long time? How long, then – months? Years?'

'Years, at least.'

'Gods, how long have I *been* here? What's the date?'

'It's the . . . let me see . . . the fourteenth of Harvest, or maybe the fifteenth by now; I don't know how long I've been here.'

'What *year*, you idiot?' Karanissa shouted.

'Fifty-two twenty-one, by Ethsharitic reckoning.'

She stared at him, dumbfounded, then demanded, 'Is this a joke? Are you playing some sort of trick on me? Is Derry in on this?'

Taken aback, Tobas said, 'No, of course not!'

'It was the twenty-seventh of Leafcolor, in the Year of Human Speech four thousand seven hundred and sixty-two, when Derry and I came in here for a private evening together! Are you trying to tell me I've been sitting here waiting for that damn wizard to come back for *four hundred and fifty-nine years*?' With her final words she rose from her chair, shouting directly into Tobas' face.

Tobas simply stared back, unable to think of any reply.

After a moment the witch sank back into her chair and

stared at the ceiling for a long, slow breath. 'Derithon of Helde,' she announced, shaking a fist at the air, 'if you weren't already dead, I'd kill you myself for getting me into this!'

Chapter 20

As the two sat glaring at each other, a tray appeared through one of the doorways, wafted into the room as if it weighed nothing and were merely drifting on the wind, like a falling leaf in the autumn. Karanissa, thus distracted from her fury, plucked it out of the air and offered it to Tobas.

It held exactly the food and drink she had requested. After a brief hesitation, Tobas helped himself generously; he was just as hungry in this eerie otherworldly castle as he had been back in the mountains of Dwomor.

The wine was not good at all, very acid and laced with gritty sediment, but after four hundred years that was to be expected. Tobas was too polite – and too unsure of his situation – to complain to his hostess. The bread and apples were fresh and tasty, however, and the cheese only slightly overripe.

When both had eaten their fill and calmed down somewhat, it was decided that Karanissa would first tell her story all the way through, and Tobas would then tell his, rather than both of them asking questions back and forth and confusing matters.

Karanissa maintained that her tale was very short and simple. Not long after she had completed her apprenticeship and been drafted into the army as a military witch, she had met Derithon, then two or three hundred years old and semiretired from his duties, but still on call for special missions and still training new combat wizards. They had, as she put it, become very good friends, but had not considered marriage because of the two-century difference in their ages, the gross disparity in their ranks – Derithon a reserve general, she a mere lieutenant – and the usual difficulties attendant upon marriages between magicians of different schools.

Tobas was not aware of any such difficulties, but said nothing.

The two of them had had good times together, Karanissa went on, and Derithon had her transferred from her reconnaissance post to 'special duties' under his own command. He had even put a spell of eternal youth on her.

Startled, Tobas interrupted at that point. 'Are you serious?' he said.

'About what?' she asked, startled.

'That eternal youth spell. Do you mean that spells like that really exist?'

'Certainly they do! How did you expect me to believe that I've been here four hundred years if you didn't know about youth spells?'

'I don't know; I thought that maybe time was different here. I was always told that eternal youth spells were just pretty stories for children.'

'No, they're real, all right, and, so far as I know, there isn't any difference between time here and anywhere else. Youth spells are a military secret, but I thought just about everyone knew about them, all the same. Haven't you ever met any powerful wizards who look as if they've just finished their apprenticeships? It always seemed to me that the military can't be very serious about keeping these things secret when they let people like that wander around openly.'

Tobas began to explain that he had never had anything to do with the military or any wizards except Roggit, but decided that could wait. The witch was telling her story. He would hear her out first and then worry about details. 'All right,' he said. 'He put an eternal youth spell on you. Then what?' He wondered for a moment why, if eternal youth spells really did exist, wizards ever allowed themselves to grow old and die, as Roggit had. He immediately realized the answer, though; not all wizards knew the spells. As he had learned himself, wizards did not share spells. Besides, the secret might well have become lost entirely by the time the Great War was over, as the methods for making flying castles had.

Karanissa shifted on her chair, brushed back her hair, and went on with her tale.

She and Derithon had become very close, and finally, one day, after swearing her to secrecy, he had brought her through the tapestry to this castle, his very special, very private retreat of long standing that no one else knew about, where they could be alone together without worrying about gossiping servants or troublesome officers. These were his most prized personal possessions, the tapestry and its castle, and she had felt honored when he chose to share them with her, as he never had with anyone else.

She was a witch and she knew that he was speaking the truth when he told her that and not just giving her a line. Either that, or he had some spell she had never heard of that let him lie so well even a witch couldn't detect it.

They had come here three or four times for brief visits, when time permitted, and each time, when they felt they ought to, they had then stepped back through the *other* tapestry to Derithon's second castle, the flying one in the ordinary World.

Then, one night, at a most inconvenient time, one of the magical emergency alarms Derithon had set back in the real World had been triggered somehow – she didn't know how, or what the alarm was, or how Derithon had known, since she had seen and heard nothing. Assuring her that it was probably nothing and he'd be right back to get her to safety, he had left. She had really not felt like going anywhere just then; neither had Derithon, but he had quickly thrown on a tunic and breeches and gone, all the same, leaving her alone in the castle.

And that was the last time she had seen him – or, for that matter, any human being but herself and Tobas – for what Tobas now told her was a few sixnights less than four hundred and fifty-nine years.

'He *tried* to get back to you,' Tobas said when she began crying. 'He was reaching for the tapestry when he died; that was how we found him.'

She glared at him through her tears. 'How could you have found him,' she demanded, 'if he was dead four hundred years ago?'

'We found his skeleton – at least, somebody's skeleton – with a silver dagger and several rings, wearing an embroidered tunic. That was him, wasn't it?'

'Aaagh!' She burst out in renewed weeping, and Tobas realized that he had been tactless. He waited for her hysterics to subside. She seemed to be struggling to control her reactions, and Tobas had enough sense to see that his arrival and the news he brought must have come as quite a shock; after centuries of isolation he could not fault her for her display of emotion. He thought no less of her for it. In fact, he was quite impressed by her; not only was she beautiful, but she spoke well and had already begun adjusting her accent so that it was closer to his own, making her speech more easily understood. Furthermore, if her story was true – and he had no reason to doubt it – she had lived here alone for centuries without losing her sanity or otherwise visibly degenerating. He was unsure he could have done that.

When she had at last regained control of herself, she went on with her story.

At first she had simply stayed in bed, waiting for Derithon to return. When she was quite certain that several hours had passed, she had gotten up, gotten dressed, and puttered about the castle, tidying up and poking around, waiting for Derithon to return.

Eventually she had gotten worried and had tried to use her witchcraft to establish contact with him, but without success. She had put that down to being in an entirely separate reality.

Finally, she had decided to go and see for herself just what had happened and had gone to the tapestry that was supposed to lead back to the flying castle. Then she had discovered that it did not work. She was unable to step through it.

This was something of a shock; up until then, returning to the World had simply been a matter of walking right through the tapestry into the private chamber of Derithon's flying castle. The thought that she might be trapped in this strange other world had never occurred to her.

However, it became quite clear that she was, indeed, trapped.

Eventually, she had gotten up her nerve to consult Derithon's great Book of Spells to see if she could get the tapestry to function again. She had found the spell that created it but had been unable to use it to get the tapestry to work. She had then experimented with other spells, right down to the elementary little training exercises for beginners, and had not yet found *any* that she was sure she could use. There were one or two that *might* work, but required items she did not have in order to be sure –

such as living subjects. A hypnotic spell she had attempted had given her an eerie feeling that *something* was happening; but without someone to test it on, she couldn't be sure she wasn't simply imagining things.

And nothing she had tried with wizardry, witchcraft, or sheer random experimentation had gotten her back to Ethshar. She had simply lived on, waiting, talking to the invisible servants Derithon had left to take care of her – even though they could not speak to answer her – tending the magical garden that provided her food, and trying to keep from going mad with loneliness. She had taken to sleeping for days at a time; she knew spells that allowed her to do that without harming her health. Several times she had tried putting herself in a trance that would last until Derithon returned or until her body needed food desperately, and each time she had awoken on the verge of starvation, with Derithon still absent.

And now, finally, Tobas had come pounding on the door.

'There's another tapestry?' Tobas asked when it was obvious that she was done.

'Yes, of course,' she answered. 'Each one only works one way.'

'Could I see it?'

'First tell me who you are and how you got here.'

Tobas started to explain, describing how his father's ship had been sunk, and almost immediately Karanissa interrupted.

'Do you mean you're a Northerner?' she asked, shocked.

'A what?'

'A Northerner? An Imperial?'

'No, I don't *think* so,' Tobas answered, confused. He had never considered the matter, since the only Northerners he had ever heard of had supposedly been wiped out to the last man centuries before. Caught off guard, he did not realize at first that Karanissa had been out of touch since before that extinction happened; instead, he thought she was using the word 'Northerner' in some unfamiliar way.

'Then why would an Ethsharitic demonologist sink your father's ship?'

Comprehension dawning, Tobas answered, 'Because my father was a pirate – or a privateer. The Great War ended two hundred years ago, my lady; the Northern Empire was completely obliterated. There are no more Northerners, as you mean the term. But Ethshar doesn't rule everywhere; part of the western coast threw off the overlords' rule and became the Free Lands of the Coast – or the Pirate Towns, as I believe they're known in Ethshar and the Small Kingdoms.'

'What are the Small Kingdoms?' she asked, puzzled.

'Oh, well, Old Ethshar fell apart toward the end of the war. The generals set up the new Ethshar – the Hegemony of the Three Ethshars, as it's properly called – and the old Ethshar fell apart into the Small Kingdoms.'

The witch stared at him. 'Are you sure?' she asked.

'Of course I'm sure!' Tobas found it difficult to deal with someone who questioned the most elemental historical facts.

She sighed. 'I can see you mean it, unless my witchcraft has deserted me completely. But it's all so hard to believe! The war over? The Empire gone? Ethshar gone? I knew that the civilian government was in disarray, but I didn't think . . .' Her voice trailed off into uneasy silence; she shook her head to clear it and said, 'Go on with your story.'

Tobas explained how he had talked Roggit into accept-

196

ing him as apprentice, how the old man had died after teaching him a single spell, and how he had gone off adventuring. He did not bother with any of the sordid details of signing up to kill a dragon; instead, he merely said that he had come to Dwomor hoping he might find himself a place and that he had wandered up into the mountains and found the fallen castle. He mentioned the strange lack of magic and explained how he had been sure the tapestry was valuable and had hauled it back down toward Dwomor.

And finally, he explained, he had taken shelter in a deserted cottage waiting for a dragon to move on and had decided to take a closer look at his prize – and here he was.

'Dwomor is a *kingdom* now?' Karanissa asked, bemused.

'Yes,' Tobas replied. 'One of the Small Kingdoms. There are a lot of them.'

'Dwomor isn't just a military administrative district under General Debrel?'

'No, it's a kingdom, ruled by his Majesty Derneth the Second.'

She sighed again. 'How very strange.' She stared off into space for a moment, then shook her head and looked at Tobas again. 'And you're a wizard, you say?'

'Well, sort of.'

'Do you know the Guild secrets?'

'Well, not all of them, certainly . . .' Tobas began cautiously.

'I mean, do you think you might be able to use some of the spells in that book, where I can't?'

'I don't know,' Tobas admitted. 'I might; I'd have to see it. I don't know whether wizardry would work the same way here as it does in the World.'

'Do you think you could get the tapestry working again?'

'I don't know; I'd have to see it and study the spell first.' A horrible thought occurred to him. 'For all I know,' he added, 'wizardry won't work here any more than it did in Derithon's other castle.'

'But *some* wizardry still works; I'm still young, and the garden still bears its fruit, and the servants still do what I tell them to.'

Tobas nodded, greatly relieved. 'You're right; that shouldn't be a problem.' He resolved, however, to test his own spell at the first opportunity. 'Could you show me this tapestry that's supposed to take you back?'

'All right.' She stood, and Tobas followed suit.

As she led the way through the castle, he quickly became lost in the maze of rooms and corridors; there was nothing traditional whatsoever about the layout of the fortress, and it was far larger inside than it had appeared from the outside. The walls were all of gray and black stone, some hung with drapes or tapestries, but the majority bare. The carved faces were only in a few passageways, not everywhere. Most of the corridors were dark and gloomy; Karanissa carried a torch so that they could see their way. The windows they passed were not particularly comforting, as the light that poured in was the now-familiar red-purple glow that seemed to have no source, but permeated the void around the castle.

At least the wind could not penetrate; the interior of the castle seemed a trifle warm and dry, but not truly uncomfortable, and a welcome change from the cold and damp of the hills of Dwomor.

Finally, when Tobas had lost all idea of where they were, they arrived in a small room on an upper floor where one wall held a tapestry that was just as odd, in its own way, as the one Tobas had taken from the downed castle.

The scene depicted in this tapestry was so utterly simple as to be almost an abstract design; it was done entirely in black and dark gray and showed a bare stone chamber that Tobas recognized, with a start, as the room where the other tapestry had originally hung, seen from a point two or three feet in front of the tapestry's wall, looking back toward the passageway that led to the wizard's study.

Looking closely, Tobas could make out the patterns in the stonework and other details that established it beyond question as the same room. The scene was exactly as he had seen it when taking down the tapestry, save that Derithon's skeleton was missing.

He reached out and ran a hand over the tapestry and felt only cool, smooth fabric. He had hoped that he might be able to use it, that some protective spell prevented only Karanissa from stepping through, but that was obviously not the case.

After another moment's study, he shrugged and turned away. He could see nothing odd about the tapestry that might explain why it had stopped functioning.

'Well,' he said, 'I guess I'll need to see that Book of Spells.'

He tried very hard to sound calm, but it was difficult, very difficult, when he realized he might at last be about to achieve his long-sought goal of learning more magic. If he could learn a few of the enchantments from Derithon's book and somehow return to the World, he would be ready to start a career.

These, however, were no circumstances he had ever imagined that achievement might be made under. He was trapped in an otherworldly castle with a beautiful witch

199

four or five hundred years old, trying to make an unfamiliar spell work in order to return to the real World.

What a strange way he had found finally to see a powerful wizard's Book of Spells!

Chapter 21

As he followed her along the dim corridor to Derithon's study, Tobas watched the way Karanissa walked, her long black hair swirling about her. He had already noticed, on the way to the tapestry, that she moved with grace and confidence. It was obvious that she knew every inch of the castle intimately – but then, that was hardly surprising after she had spent more than four hundred years trapped in it.

It was also obvious that that four hundred years hadn't affected her beauty at all; Tobas could see why Derithon had taken an interest in her. She was probably the most beautiful woman he had ever seen.

He wondered if her witchcraft, or Derithon's wizardry, had contributed anything to that.

At first, when she had led him into the castle, she had seemed a trifle hesitant and unsure, presumably because of Tobas' startling arrival and unfamiliar presence – but she was over that now. She had already outwardly adjusted to the abrupt change in her circumstances.

Karanissa opened the heavy door of the study and ushered Tobas inside; he paused for a moment to stare around at the shelves upon shelves of jars, bottles, boxes, and apparatus before reaching for Derithon's Book of Spells.

The book had a place of honor, centered on one end of the long worktable in the vast cluttered study. It was big and thick, bound in black hide, and a heavy metal clasp lay unlocked and open. Tobas hesitated just before his hand touched the cover. 'Are you sure there aren't any protective spells?' he asked Karanissa.

'No,' she replied. 'I'm not sure of anything about it, but *I* never had any trouble opening it. I just couldn't get the spells to work.'

That, Tobas thought, might mean that Derithon had attuned the protective spells to accept her, and her failure to make any of the magic work might indicate that some sort of confusion spell was in use; the book could still be dangerous, but he decided to risk it. He reached down and lifted the cover.

Nothing happened. The book opened as easily as any ordinary volume, revealing the blank flyleaf. A faint musty odor reached Tobas.

He lifted the flyleaf in turn, revealing the title page, which read, in sprawling, awkward runes, 'Derithon of Helde, His Spells, Begun in The Thirteenth Year of His Age, The Four Thousand, Five Hundred, and Twenty-Third Year After the Gods Taught Men to Speak, During the Great War Against the Northern Empire.'

Tobas marveled at that for a moment; this book was almost seven hundred years old. He guessed that it must bear some powerful preservative spell, as the paper was still white and supple and the ink only slightly faded.

Carefully, handling the book with great respect, he turned past two blank pages. The next page was smudged and indecipherable; he skipped over that to the next.

The writing on this page was still sharp and clear, and Tobas stared at it for a long moment, a smile gradually spreading across his face.

The page was neatly headed 'Thrindle's Combustion' and described that familiar spell accurately and succinctly. There was obviously no confusion spell at work.

A footnote at the bottom of the page caught his eye;

the handwriting and ink were slightly different, leading him to assume it had been added later. It read, 'Use caution! Application of the Combustion to anything already burning seems to result in an explosion out of all proportion to the materials involved.'

He had more or less found that out for himself back in Roggit's little cottage, but it was somehow reassuring to see it confirmed independently.

A moment's study also revealed why Karanissa had been unable to make the spell work. Under 'Ingredients', Derithon had listed only brimstone and a small cross-shaped mark that appeared to be a mere decoration or space holder. Similarly, in describing the two motions that the spell required, one was also marked with the little cross.

No mention was made anywhere of an athame or even of a dagger; the gesture marked with the cross was the one made with the athame, while the unmarked motion was, as Tobas well knew, made with the free hand while flinging a speck of brimstone.

Even in his private Book of Spells, Derithon had done his best to keep the Guild's secrets. Karanissa, being a witch, would have no athame – at least, so far as Tobas knew, no equivalent to the athame was used in witchcraft – and would not have guessed at the little symbol's meaning. She would have no reason to think it *had* any meaning; Derithon had done a good job of making it appear to be no more than a flourish.

Not every wizardly spell required an athame, though – or, at least, so he understood. He flipped quickly through several pages, however, and found the little athame symbol on virtually every one. Derithon had apparently not cared for spells that did not use the athame – or perhaps he had simply never come across many.

Tobas did find one; but as it was indeed a hypnotic spell, he could see how Karanissa would have had great difficulty testing it, as she had said. Much farther on he found a love potion that did not call for an athame, but she would have had little use for that, either.

He wondered for a moment, though, whether Derithon had often used such a potion – perhaps even on Karanissa.

Quite aside from his discovery of the athame symbol, he found an amazing and fascinating variety of spells, more than he had known existed; the book was a fat one, several hundred pages long, perhaps even a thousand. After the few blank pages at the front, it was solidly filled with spells until a mere five pages from the end. Had Derithon lived to learn more spells, he would have needed a second volume very shortly.

If Tobas were to keep this book for himself and master every spell in it, he realized, he would, beyond any possible doubt, become one of the greatest wizards in the World. That was a very tempting thought. He would not need to eke out a living selling charms and removing curses; he would be able to conjure up almost anything he pleased or sell single spells for roomfuls of coin.

He noted with mild interest that the handwriting had changed from the boyish scrawl of the earliest pages to a smaller, neater, more legible hand as Derithon had aged. Learning and recording these spells had obviously taken the mage a long time; Tobas guessed that Derithon had kept on adding new spells long after he completed his apprenticeship, though it was not clear how he had come by them. From a comparison of the lettering, he judged that the footnote to Thrindle's Combustion had been added at a time when Derithon had filled fifty or sixty of the book's pages.

The spells described in the volume varied from 'A Fine

Blemish Remover' to something called 'The Seething Death' that bore a small warning at the bottom: 'The full potential of this spell is not known. Its inventor believed that, unchecked, it could destroy all of Ethshar and perhaps the entire World. It has been attempted only twice in all of history and was stopped both times by a countercharm, now lost.' Below that, scribbled in the margin in red ink, a single line of runes read, 'DON'T TRY IT.'

Tobas chuckled nervously when he read it. He had no intention of trying anything of the sort.

On the next page after the Seething Death, near the back of the book, he found 'The Transporting Tapestry'.

The entry was a long one, the spell complex, with three pages of notes following the actual procedure. Tobas looked around for a chair and noticed for the first time that Karanissa was still in the room, quietly watching him.

'You don't need to wait,' he said. 'This may take a while.'

She shrugged. 'I don't have anything better to do, do I?'

'I suppose not,' he agreed. 'Could you pass me that chair?' He pointed at the one he wanted, standing in the nearest corner.

Karanissa turned and looked at it, and the chair walked, stiff-legged and awkward, over to Tobas. He stared at it uneasily for a moment before sitting down, making sure it was no longer moving.

'I *am* a witch, you know,' Karanissa remarked. 'You wizards aren't the only real magicians around.'

'I never said we were,' Tobas answered.

'Derry did.'

Tobas could think of no good answer to that; instead, he turned back to the Book of Spells.

The Transporting Tapestry required thirty pounds of gold and thirty of silver, he noticed; he had made the right decision in taking the tapestry rather than any of Peren's small heap of household furnishings. It also required all the usual makings of a tapestry as well as three fresh pine needles, three candles – one white, one black, one blood-red – a white rose, a red rose, a peculiar sort of incense – a footnote referred him to another book that gave instructions on preparing it – and, if he understood the little cross marking correctly, as he was sure he did, an athame.

The athame symbol appeared after each mention of cutting the yarn or spun metal for the tapestry; Tobas interpreted that to mean that every thread used in making the tapestry had to be cut with the athame rather than with scissors or an ordinary blade. Obviously, no one but a wizard could possibly make the spell work.

The initial ritual required one day, from midnight to midnight, and the making of the tapestry called for one full year, though it could be started at any time.

There were no instructions for repairing or renewing a tapestry that had ceased to function.

He stared at the page for a long moment, considering the prospect of spending a minimum of a year in this mysterious castle, with the beautiful Karanissa as his only companion.

Or rather, remembering the way the tray of food had been delivered, his only *human* companion.

The idea was not wholly unpleasant, actually; he was not particularly eager to go on wandering and he could think of far worse places a man might call home. However, he would have preferred to have a choice. The castle seemed comfortable enough, but he had never pictured himself making a home in another world, cut off from the rest of the human race.

Besides, the wine was terrible.

He looked over the spell again, to see if he had missed anything, and realized that he had badly misjudged the situation. If his only way out was to make an entirely new tapestry, he would be here far longer than a single year; the spell was a high-order one, requiring that every second of that twenty-four-hour ritual be absolutely perfect. He had learned enough from Roggit to know that his chances of performing the spell correctly on the first try, with no other preparation, were very, very slim indeed, In fact, he guessed that it was far more likely the spell would backfire and do something completely different from what he intended it to do, quite possibly something fatal.

Most likely of all would be for it to do nothing whatsoever.

Eventually, of course, he could study and practice and work his way up through the other spells, as any apprentice wizard would do – though he would not have the benefit of a master's advice and encouragement, so it would probably take a good deal longer than the traditional six years. A good journeyman wizard might manage to make a functioning tapestry if the spell was, say, fifth- or sixth-order, and would probably be safe from any real chance of a serious backfire.

If it were of a significantly higher order than that, as it well might be, well, a journeyman usually took another three years of study to rate as a master, and another nine usually conferred sufficient expertise to use the term 'mage'. Some were said to attain Guildmaster status before they were forty, but Tobas understood that to be due as much to politics as ability, and Roggit had once said – enviously – that the youngest grand master was only fifty-eight.

He might be here for a very long time.

Or, looking at the list of ingredients again, he might be here forever if the castle garden did not include roses or pines. Even if Derithon had kept those ingredients somewhere on his shelves, after four hundred years pine needles could not possibly be 'fresh', and roses would have withered. Furthermore, he had no way of knowing when midnight was, and the ritual had to be begun exactly at midnight. There might *be* no midnight in this void. He might live out his entire life in this castle.

Unless, of course, he could determine why the return tapestry was not working and remedy it. He began turning pages, looking for a low-order divination that might tell him what was causing the problem.

He found none; Derithon had apparently not gone in much for divinations. He did come across Varrin's Greater Propulsion, which he guessed had been the means by which Derithon got his flying castle off the ground, and spent several minutes admiring it, but after that he refused to be distracted further.

With no divination possible, he realized he would have to figure the problem out for himself. He turned back to the description of the Transporting Tapestry and the three pages of notes, and read through them all carefully.

If the tapestry was cut, even so much as a single thread, it was as good as destroyed and would never function again; he would have to check that and hope that was not the cause.

If the tapestry was unraveled, even a single thread out of place, it would stop working, but reweaving the damaged portion in accordance with the spell's directions would repair it and restore it to operation.

That he thought he might manage; that would require none of the daylong preliminary spell. The actual weaving of the tapestry did not seem to call for anything much beyond his capabilities.

He would have to inspect the tapestry very closely for cuts or raveling – even a snagged thread might count.

The notes explained that each tapestry worked in only one direction and recommended making them in pairs, one for each way; Tobas grimaced ruefully at that advice. Derithon had followed it, but that did Karanissa and himself little good now.

Derithon's comments also emphasized the absolute necessity that every detail in the tapestry match exactly with every detail in the actual place. The slightest error could result in a tapestry that led to someplace else entirely from the desired arrival point.

This was followed by a paragraph of what Tobas at first took to be theoretical musings, suggesting that intentionally creating a faulty tapestry might make an opening out of the everyday World entirely; it was only with a sudden shock as he read that section through for the second time that he realized that that must have been the method by which Derithon had conjured up his private, otherworldly castle. He had not built the castle and then created a tapestry that would transport him to it; he had created the tapestry first, and the tapestry, compelled by its magic to transport Derithon someplace, had created the castle!

That concept was almost too much for Tobas to deal with; he sat back in his chair and thought it over very carefully before looking at the book again.

The Transporting Tapestry could create entire new worlds, if he understood it correctly; that was far more than sixth-order! Was he ready to deal with something like that?

'Gods, no!' he answered himself, inadvertently speaking aloud.

'No what?' Karanissa asked from behind him.

He started. 'Oh, nothing,' he replied. Unable to resist, he added, 'But I think I just figured out how Derithon conjured up this castle.'

She looked suitably impressed as he turned back to the book.

He wondered how Derithon had ever had the nerve to try such a thing; the wizard had, according to his own notes, no way of knowing that the castle he created would not already be inhabited by something or other. The old man had obviously not lacked for courage and self-confidence.

So the tapestry had to match the actual scene exactly; that did not seem to be the problem here, however, since the tapestry he wanted to know about had worked at one time. The lighting had to be exactly right; presumably it was. The Book mentioned, cryptically and without further explanation, that this could affect travel time; Tobas was puzzled by that, since using the tapestries virtually eliminated travel time altogether. He guessed it had something to do with the angle of the sun's light, but could not imagine how it would work.

The tapestry would transport anyone and anything; selectivity was not the problem. The spell was not known to wear out or need renewal.

He wondered if the problem might be related to the fact that the flying castle had crashed in an area where wizardry did not function; since the magic was on the sending end, rather than the receiving one, that did not seem reasonable; but then, as every magician knows, magic is often unreasonable.

Could the tilted floor of the flying castle affect something? After all, the tapestry depicted the room as level, while it was actually sloping rather steeply. But the picture did not specifically show up or down; there were no hanging objects out of place, or anything of that sort. Tilting the tapestry to the angle of the fallen castle might be worth trying, but he doubted it would make any difference.

None of those sounded like a sufficient reason for the tapestry's failure, though any of them might be involved somehow.

He closed the book and sat back, thinking. He had the feeling that, in time, he would be able to figure out what the problem was, and possibly even right it, but at this particular moment he did not feel himself to be up to further study. He was utterly exhausted. The explanation would have to wait.

Whatever it might be, unless it proved to be simply a pulled thread or the tapestry's angle, he was certain he would be in this castle for several days, at the very least, and perhaps for the rest of his life.

Chapter 22

Karanissa gave him the use of a comfortable, richly furnished bedchamber near Derithon's study and provided him with a few of Derithon's clothes; these fit loosely, but were far better than the worn and filthy outfit he had been wearing constantly since leaving Dwomor, the only clothes he had owned since Roggit's hut burned.

The witch also ordered one of the three invisible servants, the least of the three, to wait on him. At first Tobas found the thing unsettling – this one was no mere sentient wind, like the one he had seen her command to bring food, but something small that skittered about, making nasty little squeaking noises and leaving wet spots on the floor. It would, however, fetch him small objects or run to bring Karanissa when he told it to.

He was unsure which spells had created the three servants; there were several in Derithon's book that seemed as if they might apply, from someone-or-other's Homuncular Animation to Lugwiler's Haunting Phantasm. He wondered whether he might find a way of conjuring up something more agreeable; he did not care for his servant's way of tittering unexpectedly at odd moments, startling him. One such uncalled-for giggle had caused him to spill a chamber pot, and when he had, in righteous anger, ordered the thing to clean up the mess, he was fairly certain it had *licked* up most of it, which was downright nauseating.

After that he did not ask it to clean anything.

For some time – he had no way of knowing just how

long – he simply rested, eating and sleeping and studying Derithon's books or talking to Karanissa when he was neither tired nor hungry.

He also took a few hours to acquaint himself with the castle; it was larger and more complex than he had thought. In fact, it was larger and more complex than he had thought possible; it seemed significantly larger inside than out.

Of course, he knew nothing about this alternate reality in which it hung. Perhaps it *was* larger inside than out.

Karanissa used about a dozen rooms ordinarily, and those were pleasant enough; she had the servants keep them supplied with lamps and candles, and the windows, with their unsettling purplish glow, were kept shuttered. The routes to important areas – gate, kitchen, tapestry room, and garden – were stocked with torches that the servants could light on a moment's notice when needed. In the gate itself a pair of torches were kept lit at all times; Karanissa explained that she had originally insisted on this as a sign of welcome for Derithon when he returned, and Tobas, seeing her expression, did not point out the obvious fact that Derithon was never coming and that there was, therefore, no more reason to maintain them.

The rest of the huge structure was left unlit and empty, but even the darkest, most obscure little cubbyhole was clean and dust-free; when not waiting on their mistress, the servants spent their time blowing away dust and cobwebs. Since they never slept, and Karanissa slept as much as possible, they had plenty of time for routine maintenance.

Perhaps it was something about the air or the light, but Tobas could find no trace of decay anywhere in the castle proper. Nothing was mildewed or rotting, despite the extreme age of the place, so that it was hard to believe that it was all actually four or five hundred years old.

The entire structure was fraught with magical curiosities, such as the corridor that led to one room if one walked down the center and an entirely different one if one walked along either side, or the tower window that gave an inverted view of the rest of the castle. Tobas wondered whether Derithon had planned any of these quirks or whether they had simply happened as a side effect of the castle's magical creation; Karanissa had never given the matter any thought and could give him no answer.

He discovered the castle's vast magical gardens almost by accident in the strange spiral-sloped courtyard behind the kitchens. The outer part, where flowers grew, he found quite pleasant, despite the way the colors were distorted by the unnatural glow of the void and despite the way Karanissa had to warn him away from some of the more poisonous or otherwise dangerous blossoms. The inner part also seemed nice enough at first – the tiny apple trees almost buried beneath their own abundant full-sized fruit, the stalks of corn that threw their own shucked ears into his hand if he held it out – but when he came to the source of the castle's endless supply of beef, he became quite queasy. The beef plants did not bother to recreate the head, hooves, or hide, but did possess all the other anatomical attributes of the cattle they mimicked – though not necessarily in the same arrangement real cattle used. The sight of beating hearts and breathing lungs atop fleshy purple-green stalks, with rich blood coursing through the arteries that were strung about like vines and the smell of fresh, raw meat billowing forth like perfume, thoroughly unsettled him, especially in the ruddy light.

Tobas spent a few futile hours trying to figure out what combinations of spells had produced the various monstrosities, but eventually gave it up. It sufficed that the garden was there and functioning.

Except, Karanissa pointed out, it was not functioning perfectly; here time had taken some slight toll, and some of the plants had died, withered, or become diseased, so that over the years her diet had become less varied. She had beef, corn, apples, and a variety of other grains and fruits, as well as an assortment of vegetables and cheeses; but except for one small and not very productive chicken bush, the fowl were all long since vanished; the lamb, mutton, and pork had become inedible, and the candies and cordials that had once been her special delight were dead and gone. Any sort of food or drink not provided by the garden had run out long ago, save for the vast wine cellars, and those were reduced to half a dozen bottles of ancient, barely potable stuff that she saved for special occasions.

If Tobas were unable to find a way back to the World, she hoped he would be able to restore the gardens to their former splendor. Otherwise it was entirely possible that they might eventually starve.

Tobas found the incredible profusion of magic in the castle daunting; Karanissa explained that Derithon had spent most of his free time for a hundred years or so in embellishing the place and that she, with her witchcraft, had added a few touches of her own as well. She had never reached the upper echelons of her craft, however, and witchcraft was always less permanent and less inherently powerful than wizardry – an admission that startled Tobas – so that most of her work was minor by comparison, and she had been unable to maintain some of Derithon's spells.

215

'I hadn't realized that wizardry was necessarily that much more potent,' he remarked, which was polite but not exactly true. He had not known it absolutely, but he had certainly suspected it.

'Oh, yes,' she said. 'Of course, it's also much more dangerous. Derry told me once that wizardry somehow taps into the pure chaos underlying our reality, so that the effect can be completely out of proportion to the cause, completely unrelated to what the wizard actually did to bring it about. Witchcraft isn't like that at all; a witch's power comes from his or her own body and mind. Oh, it's free of the limits of space and time and physicality, to some extent, but it's still human energy. If I tried to work a spell that needed more energy than I have, it would either fail or kill me, but you wizards do things like that all the time without even thinking about it.'

'*I* don't,' Tobas said.

'Oh, but you could; you could light a hundred fires and it wouldn't tire you out at all.'

'My wrists might get sore,' Tobas argued. 'From all that gesturing, you know.'

'That's nothing. If I lit a hundred fires by witchcraft, I'd be exhausted. I could probably do it; lighting a fire with witchcraft takes about as much effort as starting a fire by rubbing two sticks together, and a hundred of those – have you ever lit a fire by rubbing sticks?'

'No, I haven't. I've heard of it, but never tried it.'

'Well, it works, but it takes about, oh, ten or fifteen minutes, usually, and your arms get tired and sore. A witch can light a fire instantly, and her arms won't hurt, but she'll be just as tired as if she'd taken the ten minutes – do you see?'

'I think so.'

'Of course, I don't need the brimstone and gestures

that you use; I don't need any ingredients or ritual for my spells.'

Tobas nodded. 'Only wizards use all that stuff, I guess,' he said. 'The warlock on my ship never used any.'

Karanissa stared at him blankly for a moment. 'What's a warlock?' she asked finally.

Embarrassed, Tobas remembered that warlockry hadn't existed in her day, and tried as best he could to explain the mysterious new magic, but without much success. He knew very little about it, after all.

After a time, when he had slept several 'nights' in the castle and discovered beyond question that tilting the tapestry to various angles had no effect, he felt sufficiently secure in his surroundings to attempt a few of the spells from Derithon's compendium. The first interesting and easy one he came across, Tracel's Levitation, he had to pass by; it called for a raindrop caught in midair, and he could find nothing of the sort anywhere in the castle. If Derithon had had one, it had long since evaporated; Tobas found an empty vial marked 'Rain' on one shelf. And of course, it never rained in the void surrounding the castle.

That started him wondering where the water came from. Karanissa pointed out the well; after a glance into its seemingly bottomless depths, he decided not to enquire further and returned to the study.

Reminded of the problems of supply, he used Derithon's big jar of brimstone to replenish the little vial he still kept on his belt.

The next spell after Tracel's Levitation was something called the Sanguinary Deception, requiring nothing but his athame and his own blood; a prick on his arm, a few gestures, and his appearance, as confirmed by a glance in a mirror and by Karanissa's appalled reaction, was that of a bloody, decaying corpse.

She refused to eat dinner with him while he retained his ghastly aspect, and he could find no countercharm he felt competent to use, but fortunately the spell wore off in time.

He decided against repeating that spell to get it down pat; once was enough. He could see its usefulness in fooling one's enemies, but did not care to spend any more time than necessary having Karanissa avoid his company.

The Spell of Prismatic Pyrotechnics was another matter; he was able to work that one over and over without upsetting anyone, sending showers of colored sparks everywhere, glittering and bursting and whistling and hissing, without ever even singeing a tablecloth or tapestry. All the ingredients for that were on hand in plentiful amounts.

He found a recipe for an explosive seal; remembering Roggit's Book of Spells, he decided against experimenting with that.

The Polychrome Smoke worked well enough, but the resulting cloud hung around stubbornly until he finally asked Karanissa to herd it out a window into the void; he decided not to repeat that one, either.

A spell for the removal of blemishes proved untestable when he discovered that neither Karanissa nor he had any blemishes to remove. He had to skip over a series of spells that called for either sunlight or moonlight, since the surrounding void provided neither one.

Galger's Lid Remover frightened him out of his wits, despite the laconic warning at the bottom of the page that it was noisy and required a certain amount of working space. He had expected the jar to jump about the room; he had not expected a demonic eight-foot *thing*, glittering

218

like crystal and ablaze with white fire, with razor-sharp claws and fangs and horns, to appear out of nowhere with a banshee wail, snatch the jar from his hands, twist off the lid with a scream of tortured metal, and then vanish with the sound of shattering glass, leaving jar and lid on the floor at his feet.

When the performance was over, he stared at the open jar for a long moment, then gathered it up, closed it tightly, and returned it to the shelf where he had found it. That done, he sat and stared at it for a long time, a slow smile working its way on to his features. 'Hey, Nuisance,' he called at last, 'go find Karanissa for me, would you?'

His servant chittered, made an obscene slurping noise, and ran out of the room; he listened to the wet patter of its footsteps fading down the hallway, then got the jar down from the shelf again.

When it returned with the witch, he made a great show of seriousness. 'I think,' he said, 'that I've found what might be a very important spell here. It opens things. I don't think it will work directly on the tapestry, but I thought you might like to see it.' He picked up his athame, the other ingredients – diamond chip, gold wire, steel rod, and small silver mirror – laid out ready on the table.

'Do you really think it will do us any good?' she said.

A moment of guilt at what he planned caught him. 'Well, no,' he admitted. 'But I thought you might like to see that at least I'm learning *something*.'

'Oh,' she said. 'Well, then, what does this spell do?'

'It opens jars.'

'Is that all? *I* can open jars, by hand or by magic.'

'Not like this; the book says it can open any container a man can carry with one hand, no matter how tightly closed. Watch!' He performed the quick little ritual.

Her reaction was all he could have asked for; when the

thing appeared, she jumped backward with a shriek, knocking her chair to the floor. Even though he knew what to expect this time, Tobas himself was again disconcerted by the suddenness, brightness, and noise of the apparition.

When the thing had vanished again, Karanissa stared for a long moment, then burst out laughing. 'That,' she gasped, 'is the silliest thing I ever saw!'

Tobas smiled. 'I hoped you'd like it,' he said.

'I never saw Derry use *that* one!' she wheezed, trying to catch her breath.

'I'm not surprised,' he replied. 'According to the book, all this spell does is open jars and bottles and the like, and there are easier, quieter methods.'

In control of herself once more, the witch asked thoughtfully, 'Do you think it might open the tapestry somehow?'

He considered that seriously, then shook his head. 'I don't think I want to risk it,' he said. 'At least, not yet. I'm afraid it would rip the tapestry apart instead, and we'd have to make an entirely new one from scratch. I don't think I'll be able to do that for a long, long time, even if we have the materials – and I don't think we do. I didn't see any roses or pines in the garden. And, unless there's a treasury you haven't mentioned, we can't get the gold or silver, either, except by melting down the old one.'

'There's no treasury; we never kept any money at all in here. There was never any reason to. The roses died long ago, and we never had any pines.'

'I thought that might be the case. We can't make a new tapestry, then; we need to make the old one work again.'

'And you haven't figured out what's wrong with it?'

'No, I've read through the spell a hundred times and I

220

don't see why it would stop working. I've inspected the tapestry as closely as I can. If there's a cut or a tear or an unraveling anywhere, I can't find it. I have this feeling I should know what's wrong, that I'll feel stupid when I do realize what it is, but I can't think of what it could be.'

'Well, *I* don't have any idea,' she said. 'You keep working on it; I'm sure you'll get us out of here eventually.' She stood, then impulsively leaned over and kissed him on the cheek. 'And thank you for trying.'

'Hey, I'm stuck here, too, remember!'

'I know – and thank you for coming.' She turned and left before he could think of anything to say in reply.

He watched her go, unsure of his own feelings toward her, then turned pages to the spell of the Transporting Tapestry and read through it again.

Chapter 23

Karanissa did not come to the study again for some time after that; she ate her meals with him in one of the lesser halls and spoke civilly when she encountered him here or there about the castle, but she carefully avoided the study and his bedchamber.

He noticed this quickly enough, but it was several sleeps before he worked up the nerve to ask about it.

Finally, though, as they ate a meal of baked chicken – picked from the last little bush in the garden and prepared by one of Karanissa's two airy servants but indistinguishable from any fowl raised in a barnyard and cooked by an ordinary mortal – he asked, 'Have you been avoiding me?'

She looked down at the table, then paid careful attention to buttering a roll for a moment before answering.

'Yes, I suppose I have,' she said.

'Why?' He could think of no tactful way of phrasing his question.

'Oh, I don't know,' she replied. 'It's just that I'm afraid I might become too attached to you.'

He had hoped for that answer. 'Why shouldn't you become attached to me, if you like?'

'I don't know,' she repeated. 'It's just that it seems unfair. I'm waiting for Derry; I shouldn't . . .' Her voice trailed off. Collecting herself again, she continued, 'Besides, it's not fair to you, either. I've been alone here for so long – four hundred years, you tell me – that probably I'd fall in love with *any* man who turned up. Once we're out in the World again, it might not last. You

222

seem wonderful now – brave and sweet and clever – but I'm not sure whether that's because you really are, or just because you're here. Besides, you're just a boy, still in your teens.'

He nodded. 'I think I understand,' he said. 'You've been avoiding me so you wouldn't get carried away, then?'

'Yes, exactly,' she said.

'Well,' he said after a moment's hesitation, '*I* haven't been alone for four hundred years, and I know that I wouldn't mind a bit if you were to allow yourself to be carried away, and I'd do my best to keep your interest once we're out, but if you don't want to risk it, I understand.'

'You *are* sweet,' she said. 'You remind me so much of Derry sometimes!'

He was unsure how to answer that and, following her example, concentrated intently on buttering a roll.

After the meal, while the servants were clearing away the dishes, he rose and announced, 'I'll go get back to work.'

'I'll come with you, if you don't mind,' she said. 'I love watching a wizard at work.'

Surprised, he smiled and said, 'I'd be glad of the company.'

It seemed perfectly natural to both of them when his arm went around her waist as they walked down the corridor. Discussing her reasons for avoiding him seemed almost to negate them.

When they reached the study, she looked around in surprise. 'It's different,' she said.

'Well, yes, a little,' he admitted. He had rearranged things somewhat to make room for his experiments and to keep his more frequently used materials close at hand and had cleared out a great many containers that were either empty or held things that had not survived the centuries of neglect unscathed. A distressing variety of common ingredients had suffered, severely limiting what magic he could attempt.

'What's this doing here?' she asked, reaching out and lightly tapping an astonishingly ugly statuette that stood on a corner of the worktable. 'Wasn't it down in the green gallery before?'

Before Tobas could reply the figure began singing, loudly and off-key but in a pleasant enough baritone, 'The Sorrows of Sarai the Fickle'.

Embarrassed, Tobas reached over and tapped it again before it could get past the opening lines. Those lines, describing Sarai's anatomy with succinct obscenity, were quite enough without letting it go on to detail her nocturnal activities.

The music stopped the instant his finger touched stone.

'Galger's Singing Spell,' he explained sheepishly in the sudden silence. 'It works better with rowdy drinking songs.'

'Oh,' Karanissa said, smothering a smile. 'What's that?' This time she pointed.

Tobas explained each of the half dozen or so relics of his recent spell-casting.

'There are some in the book that I'd love to try,' he said when he had finished his explanations. 'But even when I have all the ingredients, I don't always have any way of knowing if a spell actually works when I try it. Some of them need a subject. This one, for example.' He turned to the page he wanted. 'It's called the Lesser Spell of Invaded Dreams. If I could be sure it worked, I might be able to use this to send a message to someone back in the outside world and get him to come help us.'

She looked at the brief description. 'You could try it on me,' she pointed out.

'Oh,' Tobas said, feeling foolish. 'Yes, I could, couldn't I? I hadn't thought of that, since we usually sleep at the same time.'

'I don't know what good it would be though,' she said. 'What could someone outside do?'

'I don't really know,' Tobas confessed. 'I was thinking that perhaps a rope could be thrown through the tapestry that still works, so that we could be pulled out.'

Karanissa frowned. 'I don't think that would work,' she said. 'Would it? It sounds too easy.'

'Easy!'

'Well, not really easy, maybe. But I know that whenever I came through that tapestry with Derry, we couldn't turn back, no matter how quickly we tried. I couldn't just put one foot through and step back.'

'You couldn't?' Tobas asked, disappointed. He had hoped that his own abrupt entrance had been somehow exceptional.

'No, I couldn't. As soon as even a finger went into the tapestry, I was all the way through.'

'Oh.' He had to admit that accorded closely with his own experience. Dismayed, he stared at the book for a moment. 'Oh, well. Maybe we can try it eventually, anyway, if we can't come up with anything better.'

'Maybe,' she agreed.

Both stood silently for a moment, Tobas staring at the book, Karanissa watching him.

'What are you going to try next?' she asked at last.

'I don't know,' he admitted. 'I've been working my way up; they aren't marked, but I believe I'm working on second- or maybe even third-order spells now. I wish I knew what I was looking for, though. I've been here at least a couple of sixnights now, maybe more – maybe months – and I still don't really know what I'm doing. I'm learning more magic, certainly – and I'm glad of that –

but I'm no closer to finding a way out of here than I was a day or so after you let me in.'

'There's no hurry, really,' she said.

'Oh, I'm not sure about that. The wine is running out, and the food supply deteriorating, after all. Besides, *you* may have eternal youth, but *I* don't. I don't want to spend the rest of my life here. Oh, it's not you, the company couldn't be better, but living here doing nothing isn't what I had in mind for a career, if you see what I mean. And I'd like to get you out, too – show you the World the way it is now. You deserve better than being cooped up here forever. I don't know what the chances of someone else finding that tapestry before it's destroyed are, but they probably aren't very good; for all I know the dragon's already burned it up. If *I* don't get us out, no one will. And I haven't got the faintest idea of how to do it.'

'You'll figure it out,' she said confidently. 'I'm sure you will.'

'Not by sitting here practicing singing spells I won't!'

'Maybe you should try some of the more advanced spells,' she suggested thoughtfully, 'instead of working your way up so slowly. Derry's eternal youth spell should be in there somewhere, shouldn't it? You could use that on yourself, and then you wouldn't have to worry about time at all.'

'Oh, it's here,' Tobas replied. 'But I won't dare use it for years yet; it's *really* high-order. I'd probably turn myself into an embryo or something.' He laughed derisively.

'I think you've been working too hard at your wizardry,' Karanissa announced. 'Stop thinking about it. Why don't we just go for a walk around the castle?'

'All right,' Tobas agreed. He picked up the candle-holder from the table.

Again, as they left the study, his arm fell naturally

226

around her slim waist, and again she made no protest. In fact, this time she snuggled closer.

Together they strolled down the corridor, leaning against each other, admiring the now-familiar tapestries on the walls and the statuary in the niches. Tobas heard a familiar slobbering behind them and called, 'Go away, Nuisance.'

Damp footsteps scampered off, and the two ambled on.

After a considerable time and only a few trivial words exchanged, they came near the room where the dysfunctional tapestry hung. 'I want to take another look at it,' Tobas announced.

'All right,' Karanissa said, disengaging herself from his encircling arm.

He tried to replace his hand, but she stepped away. 'I'll wait here,' she said.

'No, come with me,' he said. 'Maybe we'll come up with an idea together that I wouldn't have by myself.'

She hesitated, but finally accepted.

Side by side, but not touching, the two entered the little room with their candle held high, and stared at the dark, empty scene the tapestry depicted. Karanissa shuddered slightly. Tobas stepped nearer, intending to comfort her, but she stepped away again.

'What is it?' he asked.

'It's Derry,' she said. 'I can't help thinking about him when I look at that. You said you found his bones lying there in that room; I can't bear that. I feel as if I ought to be able to see him through the tapestry, somehow, or that he can see us, that he's watching us.'

'No, Derry – Derithon – is dead,' Tobas said. 'He's been dead for centuries. You've mourned him long enough, even if you didn't know he was really dead. His spirit must be long gone by now.'

'But his bones are still there, in that room . . .'

Tobas looked at the tapestry. 'Yes,' he agreed. 'They are, right there . . .' He started to point to the spot where Derithon's skull lay, but stopped, his hand raised, as a sudden realization hit him.

The scene in the tapestry had to match the scene in reality *exactly*, in *every* detail; this tapestry showed an empty room, while in reality Derithon's skeleton lay in the corner, half in the room and half around the corner in the hallway.

That was why the tapestry wouldn't work!

Chapter 24

'This is fascinating,' Tobas said as he lay back on the velvet-covered couch in one of Karanissa's favorite sitting rooms. 'That must be why that room doesn't have any windows; the angle of the sunlight would have to match exactly. And a rainy day might be a real problem. These tapestries aren't as clever as I thought.'

Karanissa, on a nearby chair, shrugged. 'They're clever enough to get us stuck here.'

'The notes said something about time being tricky; that must be what he meant, the angle of the sunlight. I wonder, will a tapestry just not do anything if the light's wrong? The note said that transit time could be affected; maybe, if you step in at the wrong time, you just aren't *anywhere* until the light changes.'

The witch shuddered slightly. 'If that were it, why didn't I just vanish completely when I tried to use the tapestry? I should be in limbo somewhere, waiting for poor Derry's skeleton to disappear, and that would leave *you* stranded out front, starving to death – unless you could talk the servants into opening the door, anyway.'

Tobas thought about that. 'I don't know,' he said. 'Maybe there's a difference between predictable, regular changes, like sunlight, and unpredictable changes, like moving the skeleton. Or maybe that scene will *never* exist again – the roof will fall in before the skeleton is removed, or something – so that the tapestry couldn't work at all.'

'I don't like *that* idea, either,' Karanissa said, hunching forward.

'It's just a suggestion,' Tobas said with a shrug. He

thought for another moment, then said, 'I guess it couldn't just create a new world because the room *used* to exist exactly the way it's shown. Once the spell was established, going to one place, it couldn't switch to another; it could only shut itself down.'

The witch said nothing.

'And as far as one tapestry changing transit time while another doesn't work at all, I suppose that's possible, too. Wizardry is funny stuff. Some little variation in the original spell, something too small to detect, could make a difference – the spell would still work pretty much the same, but would react differently to special circumstances. Roggit told me about things like that, where a spell could work just the same, but would need a different counter-charm, depending on whether the wizard held his left thumb up or sideways on one gesture. With something as complicated as the tapestries, I'd guess there will just about always be a little variation – I mean, the preparatory spell takes twenty-four hours! *Nobody* can do exactly the same motions, down to a fraction of an inch, over an entire day and night. And the magic goes on into the weaving, too, so even the scene itself might affect the spell.'

Karanissa shook herself, then asked, 'Well, whatever the reason is, what do we do now?'

'I'm not sure; I guess we could put the skeleton into the scene, weave it in somehow – but I'm not sure that would work. I think I'd have to completely redo the entire tapestry – ' He stopped dead for a moment, then demanded, 'What am I thinking of? That's stupid. The tapestry's fine the way it is. What we have to do is remove the skeleton; then the scene will be right again.'

'How are we going to do *that*?' she demanded. 'We can't get back through the tapestry to move it until it's been moved!'

'Oh, come on, Kara,' Tobas replied. 'You're a witch! You don't have to reach out and touch something with your hands to move it. Can't you move the skeleton from here?'

'No, I can't!' she snapped. 'I need to know where something is relative to myself, before I can do anything to it. I can sense such things ordinarily – I have the witch-sight and the witch-smell and I can hear minds and read hearts, but not from this world into another. We aren't *anywhere* here. I don't know where to look or how to look. I tried to call for help when I first found out I was stuck here and I couldn't do it; I'm cut off.'

'Oh.' Tobas looked thoughtfully at the ceiling.

'Can't you do something? Don't you have some spell that will remove the skeleton?'

'I don't know,' Tobas said. 'I can't think of any off hand.'

'What about that dream-spell. Couldn't you – '

Tobas sat up, cutting her off. 'Sure! Of course I could! At least, that is, I *think* so. It's supposed to work no matter where the other person is. And we know wizardry works between worlds, even if witchcraft doesn't, because you said Derithon got some kind of alarm or message from his other castle while he was here with you.'

'That's right,' the witch said. 'He did. You can call someone to come and move the skeleton.'

'I have to send the dream to someone specific; that's the way the spell works.'

'Well, so what? You must know somebody.'

'It's got to be someone who knows where that castle is, though; I can only send a message a few minutes long, and I couldn't give clear directions. Not in a dream, anyway. I don't know how much anyone would remember of one of these dreams when he woke up, either. The Lesser Spell doesn't work in both directions; it just sends, it doesn't receive, so I can't check, can't be sure I'm getting through.' He hesitated. 'There's only one other person who knows where the castle is; it'll have to be him. I hope he hasn't gone and fallen off a cliff or something.'

'Who?'

'His name is Peren the White; we met in Dwomor – no, in Ethshar, really. He went off eastward when we split up, across the mountains. I hope I can talk him into coming back.'

'Well, you'll certainly have to try.'

'I suppose I will.' He lay back again, running the plan through his mind to see if there was anything obviously wrong with it.

It seemed sound. He would call Peren with the Lesser Spell of Invaded Dreams. Peren would come and remove Derithon's skeleton, restoring the hidden room to its original condition and allowing the tapestry to work once more. He and Karanissa would be able to just step through into the fallen castle then.

It should work, he decided.

'You called it the Lesser Spell,' Karanissa remarked, breaking into his thoughts. 'Is there a greater one?'

'Well, yes, there is,' Tobas admitted. 'And it works both ways at once, both sending and receiving, and gives the user complete control of someone's dreams for up to half an hour, according to the book. But it's much harder. It uses blood and silver and . . . well, it's harder. Probably fourth-order.'

'You said you thought you could do a third-order spell; is there that much difference?'

'Oh, I suppose not, not really – but I'm not sure I've done any third-order. They might have just been tricky second-order, really.'

'Well, what harm can it do to try?'

232

'I don't know – that's what scares me.'

'*I* think you should try it,' Karanissa said emphatically.

'That's because you don't know any better. There are wizards who live their entire lives without getting past third-order spells, and you want me to go from a single spell to fourth-order in a couple of sixnights!'

'Oh, Tobas, don't get so upset! You're the wizard here; you do as much as you think you can. But fourth-order doesn't sound like so much; you said Derithon must have used something higher than seventh to have created this castle, didn't you?'

He nodded. 'It would need at least that – but Derithon was probably a very talented wizard and two hundred years old. I'm seventeen, or more likely eighteen by now, and I don't really know if I have much aptitude for wizardry or not. And these things aren't just one-two-three, really; second-order is supposed to be eight or ten times as difficult as first, and third-order ten times harder than that, and so on. First-order spells are easy for me now, and I can handle second, but *fourth* . . .'

'Oh.' Her voice was small. 'I hadn't realized it worked that way. I don't know much about wizardry.'

'There's no reason you should. I'm sorry that I'm not a more powerful wizard, but I'm not; I'm just a failed apprentice, really. I'm going to go try that spell, though – the lesser one. I ought to be able to handle that. You go to bed now and get some sleep – I want to test it on you, see if I can send you a message in your dreams.'

'All right,' she agreed. 'I could use a nap, anyway.' She rose, yawning.

They separated in the hallway without touching one another, he bound for the study and she for her chamber. Tobas glanced back over his shoulder at her departing figure and caught Karanissa looking back at him. He faced forward again, smiling.

Chapter 25

The Lesser Spell of Invaded Dreams worked perfectly every time he tried it on Karanissa, so he knew he had mastered it, but he had no way of knowing whether his repeated messages were reaching Peren across the gap between worlds.

He ran through the procedure again and peered intently into the eerie haze of dust and incense smoke that it created.

'Peren,' he said, 'I don't know if you got my earlier messages, but this is Tobas of Telven, using a dream-message-spell to talk to you. I need your help urgently. Go to the fallen flying castle, to the secret room, and move the skeleton – it doesn't matter how, or where you put it, just as long as everything is out of that room. That's all you need to do. I'll pay you back any way I can, if you'll do this for me, and I've got money and magic now.'

He paused. Saying he had money was a slight exaggeration; he had a few odd valuables from Derithon's study, mostly precious and semiprecious stones used in various spells, but no more coin than when he left Telven. That didn't matter, he told himself; he could get money easily enough once he was back in the World. 'Move the skeleton!' he repeated. 'Drag it back around the corner into the hallway – that'll do. Just move the skeleton.'

The haze began to thin, and he stopped talking. That was all he could fit into that invocation of the spell; in an hour or two he would try again.

Meanwhile, it was time to go check the tapestry again,

as he did after each sending. For all he knew, Peren had been right in the castle itself and might have moved the skeleton – or he might have wandered off and gotten lost somewhere in the eastern desert, fallen off a mountain, or gotten himself killed in a fight. All Tobas could do until he got up his nerve to try higher-order magic was to keep trying, sending messages and checking the tapestry.

Taking his prepared supplies with him, he went up to the exit room and poked at the fabric. The tapestry was still dead. He sighed.

He was still stuck in the castle. He had done what he could for the moment. He glanced about, trying to decide what to do with himself until the next attempt at contacting Peren.

His schedule had slipped out of synchronization with Karanissa's as a result of the experiments with dream messages; she was asleep just now, leaving him alone in the castle.

Alone, that is, except for Nuisance, who smeared something ichorous on his slipper as he leaned against the useless tapestry and then ran away giggling. The little monster had gotten totally out of hand of late; he was unsure why, after four centuries of obeying Karanissa, it had decided to cause trouble now, but it undeniably had. Had he been able to see it, he would have kicked it soundly.

He pulled off the slipper and rubbed at it; the stuff was sticky and foul-smelling and clung to his fingers unpleasantly.

Furious, he decided that it was time he did something about Nuisance; he returned to the study, put his bundle of supplies up on the shelf, and flipped open the Book of Spells to Lugwiler's Haunting Phantasm.

This, he was fairly certain, was a third-order spell, and as good a one as any to try out. He had gotten proficient

235

at the spells he believed to be second-order and even the ones he thought might be third; it was time to try another, slightly harder one.

When he had thought that the Phantasm might have created Nuisance or the other servants, he had not yet read through it; that was not at all what it did. It was actually a sort of curse. It created a nasty little haunt that would torment its victim by appearing in unexpected places, looking hideous and startling, while being utterly invisible and imperceptible to everyone else. The Phantasm was actually quite harmless unless it frightened someone to death, but it didn't *look* harmless, according to the instructions. It could be made to haunt the target relentlessly, randomly at its whim, or in response to a particular stimulus.

Tobas intended to have the Phantasm haunt Nuisance so long as Nuisance remained in the upper floors of the castle. He thought he could manage quite nicely without a servant – certainly without Nuisance – and, if he should later change his mind, he could remove the spell.

He could simply have ordered Nuisance to stay away; the thing did still obey direct orders. That, however, was far too dull and easy. This curse seemed a good way to proceed with his wizardly training, and he thought it might be fun to see Nuisance on the receiving end of unpleasantness for once.

Not that he could actually see Nuisance at all – perhaps, he thought, he should say that it would be nice to *hear* Nuisance being on the receiving end. A few whimpers would be a welcome change from the constant giggling and squishing about.

The spell required a mirror and an assortment of odd ingredients; he selected them carefully from the shelves, then arranged everything on the big worktable, ready for use.

He read through the spell four times; it looked tricky, very tricky, but at last he felt himself ready to attempt it. He began the ritual.

Halfway through he knew something wasn't working right; a greenish-yellow flicker of some sort was crawling around the table, and that was definitely not anything that had been mentioned in the description. Besides, the spell didn't *feel* right; he had had enough experience of wizardry by now to know that. He had made an error somewhere. He was unsure whether it would be better to stop or to continue, and he felt his instant of hesitation damage the spell further.

Grimly, realizing that he had now botched it completely, he continued, hoping to minimize the damage. There was no telling what he had done until he finished it; perhaps nothing would come of it.

He completed the spell as best he could, then laid the small round mirror down on the table.

The yellow flicker was gone; he could see no sign of magical activity. Perhaps nothing *had* come of his bungling. Perhaps he had not actually bungled it at all; he had never placed a curse before, and the odd feeling of wrongness might be normal with curses. Somewhat reassured, he was about to call for Nuisance to see if the Phantasm had appeared, when something climbed up out of the mirror.

He stared at the little creature, horrified. It stood on the tabletop and stared back at him.

It was no more than eight inches tall; its glossy hide was a muddy greenish-brown color, and it was shaped something like a man, something like a frog. It stood upright on two bow legs, long-fingered hands on its hips, staring back at him with bulging popeyes, its big, pointed ears cocked forward. He could see no sign of any sex, but then, many magical creatures were said to be sexless.

237

It was not the Phantasm; there was nothing very horrific about the creature, and it was indisputably solid. He reached out and poked it in its fat little belly.

It squeaked with alarm and stepped back, away from the mirror.

'And what in the World are *you*?' Tobas asked aloud.

It puffed itself up proudly, then pointed a thumb at its narrow chest and said in a ridiculous little voice, 'Spriggan.'

Startled, Tobas said, 'What?' He had not expected it to be able to talk.

'Spriggan, me!' it squeaked.

'Oh,' Tobas said. Curiously, he reached out to pick it up.

It squealed again, and scampered away; before he could catch it, it had bounced off the wall, dived off the table and vanished out the doorway.

Oh well, Tobas thought. It seemed harmless enough, and it might not be permanent in any case. In time it might well vanish of its own accord.

So much, though, for trying any high-level spells in the near future. He reached out to pick up the mirror.

Another spriggan, identical to the first, climbed out of the glass before his hand reached it.

'Hello,' he said, surprised.

'Hello,' it squeaked in reply. Its voice was pitched lower than the first, but was still somewhere well up into soprano range.

'You're a spriggan?' Tobas asked, slightly worried; he had not expected a second to appear and feared that more of these mysterious little creatures might be forthcoming.

'Yes, yes!' it said, smiling up at him. 'Spriggan!'

'Where did you come from?' Tobas asked. Its origin might give a clue to its abilities or purpose.

It looked puzzled for a moment, its face contorted into

238

a ludicrous parody of perplexity, and then suddenly smiled again. 'Here,' it yelped, jumping up and down and pointing at the mirror. 'Here! Here!'

Tobas stared at it for a moment. The thing did not seem very intelligent, but he had no one else to question. 'Is there a reason you're here?' he asked cautiously.

'Fun, fun,' it said. 'Have good fun, yes?' It grinned toothlessly up at him.

'I suppose you will,' Tobas answered doubtfully. He wondered how many of these things were going to emerge from the mirror before the spell wore off. Were these two all of them, or would the castle soon be crowded with these little creatures?

The second spriggan suddenly scampered to the edge of the table, yipped, 'Bye-bye!' and jumped to the floor; before Tobas could stop it, it had, like the first, dashed out of the door and out of sight.

Quickly, before another could appear, he snatched up the mirror and threw it into a convenient wooden box. That, he thought, should keep any more spriggans from getting loose in the castle.

He watched for several minutes, but no more appeared; he closed the box and turned the key in the lock, just in case.

No more tricky spells, he promised himself. He would work his way up gradually. The Lesser Spell of Invaded Dreams would have to do. If he couldn't reach Peren with it, he might try Arden or Elner or Alorria.

He felt suddenly tired; all this magic, and the stress of trying to arrange an escape from the castle, was wearing on him. He had no idea how long he had been awake; he had no way to tell time without the sun. The castle contained no hourglass, water clocks, or other timepieces.

He packed away his books and tools and went to bed.

A moment later, behind him, behind the closed door,

inside the wooden box, a spriggan emerged from the mirror and began whimpering dismally upon realizing that it was confined.

Chapter 26

'There must be dozens of them!' Karanissa wailed as she swatted ineffectually at a spriggan, sending it scampering out the door and down the corridor.

'I know,' Tobas said. 'I know. It must have taken at least four or five of them to break open the box, and that was days ago.'

'Can't you do something?'

'If I could find the mirror, I'd smash it; at least that would stop any more from appearing. Then maybe we could throw some out into the void – except that seems awfully cruel.'

'When the tapestry works again, we can herd them out though that,' Karanissa suggested. 'There's room enough for them in the World.'

Tobas nodded. 'Good idea. First though, we have to find the mirror. They're not completely stupid; they must have hidden it somewhere.'

Karanissa started to say something, then stopped to pick a spriggan off a nearby chair and fling it out the door into the hallway. It ran away squeaking; she watched it go, then looked intently around the room.

'There aren't any more in here, so we can make plans.'

'Are you sure? I do have an idea, but I don't want them to hear it.'

'Of course I'm sure! I'm a witch; I can tell when someone's listening.'

'Good. Kara, I don't think we're going to be able to get the mirror; we're too big and obvious. But I don't think they can see any better than we can; the servants should be invisible to them, just as they are to us – '

'To you, maybe,' she interrupted him. 'I can see them if I try.'

'To me, then, or anyone who doesn't have witch-sight. Anyway, if you order the servants to find the mirror and bring it to us – or just to smash it – I don't think the spriggans will be able to stop them. We'll have the problem halfway solved.'

'That's a good idea – except how will they know which mirror to smash? I don't want them breaking every mirror in the castle!'

'How many mirrors could be lying around out of place? Just to be sure, have them bring the mirror to me; I'll know the right one when I see it.'

'All right, I'll tell the sylphs; you can tell the little one.'

'Nuisance, you mean.'

'Nuisance, yes. I still can't get used to calling it that; Derry and I never had names for any of them.'

Tobas shrugged. 'It's useful, sometimes.'

'I know it is; I should have thought of it years ago, really. I've wasted so much time. I know I couldn't have gotten out of here without a wizard, but it seems as if I could have done more while I was here. You've done more to the place in a couple of sixnights than I did in four hundred years – learning those spells, conjuring up the spriggans, and so forth.'

'Oh, it's been more than a couple of sixnights – it must be more than a month by now, I'm sure.'

'Well, all the same, these spriggans hiding everywhere and getting into everything – they've reminded me what a mess this place is, all full of clutter that Derry left around. The servants deep it dusted, but they don't know enough to put things away or keep cabinets and doors locked, and the spriggans have been all over the place.'

'They're harmless, really,' Tobas said, hoping it was true. It seemed to be, so far.

'I know that, but they get into *everything*! Damn them anyway! If I see one more little footprint in my dinner, I swear I'll start killing them – I'll burn their slimy *guts* out! And when they spilled everything out of the drawers in my bedroom . . .'

'They were just exploring, I guess.'

'I know – exploring through all my private things! Scattering my clothes everywhere!'

'They don't know any better.' Tobas hoped that was the reason and that the creatures didn't have a malicious streak.

'I know, but my clothes . . .' Her voice trailed off, and for a moment they sat silently across from each other, Karanissa staring at the tabletop, Tobas letting his eyes roam about the room, but always coming back to the witch, her flowing black hair, her fine, dark features, her slender figure.

'Tobas,' she asked, looking up again 'what do the women wear in Ethshar of the Spices?'

Startled, he answered, 'I don't know – just clothes. Tunic and skirt, mostly; the fine ladies and some of the magicians wear gowns.'

'Tunic and skirt.'

'Certainly, the same there as anywhere else.'

'What do they look like?'

Tobas began to laugh, then realized that her question was serious, that he had never seen her wear anything but gowns and dresses. 'It doesn't matter,' he said. 'Your clothes are fine as they are; most women can't afford any so fine.'

'I don't want to seem strange, though. Four hundred years – styles must have changed.'

'I suppose they have, but really, you'll be fine as you are.'

'What about hair? Do the women wear their hair long? Do they put it up?'

'I don't really know,' Tobas admitted. 'I mean, I never really thought about it. They don't wear it *short*, but I've never seen any as long as yours.' Karanissa's hair, worn loose, reached her waist. 'I guess they trim it a little below the shoulders, or tie it up in back.'

The witch reached up and tugged at her hair. 'Should I cut mine, then?'

'No, don't! It's beautiful just the way it is, really!' He half rose and reached out, taking the hand that held the hair.

'I want to fit in, though. I've been listening to you and working on my accent – not just with witchcraft – because I want it to stay even when I don't think about it. Had you noticed?'

Tobas grimaced. 'I didn't realize it was intentional,' he said. 'But I had noticed, and I had meant to warn you about it. I have a Pirate Towns accent, as it's called; you don't want to talk the way I do.'

'But the language must have changed . . .'

'Oh, yes, it certainly has – in Dwomor it's an entirely different tongue now. But your accent is lovely; it's old-fashioned, elegant.'

'I don't want to be old-fashioned, though; I want to fit in.'

'You'll never fit in; you're too beautiful. You'll always stand out.'

'Oh, you're just being silly!' She pushed his hand away.

'No, I mean it!' He took her hand again, then leaned forward and kissed her, more to his own surprise than hers.

The table lifted slightly and slid out of the way, which Tobas took as encouragement; witchcraft could be handy.

Almost an hour later a spriggan glanced in the door and squealed; Tobas heaved a convenient boot at it, and it ran off.

Karanissa giggled.

'What are you laughing at, woman?' Tobas demanded.

'Oh, I don't know – the spriggan, I guess. They *are* kind of cute.'

'A little while ago you were threatening to flash-fry the little monsters.'

'A little while ago I was frustrated and angry.'

'Well, I'm glad I was able to help with that; now, if I could get rid of the spriggans' mirror and find us a way out of the castle, we'd be all set. Nuisance! Here, Nuisance!'

Wet footsteps pattered into the room, and something foul began dripping on the carpet. 'Nuisance, I want you to find the mirror those spriggans took from the study and bring it to me; got that?'

Nuisance made a noise like a strangled cat and scampered away. Tobas sighed. 'Do you think he understood?'

'Oh, probably,' Karanissa said. She turned and addressed empty air, giving the two sylphs the same instructions Tobas had given Nuisance. The air stirred slightly, and they were gone.

'You know,' Tobas said, 'I wonder whether Derithon made Nuisance intentionally, or whether it was an accident like the spriggans. I can't find any spell in the book that would produce something like that.'

Karanissa shrugged. 'I really don't know; it was in the castle when I first came here, and I never thought to ask. I just took it for granted – another little bit of wizardry, as incomprehensible as the rest.'

'Wizardry doesn't all have to be incomprehensible – at least, I don't think it does.'

'Compared to witchcraft, it's all madness, if you ask me – remember, wizardry uses raw chaos.'

'Well, maybe, but it makes order out of it – sort of.'

'Oh, it does, does it? Like that jar-opening spell? That's so orderly and efficient.'

Tobas grinned. 'You argue well, witch.'

She punched him in the ribs; he retaliated by grabbing her around the waist and pulling her toward him, and the two of them rolled, giggling, across the carpet.

They ended up against a wall, Karanissa on her back and Tobas sitting astride her. 'Aha, wench!' he said. 'You're in my power now!'

She laughed, then put the back of one hand to her forehead. 'Oh, mercy, master! What will you have of me?'

'What have you got?' he asked wryly.

'Only my poor self, you fiend!' She burst out giggling.

'Oh, that's good enough,' Tobas said. 'I'll take it.'

'You already have,' she pointed out.

'Oh, but I mean to keep it!' He turned serious, and asked, 'Karanissa, would you marry me?'

Her giggling subsided. 'I don't know,' she said. 'How do you mean that?'

'Is there more than one way?'

'There were in my time – civilian marriages were different from military marriages, and there were various more casual affairs as well.' She pushed him off and sat up. 'That doesn't matter, though. Tobas, I like you – maybe I love you, I'm not sure – but I am not going to marry anyone until we're out of this castle.'

'Good enough,' he replied. 'We don't have the witness we need here, anyway.'

'Only one? In my day you needed three.'

'Well, more are better, but one will do.' Tobas got to his feet and retrieved his boot from the hallway, where it had landed when thrown at the spriggan.

'What do you want your boots for?'

'I don't like walking around barefoot – especially not with the spriggans around – and Nuisance did something to my slippers so that they're all sticky.'

'Well, tell it to clean it off! Or have one of the sylphs do it!'

'The sylphs won't obey me – you never told them to. And it never occurred to me to tell Nuisance to wipe it up.' Since the incident of the spilled chamberpot he had avoided telling Nuisance to clean up anything.

'No wonder it gives you so much trouble! You let it get away with making a mess. If you made it clean up after itself, it would behave itself better.'

Tobas shrugged. 'Maybe that's it.' He settled in a chair and began pulling on the boots.

'You still haven't told me why you need anything on your feet; where are you going?'

'Well, if you won't marry me until I get us out of here, I thought I'd go check on the tapestry again and, if it's still not working, try sending Peren another dream.'

'Wait a minute. I'll come with you.' Karanissa stood up, straightening her crumpled skirt and pulling her bodice back into place.

Tobas waited, and a moment later the two of them were ambling slowly down the hall toward the tapestry, arms about one another. They paused while Tobas opened the door to the chamber, and he took advantage of the opportunity to kiss her lingeringly.

Their little interlude was interrupted by a furious chorus of squeaks and squeals, and the soggy sound of Nuisance running desperately toward them, gasping out hideous noises.

Tobas turned, and saw the spriggan mirror bouncing toward them, obviously carried by Nuisance, with a horde of spriggans in hot pursuit.

'Good boy!' he called, ignoring momentarily the fact that Nuisance's gender, if any, was unknown. 'Bring it here!'

Nuisance tried, but before it could reach its master, a pair of spriggans jumped it; the mirror fell to the floor and rolled free.

Tobas dived for it and snatched it up, but a spriggan was in the process of climbing out of it and let out an earpiercing shriek of sheer terror. Tobas ignored the creature as he tried to dash the glass against the wall.

The spriggan wrapped itself around his hand, clinging for dear life and incidentally forming a very effective cushion. Tobas started to pry it loose with his other hand, but after a glance back down the hallway he thought better of it.

Every spriggan in the castle, three or four dozen of them, was charging directly toward him. Clawless and toothless they might be, but that many of them could still be formidable. He got to his feet and scrambled into the tapestry chamber, dragging Karanissa with him, and then slammed the door in the faces of the onrushing mob.

The latch did not engage, and an instant later he was swept off his feet by a wave of squirming, squeaking spriggans.

He rolled over, trying to force them to drop off to avoid being crushed; most of the little creatures panicked and jumped clear. Holding the mirror high, he tried to get to his feet once again.

A dozen spriggans jumped him. With others close underfoot, he lost his balance and staggered backward. He wobbled, then fell.

The lights went out, and he felt a sudden rush of cool

248

air about him. When he hit the floor, it was at a steep angle, so that he rolled involuntarily. Startled, he loosened his grip and felt the spriggans pry the mirror from his grasp.

That goal achieved, they ran off in every direction, squeaking like an entire castle's complement of rusty hinges, all swinging at once.

Tobas got slowly to his feet, discovering as he did so that the floor had tilted somehow. His eyes gradually adjusted to the darkness, and he realized that Karanissa was not in the room; he was alone.

Only then did it register that he was not in the room he had been in, and, after a moment of wild fancies about secret doorways and trick walls, he realized that the tapestry was working again. He had gone through it! The sloping floor told him immediately where he had landed – the bare, empty chamber in the downed flying castle where his tapestry had once hung.

He had been afraid of that. He had hoped that the tapestries, being a pair, were somehow linked, so that he would emerge in the little cottage a good distance closer to Dwomor Keep; but since this was the chamber the tapestry showed, he was not surprised to find himself in it.

He had half expected to find Peren waiting for him, though. 'Hello?' he called.

No one answered. He felt his way forward; the darkness was so complete that he could see almost nothing of his surroundings. He found a wall and groped his way along it, rounding a corner.

The instant he had cleared the corner, he heard a footstep behind him. A familiar female voice called, 'Tobas?'

'Kara?' He realized that she had been unable to use the

tapestry until he had removed himself from the scene and cursed himself for not doing so more promptly.

'I'm right here,' she replied. 'Why is it so dark? Where are we?'

'In the flying castle. I'm not sure why it's dark.' His eyes were still adjusting; he could see now that he was in the narrow, vaulted corridor leading to Derithon's study. Turning around, he could make out, dimly, Karanissa, standing unsteadily on the slanting floor.

'I don't suppose you went back to the study and got the pack of supplies I had prepared,' he said.

'No,' she admitted, 'I didn't think of it. I didn't bring anything.'

He could see that she was still wearing the light gown she had on when he fell through the tapestry; that was hardly surprising, since she had had no time to change.

They were poorly dressed for the journey to Dwomor, all their supplies were back in Derithon's study, and they had made no definite plans beyond this point, but the tapestry was working again.

'Well,' he said aloud, 'at least we're out.'

Chapter 27

The flying castle's outer study was not as dark as the tapestry chamber, but was still dim and gloomy; Tobas realized that they had emerged either at night – or at least dusk – or during a heavy rain. He heard no rain and decided it must be night. He tried to flick a fire into existence, then remembered that wizardry did not work here.

'Can you make a light?' he asked Karanissa.

She responded by raising a hand that glowed dimly. 'I'm out of practice,' she apologized. 'I'm better with fire, if you can find me something to burn.'

Without regard for whatever respect might be due the dead Derithon's property, Tobas picked up the nearest length of shelving. 'I've got some wood here that should burn; light one end, and I'll hold the other.'

The witch complied; in a second or two a blue flame sprang up from a corner of the ancient plank, then spread across one end and brightened to a cheerful yellow.

Karanissa looked around at the wreckage of her long-dead lover's library and murmured, 'Gods!'

'What's the matter?' Tobas asked.

'This place – last time I saw it . . .'

'The last time *I* saw it, it looked just about as it does now.' The burning plank was awkward to hold and was burning faster than he liked; he did not care to take the time to indulge Karanissa's nostalgia. 'Let's get out of here,' he said. He took her hand and led her into the bedchamber.

She stared about, horrified, at each of the rooms as they passed through, but said nothing further.

When they reached the balcony above the Great Hall, Tobas noticed a light at the far end of the hall; he held his own light away from himself for a moment to get a better look.

A fire was burning somewhere outside, its glow visible through the crumbled gate. He hurried Karanissa down the steps and across the debris.

As the pair emerged into the cool night air, Tobas called, 'Peren? Is that you?' He looked down over the edge of the stone disc on which the castle stood.

A lone figure sat crouched beside a campfire; at the sound of Tobas' voice he arose and called, 'Tobas?'

'Yes!' Tobas answered, all doubts dispelled by the yellow gleam of firelight on white hair. 'Thank all the gods you came! No, not the gods; thank *you*, Peren! Thank you for coming!' He flung aside his burning piece of shelf and began half climbing, half sliding down the stone, Karanissa with him, in his eagerness to join his companion.

Peren came around the circumference to the lowest point to help the two down; he clasped Tobas' hand warmly and tried to hide his surprise at Karanissa's presence.

When all three were on the ground, Tobas, still catching his breath, announced, 'Karanissa, this is Peren the White; Peren, this is Karanissa of the Mountains; she's a witch.'

'I'm pleased to meet you,' Peren said.

'And I you,' Karanissa replied with an odd salute that reminded Tobas that she had been in the military.

A moment of awkward silence followed; then Tobas took the initiative and began walking toward the campfire, asking, 'How long have you been here, Peren?'

'Not long; I arrived around noon.'

'What time is it now?'

'The sun has been down less than an hour.'

'What did you do with the skeleton?'

Peren hesitated before replying. 'I buried it. It seemed the best thing to do, since I had no way of making a proper pyre for bare bones. The spirit must have been freed long ago.'

Tobas glanced at Karanissa, worried that Peren's words would upset her, but she seemed undisturbed. 'That's good,' he said. He hesitated, then asked Karanissa, 'Do you think we should make a marker of some sort?'

'I don't know,' she said. 'Derry never mentioned anything about it. He didn't intend ever to die, after all. I think he'd like something, though.'

'Derry?' Peren asked.

'Derithon the Mage,' Tobas replied. 'Those were his bones you buried.'

Peren nodded.

They had reached Peren's little camp and all three settled to the ground by the fire; Peren, observing that Tobas and Karanissa were sitting as close together as humanly possible, quietly made sure that he himself was several feet away. He could see well enough that three together would be a crowd.

'What about the spriggans?' Karanissa asked suddenly.

'What about them?' Tobas asked.

'Where are they? Some of them went through with you. And what about the mirror? Did you break it?'

'No,' Tobas admitted. 'They got it away from me when I fell down the sloping floor. They're all in the castle somewhere, I suppose, and the mirror with them.'

'Should we do anything about it?'

'I don't think we need to,' Tobas replied, then hesitated. 'Kara, are any of them listening?'

She peered around carefully. 'No,' she said at last. 'There are a few animals over there – chipmunks, maybe – but no spriggans.'

'Good, Kara, wizardry doesn't work around here; we think that's why Derithon's castle fell. I told you about that. The mirror's harmless unless they take it out of the dead area, and I don't think they're smart enough ever to figure that out unless someone tells them. So there won't be any more spriggans appearing. And I don't think they can reproduce any other way. A few dozen spriggans won't hurt the World; we don't need to worry about them anymore.'

'Oh,' Karanissa relaxed slightly. 'Oh,' she said again, 'that's good.'

Peren said nothing, but glanced curiously at Tobas.

'Oh, you don't know what a spriggan is, do you?' Karanissa said, noticing the glance. 'I didn't mean to be rude.'

'It's all right,' Peren said.

'No,' Tobas said. 'I don't mean to shut you out. I'll tell you the whole story.'

He described his adventures since their parting. By the time he had finished, Karanissa had dozed off, her head on Tobas' shoulder, and the greater moon had risen halfway up the sky.

'. . . And we didn't bring any supplies at all, I'm afraid,' he concluded. 'Just what we were wearing. I've got my belt and a few precious things, but no food, no other weapons, no blankets. I'm sorry to be so careless.'

He did have his athame – he never went anywhere without it – and the little vial of brimstone was still on his belt because he had never bothered to remove it, but he had no other magical ingredients, no Book of Spells. He was glad that he had happened to have boots on when he tumbled through the tapestry.

When he stopped speaking, he shivered; the night had turned cold. Despite the fire they had kept up, he felt a sudden strong chill. 'What's the date?' he asked, suddenly curious.

'The fourth of Snowfall,' Peren replied. 'We're having a warm spell, and the snows are late this year.'

'Snowfall?' Tobas stared at the flames. 'That's almost three months. Where have *you* been, all this time? Did you get over the mountains?'

'It's late,' Peren said. He pulled a blanket from his pack and wrapped it about himself. 'We all need sleep. You and your woman take the tent; I'll stay out here.'

'But . . .'

'I'll tell you in the morning,' Peren said. 'Now, go get some sleep.'

Reluctantly, Tobas obeyed. Karanissa never stirred as he carried her into the tent.

Chapter 28

The sun was well up in the southeast when Tobas awoke, its light filtered by the leafy treetops.

Karanissa was still lying beside him, but her eyes were open, staring up at the light that seeped through the tent's fabric. When she saw that he was awake, she turned and smiled at him. 'We're really out of the castle?'

'We really are,' he said, smiling in return.

'It's hard to believe that after so long – I'm afraid I'll wake up again and discover it's all a dream. Even you – maybe this whole time with you is a dream.'

'Oh, it's all real enough; come on out of the tent and I'll show you.' He opened the flap, and sunlight streamed in.

'Oh!' Karanissa said. 'It's so bright!'

'It's not so bad,' he said as he crawled out, blinking.

Karanissa followed him, one hand shielding her eyes. 'That's easy for you to say,' she retorted, 'but I haven't seen the sun in four hundred years!' She shivered. 'And it's cold, too.'

Tobas spotted Peren, sitting quietly on the far side of the remains of last night's fire, stirring the ashes with a stick to get out the last bits of warmth. 'Good morning!' he called.

Peren nodded acknowledgment, then stood up, brushing ash from his breeches. 'We should get moving,' he said. 'I've packed up everything but the tent, and I scratched out a stone for the grave. Derithon the Mage – that was the name?'

'Yes,' Tobas said.

'I thought so,' Peren replied, nodding. 'Well, are we heading for Dwomor, or hadn't you decided?'

'Dwomor, by way of the cottage where I left the tapestry. What's your hurry, though?'

Peren stared at him for a moment, then said, 'Tobas, today is the fifth of Snowfall, and we're leagues away from anywhere, in the middle of the mountains. I don't care to stay up here any longer than necessary; even if you and your witch can keep us from freezing, we would still starve if a real storm caught us here.'

'Oh,' Tobas replied sheepishly. 'You're right. What should I do?'

'You and she can eat breakfast while I pack up the tent,' Peren said, holding out a sewn pouch of dry salt beef. 'I'm afraid it's cold, but I didn't want to waste time building another fire and then burying it again.'

'That's all right,' Karanissa said. 'I can warm it up.' She took the pouch and held it.

After a moment it began to steam; she ripped open the pouch and handed a strip to Tobas.

They ate in silence while Peren took down the tent and folded it away. As he finished, Tobas remarked, 'It's too bad I hadn't got as far as making a bottomless bag – Derithon had a spell for one in his book.'

'Well, you didn't,' Peren said. 'So you'll have to carry half the supplies.'

'I can carry a share,' Karanissa interjected.

'All right then, all the better; we'll split them three ways. Let's do that and get moving.'

Ten minutes later they were on their way south through the forest, toward the familiar path around the end of the great cliff, with Peren's supplies divided more or less evenly. When they had walked far enough to settle into a comfortable rhythm, Tobas reminded Peren of his prom-

257

ise. 'You said you'd tell me what happened to you these past three months,' he said.

Peren was silent, and Tobas added, 'I thought you'd have rich clothes and servants by now, but that tunic you're wearing is one of the ones you had when we met. I don't even see your sword.'

Peren nodded. 'I was robbed,' he said.

Tobas had thought that Peren had seemed more irritable, less pleasant, and even quieter than before and had suspected that he had had a hard time. 'Tell me about it,' he said.

They marched on another dozen paces before Peren began. 'I'm not the hunter I thought I was; after we split up, I didn't catch much. Oh, I could hit what I aimed at – I *am* good with a sling – but finding anything to throw at is harder than I thought. I ate everything in my pack and only caught a couple of rabbits and once, when I was desperate, a chipmunk. I was hungry – really hungry! – when I came down out of the mountains in Aigoa.'

'You did reach Aigoa, though?'

'Oh, yes. I came across cottages as soon as I was past the last of the true mountains – or maybe those hills are still mountains; I suppose it depends on how you look at it. I was past the last of the peaks that break the timberline, put it that way.' He paused for a moment, remembering, then continued. 'I was hungry. I stopped at the first cottage I found, the home of an old shepherd, and traded him a gold candlestick for a good dinner, a night's lodging, a hearty breakfast, and some supplies to see me farther down the road. While I slept he helped himself to a few other things as well, my sword among them, but I was too weak to argue and grateful he didn't just cut my throat and keep it all. I told myself that I would hire helpers and come back later for the rest if I needed it.'

'*Did* you come back?' Karanissa asked.

'No, of course not. After that I begged or stole what I needed and kept the bag hidden until I reached the trade road between Aigoa Castle and the Citadel of Amor. I found an inn and waited there until a caravan stopped in. That was – let me see – the twenty-eighth of Harvest, I think, that I reached the inn, and the last caravan of the season arrived on the third of Leafcolor. I had kept the innkeeper happy by working for my keep – cleaning stables and the like – and by showing him that jeweled box and telling him I'd pay my bill when I sold it to the traders.'

'Which box was it?' Karanissa asked, her voice wistful.

'It was made of white shell, with a gold latch and pearls at each corner.'

'Oh, well,' she said, resignedly, 'I never cared for that one, anyway.'

'Just as well, lady. When the caravan arrived, I spoke to its master; he asked questions about where I had found the box and the other things I showed him, and I lied with every word I told him – I didn't like his looks, but I was in no position to be choosy. The innkeeper wouldn't wait much longer. The caravan master seemed to take it for granted that I had stolen it all somewhere, despite my story, but that didn't seem to bother him much. Finally, we settled on a price – a hundred pieces of silver for everything I had left. It was easily worth twice that, I'd say, probably more, but I was in no position to bargain. So he counted out the coins, and I took them, and we went to our rooms for the night.

'And when I woke up, the money was gone.

'Oh, I shouted, and I argued, and no one so much as offered a prayer of sympathy. I was just another penniless adventurer making big claims with nothing to back them up. The caravan packed up and left, saying they had a schedule to keep, and I stayed to search the inn and berate the innkeeper.

'Finally, the man would take no more; he picked me up and threw me out on to the road, with all my belongings, in the rain. Last of all he threw a silver coin after me and told me, "The caravan master gave me a tenth as my share; here's a tenth of that to go away and never come back, you lying pale-skinned little thief."

'I swore and I cursed and I called down the wrath of the gods, and then I picked myself up and ran after the caravan, determined to get my money back. I caught up to them late in the afternoon.

'I hadn't thought how I, a lone man, unarmed, and not in the best of health, would take my money back from the crews on a dozen wagons. I marched up as they pulled into the yard of the next inn and demanded my money, hoping to shame them into honesty; instead they called me a liar and a monster and beat me and threw me out on the road.

'I was still lying there the next morning when they moved on; I believe they thought I was dead. I almost was, I suppose. I had more bruises than sound skin.

'Eventually, though, I picked myself up and crawled away. No one had stopped to help me, though a dozen travelers had passed.'

Peren paused as if waiting for comment, but neither Tobas nor Karanissa could think of anything to say.

'This was in Amor,' Peren said. 'I had crossed the border when I followed the caravan. Amor is said to be one of the larger of the Small Kingdoms.'

Again they walked several paces in silence before he continued.

'I found a farmer who took me in – I promised to pay her when I could, but she didn't seem very concerned about that. I stayed there for the rest of Leafcolor and into Newfrost, getting my strength back. I thought at first that I might stay there permanently; she had no husband, seemed to take an interest in me, and was comely enough. After a few sixnights, though, it was obvious that her interest had passed; once she had realized that, despite my color, I was nothing but an ordinary man, she had no more use for me. I think she had assumed I was a magician of some sort or a magician's creation and she would be richly rewarded for helping me; when I convinced her that was not the case, she allowed me to stay, but treated me with more scorn than affection. On the tenth of Newfrost I left.

'I had no money and nowhere to go, but Desset – that was the farmer's name – had mentioned a great highway somewhere to the north that led around the mountains to Ethshar, so I headed north – or northwest, actually. I suppose I also hoped to come across members of that caravan so that I might somehow retrieve some of what I had lost, since the Citadel of Amor also lay to the northwest.

'And then, on the first night I was alone again, I dreamed that I heard you calling me to come back to the castle in the mountains.

'I thought it was just a dream, but it happened again on the next night and the next, and each time I remembered more of your message and I realized that it was magic – or I hoped it was. I had no real goal, nowhere that I had to be, so I saw no harm in returning; I had been treated better in Dwomor than in Aigoa or Amor, certainly. I had a few things Desset had given me, and I found others where I could – the thieves had never bothered to take everything from my pack, only the valuables, so I still had the tent and rope and so forth. I took odd jobs to earn money for the things I couldn't beg, borrow, or steal. When I had everything I needed, I began retracing my steps; I knew I'd never find the place if I tried taking a different route. I got here two nights ago, on the third of Snowfall, and you know the rest.'

'I'm sorry,' Tobas said. 'I hadn't realized that you would have so bad a time alone over there.'

Peren shrugged. 'You've done nothing to be sorry for; you had your own life to live, back to Ethshar with your tapestry. If I had had any sense, I would have come with you.'

'Well, I'm still sorry about the way things turned out. Do you know the names of any of the people who robbed you?'

Peren looked at him curiously. 'Some of them,' he said 'Why do you ask?'

Tobas looked at the ground for a moment, then back at Peren. 'If you want,' he said, 'I can put curses on them, once I get back into the castle through the tapestry and bring out Derithon's Book of Spells and some of the paraphernalia and supplies.'

'What sort of curses?'

'Oh, I don't know; Derithon had several. Lugwiler's Haunting Phantasm, that created the spriggans when I messed it up, for example. Or the Dismal Itch. Or once I get better, there are some higher-order ones that get really nasty. You could pick and choose.'

Peren took his time to think before replying. 'I don't know, Tobas; I appreciate the offer, certainly, but I'm not sure I want to start cursing people. I'll have to thimk about it.'

'Well,' Tobas said, 'you have plenty of time to think about it in any case.' He grimaced. 'I don't know how much use I'll actually get from that tapestry. Oh, I've got access to all Derithon's spells now, and I can make a living readily enough, but first I've got to go back through the castle and collect the book and everything else I'll need, and then come back through to the *other* castle, and then make this trip down the mountains all over again. That's not the most convenient situation, having the only exit up here. I doubt I'll be going in and out very often. I suppose it will depend on where I eventually settle down.'

'You could always just stay in the tapestry,' Peren suggested.

'Oh, no!' Karanissa said before Tobas could reply. 'No, no, no! Not permanently! Not again! After four hundred years in there, I'm not going to go live there forever. I'll be glad to visit there, perhaps live there part of the time, But I don't want to stay there permanently and give up the outside world. Look around you at all this!' She gestured, taking in the green pines, the blue sky, the bright sun. 'How could I give this up again? Besides, the garden is dying and the wine is running out. Out here it's so beautiful! Look at the sun and the trees and the dirt here – pine needles, the birds singing – I like it out here.'

Peren turned. '*You* could stay out; you're a witch, you can earn your keep anywhere.'

'You think I would let Tobas go back there alone? I don't intend to let him get away that easily.' She reached out and stroked Tobas' hair possessively.

'And I wouldn't leave you,' Tobas assured her, returning the caress. 'Don't worry; eventually I'll learn enough magic to make more tapestries, and then we can live wherever we please and still get in and out of the castle at will – assuming we want to.'

Karanissa hesitated, but then said. 'Well, actually, I think we *will* want to, Tobas. It *is* beautiful out here, but it's cold and a little frightening. The castle has been my home for so long that . . . well, it's home. My home. *Our* home.'

Tobas nodded and put his arm around her. 'Yes, it is,' he agreed as they trudged onward.

He had a home again, someplace to go back to. Telven no longer mattered; he had a new place in the World – or, rather, out of it.

He still needed more, though. Like Karanissa, he did not want to be cut off from human society indefinitely. He wanted to find a place for himself socially as well as physically; he needed not just a home but a career, and not just a lover but friends.

And a goodly supply of money to restock the castle's wine cellar and Derithon's depleted and decayed supplies wouldn't hurt, either.

Chapter 29

On the afternoon of the sixth of Snowfall, in the year 5221, Tobas of Telven and Karanissa of the Mountains were married on a deserted hilltop somewhere in eastern Dwomor, in an improvised ceremony invoking whatever gods might hear, with Peren the White as their only witness and with the required document inscribed on a piece of tree bark.

'This is silly,' Peren said as they scratched their names on the inside of the bark. 'You could have waited until we got to Dwomor.'

'I didn't want to wait,' Tobas said. 'Karanissa might have changed her mind again.'

'Or you might have,' she retorted. 'You might have decided to marry that princess of yours, Alorria of Dwomor.'

'Instead of you? Never!' Tobas replied, hugging her.

'Besides, Alorria's probably married to some big, brave dragon hunter by now – and getting tired of him already,' Peren said as he started down the slope from the hilltop where they had performed the little ritual.

'If she's not, maybe she'll marry you, now that I'm taken,' Tobas suggested as he followed, his new wife at his side.

'Oh, maybe; I think I'd rather have her sister Tinira, though,' Peren replied, smiling.

'You never did have any taste,' Tobas retorted.

'Why not marry both of them?' Karanissa suggested.

'Well, I suppose I could,' Peren said. 'But I didn't kill the dragon.'

'Details, details!' Tobas laughed.

Karanissa smiled, but then shivered slightly. 'You don't suppose that we'll run into that dragon, do you?'

'No,' Tobas reassured her. 'I'm sure somebody must have killed it by now and probably married all the princesses as well.'

'Too bad,' Peren remarked. 'We could use that gold.'

'True enough,' Tobas agreed.

Peren moved on ahead, allowing the newlyweds a little more privacy; for a moment they all walked on in silence, but then Tobas could restrain himself no longer.

'Why *did* you change your mind?' he asked Karanissa abruptly. 'I asked again because you had said you wouldn't marry me until we were out, and we were out, but I didn't really expect you to agree yet.'

'Oh, I don't know,' she said. 'It's just – when we saw the whole World spread out around us yesterday morning, and I heard Peren talking about his adventures, I felt so alone. Things are so strange here. I wanted to have something safe to hold on to, something secure and permanent, something I could trust in, and I wanted it to be you. I wanted to know you'd always be there. The first time I ever saw you, standing in the castle gateway, before I knew anything about you, I liked you better than I think I could ever like Peren. I don't think I could face the world alone after so long; and with you beside me, I'm not alone. I'm a witch, and witches are taught to know things without knowing how they know them. Once I saw you out here, in the World, I knew that I could trust you to stay with me. I do trust you – and I love you, too. I *do* love you, I know that now, and I don't think that will change, after all.'

'Oh,' Tobas said, embarrassed. 'Well, that's good, then, because I love you, too. I know I do, even without witchcraft to tell me.'

After a moment of silent affection Karanissa asked, 'When will we reach the cottage where you left the tapestry?'

Tobas considered. 'Probably this evening,' he said. 'If I remember right, it's just past these next two hills and across a little valley.' He looked ahead at the landscape. 'I *think* that's right, anyway.'

The distance was actually less than he had remembered; the weight of the tapestry had made it seem far greater than it was. They topped the bare rock crest of the second hill within an hour, and saw the cottage on the far side of the valley.

Peren had let the two catch up to him. 'Where did you see the dragon when you were here before?'

'Over there,' Tobas said, pointing to the remembered rocky hilltop just a few hundred yards to their right.

'Where that smoke is?'

A sudden uneasiness swept over Tobas as he saw the smoke Peren indicated, a thin, pale wisp rising from behind a high, jagged heap of stone and thinning out to nothing in the crisp autumn air. 'Yes,' he said, reaching for his athame.

As he had feared, an instant later the dragon's head reared up from behind the jumble of rocks. It was looking directly at them; even as they realized this, it clambered out of concealment, spread its great wings, and took to the air, flapping clumsily toward them.

'Gods!' Karanissa hissed; she stepped back, tripped over a break in the stone, and fell down, landing awkwardly on one hip.

Tobas reached back to help her, but before his hand reached her, Peren yanked him upright again. 'Tobas,' the albino shouted, 'do something! It's coming right for us!' He pointed at the approaching dragon.

267

'I know that!' he shouted back, still trying to reach his wife. 'Let go of me!'

'*Do* something!' Peren insisted.

'Do *what*? All we can do is run for it!' He pulled his arm free.

'You stopped it before with that spell of yours!'

'I didn't *stop* it – and that only worked when its mouth was open.' He turned and saw that the dragon was much closer and coming much faster than he had realized; already it seemed almost upon them. Even if he could get Karanissa to her feet, even if she were unhurt and able to run, they had no chance at all of making the shelter of the trees, more than a hundred yards away. 'Oh, gods!' he said, as he found a pinch of brimstone.

The dragon's great blue-green wings seemed suddenly to block out the entire sky as it swooped upward over their heads, apparently intending to drop down right on top of them. Petrified, all three of them stared upward, certain they had come to the end of their adventures.

The monster opened its mouth in what looked almost like a mocking grin.

Tobas guessed it was probably just baring its fangs for its final lunge, but the reason didn't matter; knowing this would probably be his only chance, he flung his spell.

The dragon's face erupted into yellow flame, and it screamed with fury, but this time it did not stop, nor even slow its attack; it folded its wings and plunged toward them, still screaming, fire dripping and spattering from its jaws.

Tobas, with a sudden inspiration, remembering what had happened in old Roggit's shack when he had tried to put out the fire there and what Derithon had written in his Book of Spells, scrabbled desperately at his belt for more brimstone, meaning to fling the spell again.

The creature opened its wings again, breaking its fall,

catching itself in midair; the sudden downrush of air knocked Tobas and Peren off their feet, and Tobas felt the heat of the flames he had kindled washing across his cheek.

The entire sky was filled with the metallic gleam of blue-green dragon wings and the yellow glare of its uncontrolled fire as he finally found his little vial and poured part of its remaining contents into his hand. The beast craned down its neck, mouth agape, saliva sizzling and flame flickering wildly as it considered which of its three stunned victims would be the tastiest morsel.

Tobas struggled to calm himself; if he stammered while speaking the spell's single inhuman word or if his hands shook too much during the passes, the magic would not work. He forced his hands to steady, made the two simple gestures, then called out the incantation and threw the Combustion upward at the dragon's still-burning jaws.

Instantly, the dragon's mouth and throat exploded violently, the flash and roar blinding and deafening all three of the humans; blood and red-hot scales spattered hissing across the rocks. Fragments of the lower jaw sprayed like bloody hail in one direction, rattling on the exposed stone, while the rest of the fearsome head tumbled wildly in another. The great body slumped to the ground, collapsing with a loud, sodden thump only inches from its intended victims. An outstretched foreclaw smashed Peren flat on his back, raking his chest, and gory scraps of dragon flesh battered Tobas and Karanissa. All three were drenched in smoking, stinking red-purple blood.

The wings thrashed once, then were still; the huge crimson eyes above the shattered jaw blinked once, then slowly glazed over in death.

Tobas found himself sitting atop the hill, Karanissa lying on one side, Peren on the other, all three of them soaked to the skin in the monster's ichor and surrounded by the thing's scattered remains.

'Ick,' he said, looking about in disgust.

Then he fainted.

Chapter 30

The lump on his head throbbed dully as Tobas sat on the rock and studied the immense carcass. Karanissa sat beside him, one hand rubbing at her bruised hip as she worked what healing she could, while Peren, his ruined tunic reshaped into a rough bandage, tried to lift the battered remains of the dragon's head.

'It's too heavy,' he admitted at last, as he came panting up to join them. 'I can't get it off the ground.'

'We could roll it down the hillside,' Karanissa suggested. 'Or I can sort of slide it by witchcraft, but I can't lift it any more than you can.'

'If we can't move it, neither can anyone else who comes across it,' Tobas pointed out. 'I say we go back to Dwomor and get men, horses, and wagons and come back for it.'

'I suppose you're right,' Peren said.

'Of course he's right!' Karanissa said. She took her hand from her hip and shifted uncomfortably, then remarked, 'I don't think I can do any more healing today; it takes too much energy.' She picked at her blood-soaked gown critically and added, 'I wish I had thought to bring more clothes.'

'Well, we did come through the tapestry a little unexpectedly,' Tobas pointed out.

'I know.' She ran her hand over her skirt experimentally, and the blood ran out in a thin stream, leaving clean fabric.

'How did you do that?' Peren asked.

'Witchcraft, of course.' She did not bother to look at

him but went on brushing at her clothes, separating fabric from gore.

'Wait a minute,' Tobas said as he saw the dark fluid spilling out on to the ground. 'Don't waste that stuff! Dragon's blood is worth a fortune; half the high-order spells use it. Wizards back in Telven pay one-fourth its weight in gold, when they can get it at all.'

She looked up for a moment, then went back to cleaning her skirt. 'Don't be silly,' she said. 'There must be gallons of the stuff in that carcass over there.'

'Besides, Tobas,' Peren said, 'you're already rich, anyway! All you have to do is go back to Dwomor and collect the reward. You killed the dragon single-handed, with your one silly spell!'

'That's right,' Karanissa agreed. 'They owe you a thousand pieces of gold!'

'That's right, isn't it?' Tobas stared at the dragon's head in wonderment. 'I killed the dragon. With a single spell.'

Then he shook himself, wishing that his clothes weren't damp and sticky and already beginning to stink. 'You were with me, Peren – I'll tell them you helped. Karanissa and I won't leave you out. You can marry a princess, if you like, and have a position in the castle and a share of the gold.'

'Thank you,' Peren said sincerely. 'A few months ago I might have turned that down, since I didn't do anything, but I've learned better now; I'll take what's offered in this world. I'll choose Princess Tinira, if you don't mind, and take however much of the gold you can spare.'

'Which princess you marry doesn't concern me in the least,' Tobas replied. 'I've got a wife, thank you, and one is all I need. As for the gold, we'll settle that later; I'm too confused right now to think clearly. A third, maybe?'

Peren shrugged. 'Whatever you two think is fair.'

'Don't spend money you haven't got,' Karanissa said

acidly, straining to reach the back of her bodice to wipe it clean. 'How do you know that this so-called king of Dwomor will actually pay?'

'I hadn't thought of that,' Peren said.

'Oh, he'll have to pay,' Tobas said. 'He announced the reward all over the known World!'

'We'll see,' Karanissa said.

Her cynicism was contagious; all three sat in gloomy silence for a moment, contemplating the gore-covered landscape, their sorry condition, and the possibility of royal treachery. The witch said at last, 'I suppose he'll come through with the jobs, though, and he's probably eager to be rid of the princesses. I have the impression from what I've seen and what Tobas has told me that things have gotten more primitive since my day, and I suppose unmarried daughters are probably not very welcome.'

'Elner told me that they aren't,' Tobas agreed. 'But I don't want a princess; I've got you.'

'Well, I know that,' she said with a trace of self-satisfaction in her voice. 'But you can at least take the job; you don't want to spend the rest of your life back inside the tapestry, living off those gardens, do you?'

'Actually,' Tobas answered, 'if we could get the gardens back in shape, I don't think I would really mind; the castle wasn't so bad at all. It was just being trapped there that was unpleasant. Once we chase out the rest of the spriggans, it'll be a nice place.'

'I'd like to see it sometime,' Peren remarked.

'You were scared of it, I thought,' Tobas replied.

'Well, yes,' Peren admitted, 'but I didn't know what it was then.'

'True,' Tobas conceded. His stomach rumbled. 'I wonder if you can eat dragon meat?'

'I don't know,' Peren said. 'I'm hungry, but I'm not hungry enough to try.'

'Are we going to sit here all night?' Karanissa asked, getting to her feet and beginning to work on cleaning the back of her skirt. Tobas watched in appreciation.

'She's right,' Peren said. 'We should at least get to the cottage and make sure the tapestry's safe.'

'And get away from all this dead meat before it starts to smell; I suspect dragons decay quickly,' Karanissa agreed.

Tobas nodded and rose.

They found the tapestry just as Tobas had left it, and the three of them carefully rolled it up so that no one would accidentally stumble into it; that done, Tobas and Karanissa settled in the cottage for the night, while Peren tactfully found himself a spot well away from the building, out of sight and hearing.

The following day they simply rested, while Karanissa used her witchcraft to speed the healing of their various injuries. They were all still exhausted. Karanissa, in particular, had put more energy into her witchcraft than might have been wise, leaving little for traveling.

On the eighth of Snowfall they headed out again, Peren and Tobas carrying the rolled tapestry on their shoulders, and on the ninth, at midmorning, they came in sight of Dwomor Keep.

Someone spotted them as they approached; by the time they neared the gate, the battlements were lined with curious people peering down at the unexpected arrivals.

The portcullis was down and stayed down despite their presence; they halted, of necessity, just outside, and the two men carefully lowered the tapestry to the gound.

A guard on the other side called out something in Dwomoritic.

Karanissa, who had listened intently, called something back, concluding with 'Ethsharitic! Speak Ethsharitic!' Tobas was impressed that she could do so much after hearing just a few words of a completely new language; he had not realized her witchcraft was that versatile.

The guard, after an instant's hesitation, called out, 'Who goes there?' in Ethsharitic, speaking with a thick, ugly accent.

'Peren the White, the witch Karanissa of the Mountains, and the mighty wizard and dragon slayer, Tobas of Telven!' Peren announced. He tried to look impressive despite the filth still marring his white hair, the tattered condition of his breeches, and the shredded near-absence of his tunic. Tobas looked somewhat better, his clothes being intact, and Karanissa had used her witchcraft during the journey to restore herself to her best appearance.

'What . . . ah, what is your business?' the guard managed in his ugly Ethsharitic.

'We have come to claim the reward due us for killing the dragon in your hills,' Peren replied.

'Dragon? Killed? Really?' the guard asked with evident surprise.

A smile appeared unbidden on Tobas' face; Peren fought his down, but did not speak.

'Yes, really,' Karanissa said, then repeated herself in her improvised witch's Dwomoritic.

'Let us in!' Tobas demanded, drawing his athame dramatically.

The guard still hesitated; Tobas gestured and spoke, setting the left sleeve of the man's surcoat afire.

The effect was quite dramatic; he could hear several of the watching Dwomorites suck in their breath. He immediately regretted his hasty, impulsive action, though; attacking the guard was no way to make himself welcome. Besides, he did not want to overuse his spell; his supply

275

of brimstone was finally running low, as he had spilled some when he exploded the dragon.

The soldier beat out the fire and stared out at the strangers, his initial surprise and wonder replaced with fear and anger. 'Open this gate,' Tobas demanded, keeping up the role he had established, 'or it'll be your beard next time.'

The guard glared out for another second or so, then turned to obey. With much cursing and creaking, the portcullis was raised, and half a dozen soldiers appeared to usher the party into the courtyard. Two started to pick up the tapestry, but Peren and Tobas stopped them, preferring to carry the precious hanging themselves.

Once inside, they lowered the tapestry and stood silently, trying to seem calm and aloof, while Karanissa looked around at the sorry state of the castle in evident dismay. At the behest of the commander of the little detachment of guards, a civilian messenger ran to report their arrival.

Naturally, they were not immediately taken in to see the king; instead, various people, presumably officials, none of whom spoke a word of Ethsharitic, came and studied them where they stood. Karanissa did not bother to strain her witchcraft sufficiently to follow what was said; instead, one or another of the three foreigners simply demanded, 'Speak Ethsharitic!' each time a new person appeared and addressed them in Dwomoritic.

After an hour of such delays, the gatekeeper they had first spoken to, whose sleeve Tobas had set afire, reappeared and instructed them in barely intelligible Ethsharitic to follow him into the castle. They obeyed. A moment later they finally found themselves seated at a table across from the Lord Chamberlain.

'So you claim to have slain the dragon,' the chamberlain said without preamble.

'We *have* slain the dragon,' Tobas replied.

The chamberlain shook his head. 'You are by no means the first to make that claim. We have sent out seventy-four self-proclaimed dragon hunters; we have good evidence that over half simply deserted. After accepting our hospitality, they simply left the country without ever trying to kill the beast. A few others, who made the attempt in good faith, were evidently killed. Another few made unsuccessful attempts and escaped alive – I believe that your former comrades were among those; in fact, they told us, if I remember correctly, that the two of you had fled eastward over the mountains rather than return to admit failure. Still others, besides all those I have mentioned, have returned claiming to have killed the monster, but none could prove their claims. One went so far as to bring back the head of a dragon – but only a very small one and not at all fresh, obviously not the right one. Now you march in here with no evidence to support your story, no details of how you slew the creature, but only with this mysterious great roll of cloth you will let no one touch, and expect us to accept you as heroes immediately. I regret that we cannot do that. First, you must prove your claim.'

'We will be glad to do just that,' Tobas replied, 'if you will provide us with the necessary men, beasts, and wagons to haul the dragon's remains back here. We weren't strong enough to lift the head after we decapitated the monster, let alone its body. Its blood you see all over us.' He held out the encrusted front of his tunic.

The chamberlain looked startled. 'Oh? Then you really did kill something? And you left the carcass untended?'

'That's right,' Tobas agreed. 'We didn't have much choice. It's about a day and a half from here. Any of us can show you.'

The Dwomorite sat back, contemplating the three, then

asked sharply, 'How big was this dragon? And what color?'

'It was blue-green, and, oh . . . what would you say, Peren? Sixty feet long?'

'About that,' Peren agreed.

'How did you kill it?' the chamberlain demanded.

'Magic,' Tobas answered.

Seeing that their questioner was not satisfied, Peren added, 'Fire-magic. My companion here, the mighty wizard Tobas of Telven, blew its neck to pieces with a single spell.'

'Forgive me if I still have reservations,' the chamberlain said, polite once again and apparently at least partly convinced. 'But how is it that you took so long to accomplish the task? You departed well over three months ago.'

Tobas shrugged. 'We found other matters to occupy us for a time.' He gestured toward Karanissa and the tapestry that lay against one wall.

'Look,' Peren said in his most reasonable tone. 'We don't expect you to pay us here and now; get some wagons, and I'll show your men where it is. Tobas and Karanissa will stay here in Dwomor as hostage for my good behavior; I'll leave the tapestry and everything else with them.'

'I don't know,' the chamberlain said. 'You could intend to lead my men into a trap.'

'Arm them, then! And if I were planning any treachery, would my companions allow themselves to remain as hostages?'

The Dwomorite considered for another moment, then nodded. 'I suppose not, not if they knew about it,' he said. 'All right, then; we shall see if you have done what you say. Remember, though, if this is some sort of trick, that you did not see all of this castle during your previous stay here; there are dungeons enough for the three of you.'

'Your dungeons don't concern us; we want nothing but what we have earned,' Peren said as he rose.

Chapter 31

The three of them were given the use of a suite of rooms on the second floor of the castle, around a corner from the princesses' wing, consisting of a small, cozy sitting room, a small bedchamber Peren appropriated that had probably originally been intended for a valet, and a large and elegant chamber equipped with a magnificent canopied bed. Although Dwomor Keep was still well populated, the departure of dozens of dragon hunters had left the place with considerably more free space than when Tobas and Peren had last seen it; and as guests who might have actually won the right to marry princesses, they rated significantly better accommodations. As best anyone could recall, a prince had shared this suite with a lesser noble during those closing days of Summersend.

Peren stayed to rest for only one night before departing again, leading a caravan of wagons, soldiers, assorted workmen, and curiosity seekers into the hills, intent on bringing back proof of the dragon's demise. Tobas and Karanissa watched him go from the battlements and then adjourned to their splendid bedchamber to make the best of his absence. Their rooms in Dwomor were far more suitable for a honeymoon than the open country or ruined cottage had been.

Despite their rather peculiar and uncertain status whenever they left their suite to roam the castle, the newlyweds thoroughly enjoyed their relative privacy for the first two or three nights after Peren left. By the time the fourth night came with no sign of his return, however, they began to worry somewhat. Their uneasiness grew steadily throughout the next day, as Peren still did not appear; quite aside from their own concern about their friend, the inhabitants of the castle, from King Derneth himself right down to the chambermaids, seemed to be treating them with mounting suspicion. They were officially still guests, but it was obvious that they were also now prisoners; guards eyed them closely any time either of them stepped out into the courtyard, and it was made plain, silently but unquestionably that they would not be permitted to leave the castle. No one spoke to them unnecessarily; on one occasion Tobas glimpsed the Princess Alorria being herded quickly away by the Lord Chamberlain, lest she might have spoken to the foreign wizard.

Alorria, judging by the expression Tobas thought he saw, was not at all happy to see him, though he was unsure whether that was because she believed him to be a fraud, because she was frightened by him, perhaps embarrassed somehow, or, possibly, because she resented the fact that he had married someone else.

Tobas and Karanissa retired early that night, too worried to enjoy each other's company properly. Simply being together in the great canopied bed was soothing, however; as an hour or two wore slowly by, though neither of them slept, they both calmed down considerably. Nonetheless, midevening of this fifth night after Peren's party had gone to fetch the dragon's head found them both still lying awake.

Shortly after their arrival they had hung the tapestry on one wall of their bedchamber, being extemely careful not to touch its surface. By unspoken mutual consent, both had wanted it hung, but neither of them intended to use it immediately. Once the hanging was securely in place, they had hidden it with the simple drapery that had covered that wall before their arrival, this concealment being necessary to prevent unwanted questions from servants or visitors and, far more importantly, to prevent anyone from accidentally touching it and winding up at the gates of their castle. Now, reaching out from the bed, Tobas had pulled the drapery back, and both of them were staring at the tapestry.

'I think I miss the place,' Karanissa admitted after a few moments of silent contemplation.

'I *know* I miss it,' Tobas replied. 'It was all ours, with no chamberlains or kings to worry about, no princesses and peasants staring at me every time I go out. And the servants did what we told them without trying to beg for favors, constantly apologizing for everything, or acting as if obeying me were beneath their dignity. If I knew my way around here better and were welcome into the kitchens, I think I'd rather not bother the servants at all.'

'It's not just the servants; everybody here is suspicious. They seem to think we're here under false pretenses – as if there's anything here we would bother defrauding them of!'

'I know. The castle in the tapestry, strange as it is, is finer than Dwomor could ever have been.'

'It was so lonely, though, before you arrived,' Karanissa said, snuggling closer to him under the quilts.

'It was never lonely for me,' Tobas answered, his arm encircling her shoulders. 'You were always there.'

'Do you think we should go back?'

'I don't know. We *can* get back out now, if we want to. Both tapestries are working.'

'But we can only get out way up there in the mountains – and it's almost winter. The snows could come any day now.'

'We'll need to go back some time, at least for a while; the only position they could possibly give me here is court wizard, and for that I'll need the Book of Spells and some of the supplies and ingredients from Derithon's study. I don't think I'm going to find hair from unborn children or mummified bat wings here in Dwomor Keep.'

'Maybe I'm just being cowardly, wanting to slink back to my refuge instead of facing the World,' Karanissa said bitterly.

'No, that's not it!' Tobas was shocked at her words. 'You survived there alone for four hundred years; you're no coward!'

Impulsively she hugged him, then nuzzled him silently for a moment. He returned her embrace. She smiled up at him, then said contemplatively, 'You know, if I did go back, I'm sure that within a month or two, at most, I'd want to get out again, to see the sun and the moons and the stars and other people and green fields and trees and mountains and streams and all the rest of it.'

'Of course; so would I. There's nothing wrong with that. Nobody wants to stay cooped up at home all the time.'

'It *is* really our home, isn't it?' Karanissa's tone was wistful.

'Yes, of course – you lived there for so long, how could it *not* be home?'

'But *you* didn't live there very long!'

Tobas shrugged. 'I haven't got any other home; I got kicked out of the one I grew up in and burned down the next. And the castle had you in it – wherever you are would be home.'

She punched him lightly. 'Oh, stop flattering! I'm trying to be serious.'

'I'm *being* serious!'

'Really, Tobas, should we just get up right now and walk through the tapestry?'

'You're asking me for advice? You're the one who's centuries old; I'm just eighteen,' Tobas said. Before she could make any retort, he quickly went on. 'But no, we shouldn't. It wouldn't be fair to Peren when he gets back. Besides, the Dwomorites might not like it, and this is the place I know how to get to from the wrecked castle; when we came back out, they might take offense. And we can use that money. The wine cellar is empty, among other things. No ale, no *oushka*, no figs or pomegranates. Some of Derithon's supplies are about used up, and others have gone bad with age. If you're not picky, I suppose the castle does have all the food we'll ever need, really, but we'll want either money or magic to add some variety, and for any number of things. And if we have children, we don't want them growing up all alone in there.'

'I hadn't thought about children.'

'Don't you want any?'

'I hadn't thought about it, really,'

'Well, you probably should,' he said, smiling. 'If we keep on as we have, they're likely to happen.'

'Let them happen, then!' She giggled. He hugged her to him for a moment.

'Then we shouldn't cut ourselves off in the tapestry,' he said. 'Not if we're going to lead a decent life and have children.'

'You're right,' she agreed. 'Besides, I want to see the World.' She paused, considering, then asked anxiously, 'It isn't all like Dwomor, is it?'

'Aha! So *that's* what's really bothering you! No, it isn't all like Dwomor. This is one of the least pleasant places I've seen, as a matter of fact. I think you'd be impressed by Ethshar of the Spices; it's not as primitive as this place. Or even the beaches near Telven . . .' His voice trailed off.

'What is it?'

'I just realized; I *can't* stay in the tapestry! I owe someone an apology and a new boat. And besides, I promised Peren I'd put curses on the people who robbed him if he wanted me to.'

'Well, it's settled, then. We'll just have to learn to deal with the World. We'll get the money, and you'll take the position here, and we'll travel and see Ethshar and Telven and buy those people their new boat – and whenever we want to get away from it all, we can just step into the tapestry.'

'We'll need to make a proper road down from the wreck if we do that – either that, or I'll need to learn to fly.' He hesitated, then added thoughtfully, 'I could do that, I suppose. Derithon had some flying spells that didn't look too difficult.'

'I think that would be fun, flying down from the mountains.'

'Oh, I almost forgot, though; we'd still have to do some hiking at first, each time. Wizardry doesn't work right around the castle.'

'Is there anything you can do about that?'

'I don't really know. I don't know anything about it. It seems as if there ought to be some use for such a place, though.' He thought for a moment, then suggested, 'Maybe we could set up a village there for people who have been cursed. The curses wouldn't work. Of course they'd have to stay up there indefinitely, and we could charge a good price for showing them where it is. Then we'd have a village right there and wouldn't need to come all the way back to Dwomor for everything.'

Karanissa shook her head. 'It won't work,' she said. 'At least, I don't think it's a good idea. Sooner or later someone would go exploring in the flying castle and mess up the hidden room, and we wouldn't be able to get out that way.'

'You're right,' Tobas agreed immediately. 'It needs more thought. I can't even put any protective spells in place, because they won't work there.' He sighed. 'Oh, well, it was an idea. Maybe eventually I'll manage to make another tapestry showing somewhere more convenient, and *then* we can set up our colony for the victims of curses.'

'You'll make another tapestry,' Karanissa said confidently. 'It can't be that hard. If Derry could do it, you can do it.'

'It may take years,' Tobas reminded her.

'Well, *I've* got forever, and they say a witch's love can keep a man young. You've got a recipe for an eternal youth spell in that book of Derry's; you can work your way up to that, and then we'll *both* have forever.' She leaned over and kissed him.

Someone knocked at the door.

Startled that anyone would be about so late, Tobas called, 'What is it?'

'Your companion has returned, my lord wizard,' announced the voice of one of the few servants who spoke Ethsharitic.

'Well, it's about time!' Karanissa said, rolling quickly out of bed on to her feet. Tobas followed suit, and both grabbed for the nearest decent clothing.

A moment later the witch and the wizard descended the staircase together and marched out to the torchlit courtyard, where a curious crowd, much of it still in nightclothes, was staring at the various fragments of the dragon that now occupied a long line of wagons.

'My lord Tobas,' someone said behind him. Tobas turned and found the Lord Chamberlain, his ceremonial robes wrinkled, obviously himself just roused from sleep. 'My apologies, sir, for doubting you. You are indeed entitled to the reward; and despite the hour, his Majesty the King is waiting in the audience chamber at this moment, eager to have the matter settled. We do not wish there to be any further delay and hope you will come now and make your choice. If you would be so kind as to follow me?'

Grinning broadly, with Karanissa on his arm, Tobas followed.

Peren was waiting at the door of the audience chamber. 'I'm sorry I took so long,' he said, speaking quickly. 'But it was hard keeping that bunch together, and it took a long time to chop the thing up. They insisted on bringing it *all* back. They wanted practically every scale and drop of blood. And then on the way back they kept stopping to rest, too! Half of them wanted to stop and make camp at sundown this evening, but we were so close, I insisted we should press on, and here we are. I'm sorry it's so late.'

'That's all right,' Tobas said. 'We thought that the delays were probably something like that. We weren't really worried – after all, we knew we'd killed dragon. Besides, we could always go through the tapestry if we had to escape quickly.'

Peren nodded, not really listening. 'Did you know that the crown is claiming the dragon's remains?' he said, clearly agitated. 'They say that since we were working for them, they own the dragon; we don't get to keep any for ourselves.'

'Well, with all that gold, we shouldn't need – ' Tobas began.

'Hush!' the chamberlain said, as the door of the audience chamber swung open.

The three adventurers obeyed and were appropriately quiet and obeisant as they were brought before his Majesty Derneth the Second, King of Dwomor and Rightful Lord of the Holy Kingdom of Old Ethshar. Tobas wondered idly whether this last title was a new acquisition or merely one they hadn't come across previously.

They noticed immediately that, in addition to a small assortment of rather befuddled advisors, the king was surrounded by his unmarried daughters. All five princesses stood to the left of the throne, arrayed in fine white gowns – though Tobas noted a few untied bows and unfastened buttons, clear proof of the hurry with which they had dressed. Zerréa was grinning behind her hand, and Alorria was visibly excited, but the older three merely seemed sleepy.

Servants were still lighting candles along the sides of the hall; about two-thirds of the racks were aglow when the king motioned for the three foreigners to rise from their formal bows.

'Hello,' he said politely when everyone was upright once more. 'We understand you three actually managed to kill that dragon.'

'Yes, your Majesty,' Tobas replied. 'We did.'

'Congratulations, my boy!' He smiled broadly, if a trifle insincerely. 'In that case, we assume that you have come here for your reward.'

'Yes, your Majesty, I – '

'Which one do you want?' He gestured at the five princesses, wasting no time on preliminaries. Tinira, somewhat more awake than her older sisters, blushed, and Zerréa giggled; Alorria licked her lips nervously. 'Pick one, and then we can all get back to bed.'

Somewhat distressed at the king's cavalier treatment of his own daughters, as well as dismayed at the assumption that he would marry one, Tobas began, 'Ah . . . your Majesty, I – '

Peren interrupted. 'If it pleases your Majesty, I would ask for the hand of the Princess Tinira. My comrade,

Lord Tobas, has voiced no objection to my choice in previous discussion.'

'Good enough, then.' The king's smile seemed suddenly more sincere. 'Tinira, step forth to meet your betrothed!'

The princess stepped forward, eyes downcast, and made her way to Peren's side. He took her hand gravely.

'Had you left the choice to me,' the king remarked casually, 'I would have offered Falissa and I do wish that you hadn't lost the other two members of your original group, but this will have to be good enough. My blessings upon you, Peren – it is Peren, isn't it? Peren, and Tinira. And now, Wizard, what of your choice?'

'Your Majesty, I'm already married,' Tobas answered boldly. 'The witch Karanissa of the Mountains is my wife as well as my comrade.'

The king stared at him for a moment, every trace of his smile gone, then demanded, 'What of it?'

Tobas stammered for a moment, then said. 'I mean only that I cannot take one of your beautiful daughters as my wife. I will be pleased and honored to accept the other promised rewards, but – '

'You don't understand,' Derneth said, cutting him off. 'You obviously don't understand the situation at all. Someone has misled you badly. You do want the reward money, don't you?'

'Yes, I – ' Tobas began.

'Well, then,' the king said, cutting him off, 'you must marry one or more of my daughters. The gold and the positions in my realm are their dowries. The sole reward for slaying the dragon is the hand of a princess; the dowry comes with that, but you can't have the dowry without the bride. If we had simply wanted to pay out a thousand gold pieces to have the dragon slain, do you think we would have gone about it the way we did?'

'I hadn't thought – '

'Of course not! That would be stupid and wasteful. For half that much, we could get a professional dragon hunter down from Aldagmor, or a really good magician of some sort from Ethshar – no disparagement of your own powers is intended, since you were obviously capable of the job, but you must admit you had no prior reputation. No, we wanted to find husbands for my daughters, husbands who would prove their worth against the monster!'

'But – ' Elner had been right all along, Tobas realized, and his own suspicions well-founded. Once again his protest was cut short by the king before it truly began.

'It didn't work out the way we planned, though, with only three of you involved and one of you a woman. We've promised the full thousand to whoever slew the dragon, and we'll honor that, but we'll be damned before we'll let you get away with not marrying at least *one* of our daughters into the bargain!' He glowered down at Tobas.

'But I'm already married!' Tobas said in almost a wail, abruptly aware of his own youth and insignificance before this suddenly formidable figure.

'And what difference does that make?'

Tobas had no good answer to that. He had certainly never intended to have more than one wife; very few men did. However, there was no law against polygamy, nor even any strong custom; Tobas had known men with two wives, back in Telven, and had even heard of men with three. The only restriction custom imposed was that a man had to have enough money to keep two families and a home big enough for them.

With the dowry a princess would bring, and living in Dwomor Keep, Tobas realized he would have both. Even if he left Dwomor, he and Karanissa owned a large enough castle for any number of families.

He did not want a second wife, though. He started to

prepare a polite little speech declining the honor, telling the king to keep the gold; after all, with Derithon's magic he was sure he could earn all the money he would need elsewhere. 'Your Majesty, I must – '

Karanissa's elbow jabbed him in the side. 'Don't be stupid!' she whispered fiercely, obviously aware of what he had in mind, whether by witchcraft or common sense Tobas could not tell. 'We can use the gold and the goodwill, and *I* don't mind having another wife around. I'm not the jealous type; I couldn't be, with Derry what he was. But I do like money. Go on and take your pick.'

Startled, Tobas stammered again, glanced at Karanissa, saw her nod firmly, then turned back to the king and said, reluctantly, 'Your Majesty, I must apologize for the delay; all of your daughters are so beautiful that making a choice is agony.'

'Take them all, then!' Derneth said, waving an arm recklessly.

'But,' Tobas said quickly, before the king's suggestion could be taken seriously, 'if choose I must, I will choose Alorria.'

'Oh, Tobas!' Alorria shrieked gleefully, her eyes widening with what Tobas could only interpret as delight; she ran to him and hugged him fiercely.

Tinira was somewhat more restrained in embracing Peren.

With that, except for the polite farewells, the audience was over; details of distributing the dowries would be settled only when the heroes were safely married. The king slipped quietly out a back door, presumably to return to his bed, and a moment later Tobas found the Lord Chamberlain at his side, discussing wedding arrangements.

Chapter 32

The wedding was to be a grand festival, the biggest event Dwomor had seen in years; it was not only a double royal wedding, after all, but a celebration of the dragon's death. The entire population of the kingdom of Dwomor was invited – which, Tobas learned to his dismay, was slightly under eight thousand people. All his life he had heard them called the Small Kingdoms, but he had never realized before just how small most of them were. He remembered the endless thronged streets of Ethshar of the Spices and resolved that, princess or no, he would not spend the rest of his life in Dwomor.

He recalled that he had once intended to spend his entire life in Telven, with its population of a hundred or so, and found it hard to believe. It was not that he had any great urge to travel, but that places such as Dwomor seemed so limited in what they might provide in the way of opportunities and comforts.

Karanissa had great difficulty in not laughing when she heard the population estimate. 'I've seen army camps with more camp followers than this so-called kingdom has people!' she remarked truthfully.

She did not think much of the attempts the castle's population made at pomp and elegance, either. Dwomor Keep simply did not have a great deal of wealth to display; most of the guests would be fed on simple wooden plates, many of them freshly carved for the event. Banners flew from every turret of the castle, and bunting was hung above the gate, but much of the bunting was faded and the banners did not match. Her own garb, repaired and enhanced by her witchcraft, was finer than Alorria's wedding dress, though Tinira, as the older sister, managed to outshine Karanissa in an ancient, vividly blue gown of some magically woven fabric one of her distant royal ancestors had somehow acquired.

Due to the time required for all the preparations and the need to spread word of the event throughout the realm, the date was set for the twenty-second of Snowfall and fervent prayers offered to the gods for continued good weather. A sprinkle of snow on the sixteenth caused minor consternation; but, as it had the good grace to melt away within a day or so, hopes remained high.

Tobas spent several evenings staring longingly at the tapestry, but Karanissa remained firm in her insistence that he marry Alorria.

'It won't bother me,' she insisted. 'And you need the money, and it will put you solidly in good with the king here.'

'But I don't want to stay here!'

'But the flying castle is in Dwomor – or maybe Aigoa, but this castle is closer and on the way to Ethshar. Until you either get the castle airborne again or weave another tapestry, or until you give up the tapestry castle for good, you're tied to Dwomor, whether you like it or not.'

'I don't like it. Kara, how can I manage being married to both of you? I'm only eighteen; one wife is plenty for someone my age.'

'Don't *worry* about it,' she insisted. 'Alorria and I will work out the details between ourselves.'

Tobas was not at all sure he liked that. 'Besides,' he said, 'I hardly know her!'

He quickly found, however, that the entire population of Dwomor Keep was determined to do their best to correct that; wherever he went, other than his own suite, Alorria was either there waiting for him or would arrive a moment later.

He found it difficult to talk to her; she was too impressed by his magic and his supposed heroism, and had led a life too different from his own. Save for a brief state visit or two to neighboring kingdoms, she had spent her entire life inside castle walls. She was educated and well-read, but clearly had little real understanding of the world.

When she heard the tale of how Peren had been robbed and beaten, she found it almost impossible to believe that the local peasants in that part of Amor had not immediately swept out of their homes in a righteous fury and hanged the entire caravan. When she heard how the wizards of Ethshar had refused to teach Tobas more spells, she assumed that it was because he had somehow been unworthy, not having proven himself yet, or perhaps he had offended them in some way, by failing to make some Guild recognition sign. And she flatly denied almost everything Karanissa said about the Great War and the nature of Old Ethshar.

Tobas found her sweet-tempered but stubborn, intelligent but naïve. She seemed far younger than himself, though he knew she was no more than two years his junior. He could not imagine living with her from day to day or taking her to his bed.

The days passed, however, and the wedding drew ever nearer.

The snow began falling around midday on the twenty-first, and on the morning of the chosen day it had reached a depth of six inches, with drifts over a foot. The Lord Chamberlain had anticipated a crowd of perhaps two thousand; a tenth of that actually showed up.

That was still quite enough for Tobas. Going through the ceremony, vowing to the gods to cherish a near-stranger, was almost worse than facing the dragon.

294

Peren seemed to be enjoying his part of it; he and Tinira made a much better couple than Tobas and Alorria, quite aside from the complications Karanissa's presence created. They both seemed very happy with their situation, and Tobas supposed glumly that their marriage would be a success. He doubted they felt any great love for each other as yet, but they did seem to like one another, which was as much as could be said for most marriages.

After the ceremony came the delivery of the promised dowry, carried out in a small locked room; Tobas and Karanissa counted out seven hundred pieces of gold as their share, and Peren took the remaining three hundred. Karanissa took charge of the large share, and Tobas did not worry about it further. He was too busy worrying about the rest of the day and night that lay ahead.

When the gold was taken care of, the feasting and the merrymaking began; three different minstrels had composed odes in honor of the dragon slayer, and Tobas found himself acutely embarrassed by all three. One singer had a trick of jamming extra syllables into his lines; another couldn't carry a tune; and the third, though his songs were well written and lovely, had embroidered the truth beyond recognition, adding a long dialogue between Tobas and the dragon wherein each listed the other's offenses against dragonkind and humanity respectively, and then went on to boast of his own prior achievements.

'But the dragon didn't talk,' Tobas insisted quietly to Alorria, while trying to keep up a polite smile. 'If it's true that dragons can learn when they grow old and wise enough, then I suppose it never had anyone to teach it a language, living alone up there in the hills – or maybe it just didn't think we were worth talking to. But in any case, it never said a word.'

'It was just a bloodthirsty monster,' Alorria agreed.

'I think that it was just hungry, really; there isn't much for something that big to eat around here, except livestock and people.'

Alorria shuddered delicately. 'Don't talk about it like that.'

'Why not?' Tobas asked, startled. 'These idiots have been *singing* about it!'

'That's different. It sounds so awful when you talk about it eating people just because it was hungry.'

'What other reason could it have? And they're singing about the same thing! Listen to that: "You have swept the fields with bloody slaughter, devouring the peasants' sons and daughters." *I* never said anything like that!'

'Tobas, it's just a song; be quiet and enjoy it.'

Tobas realized he was being unreasonable. What he actually wanted to protest was not the minstrel's songs, but that he was marrying Alorria. She, however, was not likely to be a receptive audience to any complaint of that sort; she was obviously delighted to be marrying him. Morosely, he settled back and drained his wine cup.

A servant promptly refilled it; Tobas made no protest. One good thing about Dwomor was the local wine, which was of truly exceptional quality. He had been without any wine worthy of the name for some time and intended to enjoy the stuff now that he could.

When at last the happy couple was sent off to their chamber, with much cheering and a smattering of bawdy remarks, Tobas was somewhat tipsy, though still able to navigate well enough. The combination of alcohol and an evening spent in close proximity to Alorria's beauty had worn away his reservations and left him looking forward to the night.

Their bridal chamber was the same room that Tobas and Karanissa had been using for the past two sixnights; no better accommodations were available. Alorria had, until now, shared a chamber with Zerréa, so that her former residence was not a possibility. Karanissa and Peren had tactfully been given smaller, separate rooms elsewhere.

Tobas was surprised, therefore, to find the witch waiting for them in the suite's sitting room. 'Hello,' he said, confused and embarrassed, unsure whether to keep his arm around Alorria's waist or not.

'Hello,' Karanissa said as she opened the door into the bedchamber.

'What are you doing here?' Alorria demanded, clearly upset by her rival's presence.

'I wanted to say good-bye before I left,' the witch replied. 'I didn't want Tobas to worry.'

'Left? Where?' Tobas asked. His arms dropped away from Alorria as the warm glow of the wine suddenly vanished.

The three of them had all moved on into the inner room as they spoke. 'I think you two should have some time to get to know each other,' Karanissa explained. 'So I was planning to leave for a while. I don't want to be in the way. Tobas can come and get me in the spring, when the snows melt enough for travel.' She reached for the drawstring to uncover the tapestry.

'Wait a minute, Kara!' Tobas said.

'Let her go!' Alorria said, holding him back.

"Good-bye,' Karanissa said. She picked up a case of wine she had waiting ready by the bed, stepped into the tapestry, and was gone.

'Oh, no!' Tobas said. 'You're not leaving me here like this!' He pulled free of Alorria's hands and stumbled through the tapestry after his first wife.

'Tobas!' Alorria cried. Without having any idea of what she was actually doing, she followed her hero-husband.

Chapter 33

'Now look what you've done,' Karanissa said, her hands on her hips as she stood on the bridge to the castle gate.

'You might have warned me what you had in mind,' Tobas retorted from the outer path.

'Where *are* we?' Alorria wailed, clutching Tobas' arm and staring around at the eerie, red-lit void.

'Calm down,' witch and wizard said in unison. A spriggan giggled from one of the castle windows.

After a moment, Karanissa shrugged. 'Well, we're all here until spring, so we might as well make the best of it. Come on in.' She turned, and the doors opened before her.

'Showy witch,' Tobas muttered, annoyed by the entire situation.

'They were locked from the inside,' Karanissa reminded him. 'How else would we get in?'

'Call the servants,' Tobas replied immediately.

'But, Tobas . . .' Alorria began.

'I hadn't thought of that,' Karanissa admitted.

'Ha! It seems to me that there are a lot of things you didn't think about!'

'Tobas . . .' Alorria said urgently.

'I hope most of the spriggans are gone,' Karanissa remarked.

'And I hope I have the ingredients for doing lots of dream-messages; I don't want anyone to worry about us.'

'Tobas!'

Tobas turned to Alorria. 'I'm sorry, Ali.' He waved an arm at the castle. 'This is part of marrying a wizard, I suppose; at least, it's a part of marrying me. Welcome to your new home!'

The princess gaped up at the gargoyle-covered ramparts, the bat-winged turrets, the forbidding black walls.

'And,' Karanissa said warmly, 'welcome to the family.

Hearing that, Tobas glanced at Karanissa and saw she meant it. He smiled. For the first time since he had watched Roggit's house burning, he felt that he could stop worrying about his future. He had a home, plenty of money, a career as a court wizard, and a family.

It was like no home he could ever have imagined, this castle hanging in nowhere. His money was a fabulously rich dowry, which was not something he had ever expected. His wizardry was inherited from a man centuries dead, rather than learned as an apprentice, and might almost be considered another dowry. His family consisted of two wives, a witch and a princess. Life had played strange tricks on him, certainly, but nonetheless he had a home, money, a career, and a family, and he was pleased with them all.

Any problems that might remain could only be trivial. He felt wonderful. His luck had been good after all.

Epilogue

Lador of Sesseran awoke and looked up, startled, as a shadow blocked out the sun. All he could make out was a dark shape hanging in the sky above him. He stared, unsure whether to get up and run, or stay where he was. Thera, at his side, still slept.

A head appeared over one edge of the thing.

'Hello,' a young man's voice called cheerfully. Lador was slightly relieved to hear the familiar accent of a Freelander rather than the harsher tones of an Ethsharite, but still wary.

'I don't suppose you remember me,' the voice continued. 'But no, that's foolish, of course you do. I'm Tobas of Telven; I stole your boat.'

Lador gaped, then found his voice. 'That was five years ago!'

'I know, I know,' the apparition said. 'I'm sorry it took so long, but I've been busy. You wouldn't believe some of the delays. I hope you'll accept my apology.' The young man tossed something over the side of the hovering object; it struck the ground with the distinctive clinking sound of coins. Lador stared at the purse, then back up at the thing.

Two more heads were peering over the side now; his eyes had adjusted somewhat to the bright sun behind them, and these two looked female. Both had dark hair; one wore it loose and flowing, while the other wore hers gathered up by a coronet. The object supporting them seemed to be flapping at the edges, he noticed; it was perhaps two yards wide and three long and seemed to be made of heavy fabric.

'The money's my apology,' Tobas said. 'And the boat I owe you is down on the beach. It's not actually the one I stole, but it's as close as I could make it. The chicken dinner is under the seat, but I substituted white wine; I hope you don't mind.'

'Why would he mind?' the woman in the coronet asked derisively. 'Who drinks red wine with chicken?'

'Shut up, Ali,' the other woman said. 'Let Tobas finish.'

'He *was* finished!' the first woman retorted.

'No, he wasn't,' the second insisted.

'This is all silly, anyway.'

'Will you two shut up?' Tobas roared, to no effect, as his wives bickered.

Lador simply stared for a long moment, but as the argument continued, he first smiled and then laughed aloud. The world was full of wonders, and this wizard who called himself Tobas of Telven was one of them.

Tobas looked down once more, shrugged and smiled as if to say, 'What can I do?' then turned back to his women.

The three on the flying carpet paid no further attention to the couple in the dunes; they were far too busy with their own little family squabble. After a few minutes of bemused listening, Lador woke Thera, who had somehow slept through it all. Together, the two of them went down to the beach together to see their new boat.

Notes

In Y.S. 5226, when the noted wizard Tobas of Telven consulted an oracular priest in Ethshar of the Spices, his primary purpose was to locate two people he felt he owed an unpaid debt. However, he took the opportunity to obtain answers to certain other questions as well. Those answers are provided here for any readers of this chronicle who might be interested.

Roggit knew perfectly well that Tobas had lied about his age; he was not as far gone as his apprentice believed. He was, however, a very lonely old man and took pity on the boy. Only after accepting him as an apprentice did he have misgivings, which were responsible for the delays in teaching Tobas anything useful.

The area in the mountains between Dwomor and Aigoa where wizardry would not function resulted from the second use of the spell Ellran's Dissipation. This incredibly powerful but very simple first-order spell was discovered quite by accident in Y.S. 4680, by the little-known research wizard Ellran the Unfortunate; it renders an area of indeterminate size 'dead' to wizardry, permanently. Since the military government of Old Ethshar relied heavily on wizardry, while their Northern enemies did not, the spell was deemed to be not only useless, militarily speaking, but exceedingly dangerous, and accordingly it was vigorously suppressed. It was only performed twice: once in 4680, when Ellran discovered it, and again in 4762, when Captain Seth Thorun's son, a bitter and inept former apprentice of Kalirin the Clever, himself an apprentice of Ellran's, used it to end a pointless feud with his rival, Derithon the Mage. Derithon's home was destroyed, and Derithon himself was presumably killed. A secret military outpost devoted to magical research was also rendered 'dead' to wizardry, and was consequently abandoned. This was the 'village' Tobas and Peren explored. Seth Thorun's son was tried for murder and treason by a proper military tribunal, found guilty, and hanged on the sixth day of Rains, 4763, and his Book of Spells burned, putting an end to the line of apprentices passing down Ellran's Dissipation.

Captain Istram of the *Golden Gull* could not be bothered to locate the rightful owners of the boat Tobas had left in his care, but did not feel justified in keeping it. Accordingly, he sold the boat and donated the proceeds to a theurgical hospital for injured or aged sailors.

Prince Heremin of Teth-Korun did not actually speak Quorulian as his native tongue at all; he spoke Teth-Korunese. His *interpreter* spoke Quorulian and was unaware of the distinction between the two tongues. Other than differences in the use of the subjunctive and in the genitive-case endings of proper nouns, the two languages are, in fact, indistinguishable.

Dragons were endemic to the hills of Dwomor for centuries, but none caused serious problems before Y.S. 5220 or so, because until then none ever lived long enough to grow to a formidable size. The dragon Tobas killed had resorted to eating livestock and people only when it had devoured everything else big enough for it to catch; if it had been just a little smarter, it would have moved on to a different area, instead, and gone on eating deer. Dragons have no known limit to their growth; but since young ones tend to be quite stupid and easy to capture or kill, very few ever exceed what humans consider a manageable size. They reach reproductive maturity at about six or seven feet in length, so that the tendency to get killed off when they reach ten feet or so has not seriously endangered the species. The linguistic centers of the draconic brain usually develop around the twenty-foot size, but of course, like a human infant, a dragon cannot learn to talk without someone to teach it.

The illegible page in the front of Derithon's book of spells had once held his notes on the making of an athame; they were rendered illegible when his master found them and impressed on his apprentice with a willow switch that the athame was a secret. The lesson took, and the little code symbol Derithon used thereafter was the result.

The thing that sank Dabran the Pirate's ship *Retribution* was Degorran, a little-known sea demon of the Fifth Circle. Shemder the Lame, the demonologist aboard the Ethsharitic trader *Behemoth* who was responsible for summoning Degorran, had been attempting to contact the much less formidable second-circle demon Spesforis the Hunter when he got lucky and brought up Degorran instead.

The invisible servant Tobas called Nuisance was in the castle in the void when Derithon first created it; in fact, it was arguably the castle's rightful owner until Derithon placed it under several assorted spells of constraint and compulsion, and its abuse of Tobas was as close as it could come to wreaking vengeance for its enslavement on all wizardkind.

And finally, spriggans really are harmless, except in large numbers, but not quite as stupid as Tobas hoped; it took them three years to figure out that the mirror wouldn't work in the fallen castle and another year after that to drag it somewhere it *would* work, unleashing the steady supply of spriggans that continued to plague Ethshar from then on.